Journeys
Into Possibility

TALES FROM THE PIKES PEAK WRITERS

Alicia Cay • April Benson
Robert Spiller • Jean Alfierti
D.J. Davis • Barbara Preslier
Bowen Gillings • Bill Bush
John Arthur Neal • Steven Anderson
Jeff Schmoyer • CS Simpson
KK Quinn • Wendy Oliver
Kelley Lindberg • Marlene Fabien Stiles
Veronica Roland • Jessica Mehring
Bailey Finn • Jenna MacFarlane
Catherine Dilts

CONTENTS

EDITED BY

DEBORAH L. BREWER

KIM OLGREN

KATHIE SCRIMGEOUR

INTRODUCTION

Now that the past few years are behind us it's time to come out and play! Are you ready to go on a journey to a place you have never been before? What would you like to do? Maybe a swim with dolphins, meet strange new creatures, or see John Dillinger behind bars? You could take a trip through time, visit a new planet, or hop on a train worn with memories. The possibilities are just a page away.

Welcome to the third anthology of stories and poems written by twenty-one talented member authors of Pikes Peak Writers. It has been quite a trip this past year finding our way to the end of our journey and the beginning of yours. *Journeys into Possibility* came to print with the help of Bowen, Kim O., CS, Steven, and Kim L. who pushed through the slush pile of over 200 submissions. Then, the editorial team of Deborah Brewer, Kim Olgren, and Kathie Scrimgeour (that's us!) compiled all of it to bring you these adventures in writing. We want to extend a special thank you to the cover designer, Josh Clark, whose artistic eye hasn't failed us, along with Pam McCutcheon who graciously stepped up to put it all together in a cohesive file that our distributor could work with.

So, strap in and get comfortable as we travel into the imaginative realm of possibilities. Together, we will journey into all things possible and impossible. Once you've been there and back again, you won't be quite the same.

Happy Reading!
Deborah, Kathie, and Kim

IN HER REFLECTION
ALICIA CAY

3 March 1934 – Saturday

She had that scoundrel John Dillinger right where she wanted him—sitting in her jail. Sheriff Lillian Holley sat at her desk and popped open her gold and pearl compact, a gift from her late husband, Roy. She checked her plum-red lipstick in the little mirror and sighed. There was yet another press interview today about Crown Point's most infamous prisoner.

She adjusted a sculpted wave of dark hair, mentally readying herself for the onslaught of questions, when a pair of hazel-gold eyes, big as opals, appeared in the mirror's reflection, hovering over her left shoulder.

Lillian sat bolt upright and snapped the compact shut. Her gaze darted to the long mirror in the mahogany hall tree near the door.

She launched from the wooden swivel chair as Mamie Harlow's pale face slid into view within the mirror. Mamie's thin eyebrows were drawn into a scowl beneath loose blond curls. She opened her perfectly-painted, heart-shaped mouth just as Lillian grabbed her black wool-crepe coat from a hook on the hall tree and threw it over the mirror.

Lillian stepped back, her heart dancing a jitterbug against her ribcage.

Mamie, a moll who'd run with the Dillinger gang, had been murdered last December. She'd shown up a week after Lillian had been sworn in as sheriff—a hazy memory of a wolf's face the only clue to her killing—and been wandering through Lillian's mirrors since.

The hall tree rattled, its wooden frame bouncing off the wall from the force of Mamie's pounding. "Lillian!" Mamie cried, her muffled wails audible through the thick winter coat.

Lillian hadn't seen Mamie in over a month, not since Dillinger's arrest. So, why was she back now?

The office door slammed open, hitting the wall behind it hard enough to knock bits of plaster to the floor. Lillian jumped.

Deputy Flynn stood in the doorway, his short red hair in disarray, eyes wide. "He's gone."

"Who?" Lillian asked.

Flynn's jaw muscles flexed, and he dropped his eyes to stare at Lillian's sensible black oxford heels. "Dillinger, ma'am."

Lillian bolted from the office, sweat beading on her forehead as she ran. It wasn't possible. Her heart squeezed itself into her throat; John Herbert Dillinger, Public Enemy Number One, could *not* have escaped from her jail!

The cell block was chaos. Deputies ran back and forth securing doors and prisoners banged on the iron bars, clapping and hollering to beat the band.

Lillian hurried through the master gate, skidding to a stop at the sight of the jail's custodian. He sat on the floor against the wall, a blood-soaked handkerchief pressed to his temple. She cocked an eyebrow at her deputy.

"Dillinger hit him," Flynn mumbled. "Took his keys."

Lillian groaned. "Well, go and ring the doctor for him." She *shooed* her hands at Flynn. "Now!" Then she dashed up the hallway to the only iron-barred door standing open.

She dreaded walking past this cell during evening rounds. Dillinger lying on his cot, his arm tucked behind his head. He'd smirk that roguish grin at her, deepening the prominent cleft in his chin.

"Hey, Lady Lawman," he'd drawl, his gray eyes glinting with a secret he'd never let her in on.

Lillian's gaze moved to the polished metal tray used for shaving, hung above the water basin. She dragged lead-filled feet into the cell, grabbed the sides of the basin, and stared down into the sink's rusted drain. Bank robbers, murder victims—it was all too much. She wasn't supposed to be doing this! Roy was the real sheriff. She'd only taken over to make him proud. He'd always believed in her, more than most husbands, and now he was gone. Her heart ached. Lillian gritted her teeth and forced her head level.

Mamie's melancholy eyes sparkled like shattered emeralds in the tarnished mirror. "I told you it weren't safe to bring him here, Lillian." Her voice was baby-doll squeaky and coquettish.

Lillian bit into the soft flesh of her cheek to keep the tears at bay. "No one was listening to me about your...situation, Mamie. I did it to get justice—"

Deputy Flynn skidded into the cell. Lillian spun and shifted her head to block the mirror.

"He's gone, Sheriff."

Lillian inhaled slowly. "Obviously, Robert."

Flynn shook his head. "No, I mean Edwin saw 'em taking off down Main Street from the garage. He's got Youngblood hostage, and he's stole a car."

Consarn it! Lillian took a breath, then, "All right. Get a description of the car and I'll get it on the wire right away."

"It's ..." Flynn let out a sigh. "It's a black Ford V8, ma'am."

A cannonball doused in diesel then set on fire, dropped into Lillian's stomach and rolled through her guts. "It's not?"

"I'm afraid so, ma'am."

"Frazzlin, dagnabbit!" Lillian's fists clenched as a wave of anger swept over her, pushing all of her guilt and grief straight down into her sensible shoes. Dillinger had attacked one of her men, escaped from her jail, and now that son-of-a-biscuit-eater had stolen her car.

"Run and grab my pistol, Robert, then get the van ready." Lillian smoothed sweaty hands down her black, box-pleated skirt. "We're going after him."

"Yes'm." Flynn bolted down the corridor, keys on his belt jingling.

Lillian faced the shaving mirror again. "Mamie, listen to me now. I need to get Dillinger back before those Division of Investigation boys find him. You know they'll never—"

The metal mirror's warped surface distorted Mamie's angry expression into savagery. "Yes, I do know!"

Lillian took a deep breath to steady her voice. "I need your help now to find him. I need you to think real hard."

Mamie's face fell. "I've told you, whenever I try an' think about what, you know ... happened, everything goes black and alls I see is that wolf's face." Mamie shook her head. "Big snarling teeth." Tears filled her eyes. "Scares me too much to think about, Lillian."

"I know it does, honey. So don't think about Dillinger, think about where he'd go."

Mamie chewed on her perfect bottom lip for a moment, then her eyes brightened. "He'll go to Billie, first thing. I'm sure of it!"

9 April 1934 – Monday

As soon as Billie's arrest had come across the wire, Lillian had driven the hour from Crown Point to Chicago to question her. Agent Purvis and the rest of Hoover's henchmen had greeted Lillian in a cloud of Chesterfield smoke, and when Lillian had insisted on being allowed to question her, they'd cocked their fedoras low to hide their glowering glances; a woman in law enforcement was as unwelcome as a boil on their butts.

Lillian stepped into the cramped concrete interview room. A sliver of Chicago's steel and glass skyline was just visible through a narrow window on the far wall. The room was freezing.

During their interrogation, the DOI boys had opened the wire-enforced window and taken away Billie's coat.

Evelyn "Billie" Frachette glared at Lillian with eyes as black as her tightly waved hair. "Sent one of their secretaries to try and break me, huh?" She smiled—the kind only a well-practiced woman under stress could pull off.

Lillian nodded, slipped out of her long wool coat, and held it open.

Billie's face was round with a masculine draw to her jawline. She looked every inch of her regal French and Menominee Tribe heritage. Everything about her body language wanted to refuse Lillian's offer of warmth, but in the end, she shrugged her shoulders and dropped her eyes.

Lillian draped her coat around Billie, tucking it beneath her chin. Foolish men, they should know better than to try to break a woman with the same cruelty they used on each other. The way to find out what Billie knew about Dillinger was to get inside her heart and cut it wide open—and Lillian had just the blade for the job.

She pulled her gold and pearl compact from her pocket and placed it on the table between them, then took a seat across from Billie. "You need anything? They give you enough to eat?"

Billie rolled her dark eyes.

Lillian cleared her throat. "My name is Lillian Holley. I'm the sheriff of Lake County, in Indiana."

A flash of surprise crossed Billie's features before she tamped it out.

"I fought very hard to convince the DOI to transfer John to my jail when they extradited him from Arizona."

Billie's dark-red lips curled. "My man didn't kill no cop out there, and he ain't done those bank jobs your people keep claimin' neither."

Lillian nodded. "I wanted to see justice done, of course, but I had a selfish reason too. I thought bringing him to Indiana would help a friend of ... ours, to find the peace she needs to move on." Lillian pulled the compact open and spun it around.

Mamie's pale, dead face stared out.

Billie's eyes went wide. "What the—" She scooted back, the chain on her shackled wrists pulling tight.

"Heya, Billie," Mamie said.

Billie eyed Lillian's mouth. "Are you doing this? Makin' that mirror talk?"

Lillian shook her head. Billie reached over and tapped the mirror with a pink fingernail. Mamie yelped, and Billie jerked away, her black hair flopping. This sent Mamie into a fit of giggles.

Billie looked at Lillian and frowned. "What are you playin' at with this?" She pointed a finger at the mirror.

"I'm not playing at anything," Lillian said. "You don't believe that John is a killer, so I brought one of his victims to see you."

Billie threw her head back and laughed. "Johnny would never do in a moll."

The morning I got done in," Mamie said. "I was stayin' at Cherry's place in the city 'cause I'd missed the bus home."

Billie shook her head—aggressive jerks that took her chin out over her shoulders.

"Don't shake that pretty lil' head at me," Mamie snapped. "We all knew John was on the creep with her."

The corners of Billie's mouth slammed down in violent spikes. Her black eyes blazed. "I said, John would never!"

Lillian interrupted. "He was seen circling the block in an unknown car after your arrest. One Patricia Cherrington, or Cherry as you all call her, behind the wheel."

Billie turned her firestorm eyes on Lillian.

Lillian swallowed hard and went on, "Does John have any tattoos, any animals or anything?"

"Tattoos?" Billie scoffed.

"You gotta face this, Bee," Mamie said. "Johnny was at Cherry's place that morning. He went there to be with her but found me in her bed instead. Then he done me in to keep me quiet."

Billie's head was still swinging as tears gathered on her dark eyelashes. "No." She pressed the sleeves of Lillian's coat to her face. "It ain't true."

Lillian leaned forward. "A tattoo of a wolf, maybe?"

"A wolf?" Billie stared at Lillian. "What are you asking me?"

"Does John have any tattoos, or carry around a picture of a wolf as a totem, anything like that?"

"I don't understand," Billie said.

"She's asking cause I seen a wolf when I died." Mamie's voice lowered as the memory clouded her eyes. "Big teeth, snarling. Comin' at me." She shuddered.

Billie shook her head. "Johnny ain't got no tattoos. He don't go in for stuff like that. But a wolf ..." She paused. "There's this one fella, big Irish guy, started hanging around late last year. They call him Mac Tíre."

"Tire, like on a car?" Lillian asked.

"No," Billie said. "Johnny told me back in Ireland it means something about a lone wolf."

Lillian pulled the mirror back and snapped it shut. "Where can I find this Mac Tíre?"

"Oh no," Billie said, "you don't want to find this fella. Gave us all the heebie-jeebies when he was around, even Johnny."

Lillian lowered her head. "Listen to me, Billie. Hoover's put out a big reward on John, and those men out there have permission to bring him in, dead or alive.

"My husband Roy was sheriff until he was gunned down in a shoot-out." Lillian pressed her tongue against her teeth, waiting for the knot in her throat to loosen. "There were two years left on his term, so the county commissioners offered me the job. The only reason I let them pin this badge on my blouse was to honor him and keep him close." Lillian put her hand on Billie's. "I know what it's like to love a man so much you'd carry on living his life for him if he left it behind."

Billie sniffled and wiped her nose on Lillian's coat sleeve. "I don't want him to get hurt. Stupid man, he'll try to come busting in here and break me out." She met Lillian's gaze, her eyes softer now. "Will you bring him in alive?"

"I'll do my darndest."

Tears gathered on Billie's eyelashes, glittering in the harsh overhead light. "There's a place up north John and the boys use when they need to get away. If he ain't in Chicago waiting on me, he went there."

"Up north?" Lillian asked.

"Wisconsin," Billie said. "Manitowish Waters. There's a place called the Little Bohemia Lodge."

Lillian shivered—whether from the chill in the room or excitement at getting the drop on Dillinger, she couldn't say. She squeezed Billie's hand. "Thank you."

Billie squeezed back, holding Lillian's hand firmly in hers. "Now it's your turn to listen to me. Woman or not, if you're the law, Mac won't make no bones about hurtin' you. He's a stone-cold killer, that one."

Lillian bit her cheek. A part of her wanted to rush out and tell Agent Purvis everything, to ask for his help bringing Dillinger back to Crown Point. But ... if Purvis caught Dillinger, they'd never send him back to Indiana, and they'd never investigate the murder of a lowly moll. Lillian sighed. If she ever wanted to look in a mirror again without a dead woman staring back at her, she'd have to do this on her own.

Lillian stood and returned the compact to her pocket.

"Hey," Billie called.

When Lillian turned, Billie offered her a sad smile—the kind only a woman with a broken-open heart could pull off. "Don't forget your coat, sheriff lady."

22 April 1934 – Sunday

SLENDER ASPEN-BIRCH TREES lined Highway 51, and whorls of snowflakes drifted against the windshield of Lillian's new black Ford Model 18.

Mamie's jade eyes stared out from the rear-view mirror. "We there yet?" Her voice had a smacked-gum quality to it tonight.

Lillian had needed to wait before taking this trip to Wisconsin. She'd had to shake the tails Agent Purvis put on her after she left Chicago, and there was still the fallout to deal with: telegrams, phone calls, and newspaper folk on her day and night. All clamoring to get an interview with the *woman* sheriff who'd let Dillinger escape. Lillian frowned.

"You'll get wrinkles, you keep all that frownin' up," Mamie said.

Lillian scoffed. "A murdered moll is haunting me, the most

wanted man in America escaped from my jail, and my husband was killed leaving me holding the badge. But what I *should* be worried about is wrinkles!"

Mamie stuck her tongue out at Lillian.

The sun had drifted behind the naked branches of the paper-barked aspens, casting dusky twilight hues around the cedar cabin as Lillian turned into the driveway of the Little Bohemia Lodge. She parked, spun the chamber of her .38, slid the pistol into her ankle holster, then covered it with the leg of Roy's brown tweed trousers.

"*Pssst*," Mamie hissed. "Take me with you."

Lillian tossed a glance at the rear-view mirror. "I'm not carrying around an open mirror. Stay here."

"Wench!" Mamie hollered as Lillian pushed the car door closed with a hip.

It took less than three seconds before the compact was rattling in Lillian's pocket.

A sign in the front window announced a dollar Sunday dinner special, and a healthy crowd was gathered in the main dining room.

"Spittin' possums," Lillian muttered. She tugged her rust-colored cloche hat down to shadow her eyes and crouched low as she slipped around the east side of the lodge. A patch of light spilled from a window near the back. Staying close to the wall, Lillian leaned around to peer inside.

Dillinger and two other men sat playing cards at a table in the rear of the main room.

God's wounds! Lillian's heart punched into her throat like someone had pushed the clutch in on her innards. She pressed herself back against the log siding.

The lodge's front door creaked open, then shut with a slam. Men's voices, drunk and laughing, charged into the night. Three young men sauntered through the drifting snow, got into a burgundy Chevrolet coupe, then headed out to the road.

Headlights snapped on at the end of the dirt driveway. A tight feeling of apprehension coiled in Lillian's belly. Someone had arrived after her and been waiting down there. More gangsters or—

A burst of gunfire split the night like an axe through timber. Men screamed. The coupe's doors flew open, and the three men slid out onto the gravel, fleeing the car.

Gun shots came faster and more furious. Lillian staggered forward, her heels catching on the uneven ground. She fell, icy rocks gouging into her knees, and pressed her palms over her ears. Was this the last sound Roy had heard as he entered Farmer Millford's house that day? Hot pinpricks of panic burned at the edges of her eyes.

Footsteps pounded down the driveway toward the lodge; men running, long topcoats flapping behind them. *By all the double-barreled snails!* Those monkeyshine DOI boys were here.

Lillian yanked the pistol from her ankle holster and bolted around the back corner of the lodge. Several people fled from the rear of the building; dark silhouettes that scattered through the bare-winter trees, headed toward the lake.

Then, in a slice of light from the back door, Lillian saw Patricia Cherrington, the woman Dillinger had last been seen with, with a man behind her, pushing her into the gathering darkness.

Dillinger.

Lillian stepped onto the path, the pistol rattling in her hands as she raised it at the fleeing pair. Did she have it in her to shoot him? What if he escaped again and another woman died?

"John Dillinger, stop!"

Dillinger and Cherry skidded to a halt.

There, in the near pitch of dark, Lillian could feel him grinning—so darn certain of himself. She wanted to spit.

"Well, lookie here, Cherry," Dillinger said. "If it ain't my favorite lady sheriff."

"Get on the ground," Lillian demanded.

"Thing is, Sheriff, I got a pressing engagement, and I hate being late to a party." He snickered.

"I'm not laughing, John."

"No." Dillinger stopped laughing. "I can tell you aren't at that."

With a flick of his wrist, Dillinger slipped a pocketknife from his sleeve. He grabbed Cherry's arm and jerked her in front of him, her startled laugh cut off abruptly by the blade pressed against her throat.

"Put your pistol down, Lillian, or I'll slice this moll's throat open like a fresh-caught trout."

Cherry squirmed in his arms. "John—".

Dillinger dug the blade into her neck. She squeaked and snapped her mouth shut.

Panic pealed in Lillian's head like a clapper in a bell. Agent Purvis and those DOI boys with their scornful glances loomed in her mind's eye—women belonged in offices, fingernails clicking on typewriter keys, not out in the field with dangerous men caught in their gun sights.

The compact in Lillian's pocket clattered, gold-plated edges chattering like metal teeth, reminding her why she was here. She let her finger fall from the trigger and slowly lowered the barrel. Lillian couldn't let this man kill a woman in front of her, and she didn't have the heart to take his life.

In the dark, Dillinger laughed.

Lillian bit into her cheek to keep the angry tears at bay, then slipped the pistol into her pocket, and showed Dillinger her empty hands. "Let her go, John."

"You stay right there, Lillian." Dillinger walked backward. "Don't you move a muscle!"

Cherry struggled as he dragged her by the neck. Her long heels carved gouges in the dirt. When he'd gotten far enough away, Dillinger shoved her to the ground and ran.

"Johnny!" Cherry begged through gasping sobs as she lay in the dirt. "Don't leave me!"

Lillian stumbled over tree roots toward the crying woman. She locked a hand on Cherry's shoulder. "Patricia, he's gone. Now get up before those DOI boys come and gun us both down, you hear."

Cherry's sobs quieted to sniffles, and she let herself be led around the building.

Two cars skidded to a stop in front of Lillian, kicking up loose gravel. DOI agents ran from the lodge—Agent Purvis among them. "They're headed to the lake," he yelled. "We'll catch 'em on the other side!" He jumped onto the running board of a gray Panhard, steam puffing from its tailpipe in the cold night air.

"Hey!" Agent Purvis glowered at her. "Hold that girl here till we get back."

Lillian opened the back door of her car and assisted Cherry in. "When you want to talk to my prisoner, Agent Purvis, you know where to find her." She got into the driver's seat and slammed the door. Her entire body shook like an autumn leaf clinging to a naked branch, ready to give way. She'd had Dillinger dead-to-rights, and let him go. Maybe he hadn't killed Mamie, but he was still a murderer, a bank robber, and an escapee from *her* jail. The first female sheriff of Lake County, her reputation would be forever tarnished now.

Cherry pressed her face into the leather seat in the back and sobbed.

Mamie's eyes, glittering like devastated diamonds, waited for Lillian in the rear-view mirror—tears slid down her cheeks. Lillian sighed. It was going to be a long ride home.

23 April 1934 – Monday

LILLIAN STOOD in the hallway outside her office, finished reading the telegram, folded it, and placed it in her pocket. She opened the door and went in.

Soft-pink light peeked through the front windows, spilling sunshine across her desk. Cherry lay sprawled on the brown, deco-style settee in the corner, a gauze bandage on her neck. She stirred at the smell of fresh coffee Lillian poured from the kettle on the side-board, took the offered mug, then settled back into the mohair cushions.

"Look"—Cherry yawned and sipped her coffee—"you think I know somethin' that'll bring John in, but I don't." She smoothed her fingers through her short black hair. "We're just molls to them. Lose one, pick up another. 'Cept maybe Billie. John wept like a damn baby when them G-men snagged her in Chicago." Cherry offered a smile, but it didn't send away the sadness in her brown eyes.

"You girls are close?" Lillian asked.

"We try an' help each other out. Sometimes when your man is away or he's doing a stretch, we're all each other's got, you know."

"That's good to know, 'cause I've got one here that needs your help." Lillian set Roy's chipped coffee cup on the desk and pulled her wool coat off the hall-tree mirror.

Mamie's face hovered there, hazel-gold eyes brimming with sorrow.

Cherry's eyes widened. Her mouth fell open. "What kinda chicanery you pullin'?" She speared Lillian with a dagger-edged look.

"It's me, Cherry," Mamie said.

"Mamie?" Cherry stood and ran a hand along the mirror's surface, shaking her head. "How'd you get in there?"

"Ain't quite sure." Mamie gave a half-hearted chuckle. "After I got done in, I wasn't really gone yet, it was dark, and I couldn't see nothing. There was water running in the washroom, and a man whistling. Then I see this light, real faraway." She bit at her bottom lip. "Was only the sunshine caught in the mirror over your bureau, but it was all I could see in the darkness, so I went to it." Mamie's peridot eyes filled with tears. "Been stuck in here since."

"Who was it done you in?" Cherry asked.

Lillian spoke up, "We thought it was Dillinger at first."

"No," Cherry scoffed, "why would Johnny have been at my place?"

Lillian and Mamie exchanged a glance.

Cherry looked back and forth between the other women. "No way! Billie'd kill me if she even *thought* I was making eyes at her fella." Her forehead furrowed. "That's really what you thought?" She dug clenched fists into her hips. Mamie and Lillian said nothing. "Well, to hell with that. I ain't no tramp!"

Mamie raised her voice. "Go on all you want, Cherry, but you ain't the one that's dead and gone, left with visions of the big, bad wolf to haunt you forever!"

"A wolf?" Cherry said.

"Yeah," Mamie whispered. I seen one while I ... you know. But I can't figure what it means."

"Was it a big gray head, snarling teeth with spit?" Cherry asked.

Mamie nodded. "Yeah, how'd you kn—"

The pink in Cherry's cheeks drained so quickly, Lillian had to grab her arms and help her back onto the settee.

"Mac," Cherry said. "Got himself a tattoo of it, here." She pointed at the ribs on her right side. "I seen it once when we was"—she paused —"together."

Cherry grimaced at Lillian, and Lillian's knees went wobbly. She plopped onto the sofa. After interviewing Billie, she'd wondered about Mac Tíre, that thing she'd said about the lone wolf. And now, here was the proof. Lillian put her head in her hands. She'd been so dead set on getting Dillinger as Mamie's killer, she'd gone blind to the other option—the one man Billie had warned her would kill a woman.

Lillian and Cherry jumped as the force of Mamie's voice rattled the mirror in its frame. "Dammit, Cherry! You were seeing Mac too?"

Tears flew from Cherry's eyes. "I didn't know!" she cried. "He's real jealous, found out I was still married." She looked at Lillian. "My husband, he's doing a stretch in Leavenworth. Art's been away so long, I just got lonely is all." Tears streamed down Cherry's cheeks. "I didn't mean to get no one hurt, I swear."

Lillian wrapped an arm around Cherry's shoulders. "*Shhh*, now. We know you didn't." She glanced up, fighting back her own tears. "Oh, Mamie, dear. I'm so sorry. I thought—"

Mamie looked away, her tears constant rivers now.

"If it's any consolation"—Lillian pulled the telegram from her pocket—"this came across the wire about an hour ago. Says early this morning, two men identified as members of the dangerous Dillinger gang: Lester Gillis, aka Baby Face Nelson, and Mac Tíre, true identity unknown, were shot and killed attempting to flee across state lines into Minnesota in a stolen car." She refolded the telegram. "It seems justice was—"

Mamie squeaked. Lillian's head snapped up.

A soft golden light filled the mirror, washing over Lillian and Cherry. Both women froze as they stared in wide-eyed wonder.

"Someone's here," Mamie whispered. She turned, though no one was visible behind her.

When she faced Lillian again, Mamie was a fading shadow, lingering in the light spread out around her. "It's your Roy. He says I know the truth now, and...I can go."

Her Roy.

The tears Lillian had been holding back for too long, burst from their captivity, and she pressed an arm to her face, sobbing into her sleeve.

"Don't cry," Mamie said. "You got guts, lady lawman. You done right by me, and Roy says he's real proud of you."

Behind Mamie, a head and shoulders appeared, cast in silhouette against the light. A man's voice came, faded and pocked, like a well-loved record played until worn. "Love...you...Lillian Holley..." The voice drifted away.

"Roy?" Lillian stood and touched the mirror. "Mamie, you still there?"

There was no answer.

Lillian cried harder, tears fleeing her eyes like escaped prisoners; her heart broken open—and Mamie the blade.

Dillinger was still on the loose, but with the DOI boys on his heels, he'd be locked up soon enough. She'd bumbled through this afraid and uncertain, yet somehow, she'd made Roy proud. Lillian pressed a hand against her pocket—the gold compact lay still—Mamie was finally at rest.

A shine of light, like the springtime glare of a mountain sunrise, swept across the mirror, blinding her. When Lillian's vision cleared, the dead no longer lingered in her reflection.

THE JOURNEY
APRIL BENSON

The wind whips past the train as she surges continually forward. Icy remembrance plasters itself to the cargo hull in the shapes of jagged conical teeth – teeth blackened by the soot of time and hardened by driving resolve.

How long has it been since the train has come to a screeching, shattering halt? How many moons have passed since the black icicles have melted under the fist of friction?

Too long? Perhaps.

I am told there is a time and a place for it all—that all things, both bitter and sweet, carry a purpose. Every arrival yields new passengers. Every departure summons the ghosts of those who have gone. The seats are worn with memories—a different story discovered in each soda stain. In each piece of gum, thrust on the underside of the seat cushion. In each torn seam bursting with yellow spongy fluff.

Such memories guide each train differently. Each train travels to different destinations. Some know the itinerary, while others decide along the way. Some meet delays, while others skip stops. Amidst the chaos of the stations, all trains possess the same purpose—to move onward.

The stories of one's life merge into one as the train surges onward down the tracks. These stories play upon the decision of the train as she approaches a divergence in the railway. Each fork, a single decision —irreversible once decidedly made. The train never turns back, for the tracks go only forward. She is forced to leave the past behind, even if she wistfully wishes to spin the wheels backward in time.

Thick puffs of cloud billow from the train pipe. Wisps of thought whip across the frosted windows before disappearing into the blackness behind. If one listens carefully, he may hear the passing thoughts whispering remembrance through the thin sheet of glass. Bitter and sweet, the thoughts attach to the tongues of the passengers and, in truth, are never truly lost. Shared whispers revise and shape thoughts into feelings – feelings never truly forgotten.

With both memory and feeling and thought intertwining within the hull, the train experiences the burdens and respites of life throughout the journey. At times, the train runs smoothly as butter across the railway ties—elation assuaging her strain. Upon other times, such as now, the train slogs onward—the encumbrance wearing her wheels into disrepair.

The train braves winter's fury as it restlessly beats her weatherworn hide. She watches the clouds—black as raven's feathers—stalk her and eclipse her shadow. She grimaces under the serrated teeth of frost resiliently latching onto her side.

The burden of remembrance. The pain of gnashing fear. The darkness of endless winter.

Where is hope? At these times, one asks such questions.

Where is the sun? No one can quite recall the golden hue.

Was warmth merely a dream?

But it cannot be so...for the heat of life is breathed from the chilled lips of every passenger—both big and small, dark and light, male and female—in every moment. A constant reminder that, even in the coldest regions of the journey, there is warmth and sunlight soon to come.

We need only to dress ourselves in blankets until that time. We need only share heat with one another until that moment. We simply must believe—believe that the journey will take us beyond the wasteland of the frozen tundra. Believe that the journey, though harsh and unforgiving at times, will sharpen us into the strongest of swords. Believe that the journey will draw us closer within the circle of relationship. And finally, help us understand:

Light can only be truly seen in the darkness.
Warmth can only be truly felt in the cold.
Courage can only be truly gathered from fear.
Faith can only be truly accepted in doubt.
Alas! A small light twinkles in the distance.
Is it hope? Only the journey can tell.

THE ROAD TO EL TESORO
ROBERT SPILLER

S ally and I were exhausted when I finally let the old paint have her head. She made for a small stand of saguaro cactus, which as far as I could see, was the only shade for miles.

I stroked Sally's withers. "I couldn't agree more, old girl. What say you and me take a break? I think we lost them, at least for now." In the meager shade, I got down from Sally.

It's funny how a full canteen can sometimes feel feather light when you bring it to your lips, but that same canteen weighs like a millstone when it's close to empty.

Shouldn't be true but it is.

Especially when the sun is shining down and heating the desert sand like Arizona's own slice of Hades

I avoided Sally's accusing, thirsty eyes and sat down heavy. I felt guilty drinking the last of the water. But hellfire, what did it matter? That final little sip wouldn't count a Tinker's Dam if Sally and I didn't stumble on a watery miracle and soon.

Like it had a mind of its own, my hand went straight for Grandpa Teddy's all tore up copybook I brushed my hand across the blood stains and turned to the opening page and read his words out loud.

"For my Grandson, Willard. Life ain't always fair, boy, but sometimes if you put your head down and keep pushing, it can get almost good."

About as close as Grandpa ever got to poetry. "I think I'm about all pushed out Gramps. I sure could use a big old slice of El Tesoro right about now."

I shut my eyes and let a long-ago memory swim across my fevered brain—me and Grandpa sitting on the bank of Moon Creek. I was maybe seven years old. "Ten long years ago," I whispered.

The sandpaper sound of my voice almost pulled me out of the dream, but I pushed on. That day's excuse had been to go fishing, but truth be told, I just wanted Gramps to tell me more about El Tesoro.

"The whole town hides in a deep canyon near the Mexico border. For miles around, there ain't nothing but sand, cactus, and Gila Monsters, but the town itself is paradise. And in the center—"

"Is the Grove," I shouted.

If I'd heard those opening story words once, I'd heard them a thousand times. And I never got tired of the hearing. "All full of every kind of shade and fruit tree and the Old Man."

Grandpa shot me a pretend frown like he was all put out that I interrupted his telling. I knew better.

"Who's spinning this yarn, youngster?"

"You are Grandpa." It was my turn to pretend. I wiped the smile off my face and got all sorry looking. "I won't bust in again," I lied.

"See that you don't." Gramps took his time lighting his pipe, knowing I'd be chomping hard on that bit by the time he got back to the tale. He took a long pull on that pipe, blew out a perfect smoke ring, then started up again. "Anyway, even the Comanche leave El Tesoro alone, unless..."

He paused, seeing if I'd take the bait and finish the sentence. Lord knew I wanted to. But I pressed my seven-year-old lips together hard to show the old man I could wait.

"...unless they'd been invited. Then they're as welcome as rain after a dry spell."

For the next few minutes, I let my daydream take me through Grandpa's telling how the town knew who belonged and who didn't. Townsfolks were all kinds. Mexicans, Apaches, Kickapoos, white folk, black folks, even the occasional Comanche, and all mixed together and not doing each other hurt.

Back in the here and now, a smile spread across my face in the recollecting. It almost took away the heartache of remembering that Grandpa Teddy died alone in a hospital half out of his mind.

THE MORNING GRANDPA Teddy died I woke up unable to breathe.

The sun had yet to rise. In the dark, my hands came to my throat, and I wrestled with a crazy need to hurl myself through my attic bedroom window and go running into the desert.

Maybe never stop.

Even a fall likely to break both my legs would be preferable to forcing another breath of stifling air into my lungs.

I stumbled from my bed and threw on my one set of grimy overalls and holey hand-me-down boots. By the time I made it downstairs, I was at least not feeling like a fish out of water. I stood out of sight at the bottom of the stairs 'til I pulled myself together. Wouldn't do for Uncle Norman and my cousins to see me all red in the face. The sons-of-bitches would ride me all through the workday.

Hell, Kennedy and Dwain—both grown and both a whole lot bigger than me—rode me like a quarter horse on the best of days. Never let me forget what a favor they had done me when Pa and Ma died all up and sudden of the Typhoid.

"It was the Christian thing to do," Norman told me when he thought I needed reminding. "Also, nobody else was lining up to take in the orphaned whelp of a failed preacher. Where would you be now if we hadn't opened our hearts and home to you?"

The ritual was so predictable I'd gotten my answer down to where I could recite it in my sleep. "I'd be some no-account drifter Uncle Norman. Probably dead."

I got no proof, but I think the Jensens liked hearing the 'dead' part. All the while me wanting to tell them just what I really thought of their Christian charity. But I never did. The one time I objected to

Pa being called a failed preacher—although it was true—Uncle Norman took his belt to my backside for having sass.

So, I kept my opinions to myself, the better part of valor and all that. Besides, I didn't care a mule's rear end what Uncle Norman or my sadistic cousins thought. As far as I could see, thought never entered into it whenever they opened their stupid mouths to speak.

"Grab yourself some hot cakes and coffee, boy. Got some bad news for you."

It was there in the Jensens' kitchen, over a bitter cup of coffee, I got the news about Grandpa Teddy dying. For a moment in the middle of the telling, I got that choking feeling again, but I kept it to myself.

"It's a blessing, boy. You know how he'd gotten." Uncle Norman trotted out his phony baloney sympathy, but the twins didn't even try.

Kennedy twirled a finger around his ear and whispered, "Crazy."

I know my uncle heard the remark, but since he pretty much agreed with it, he didn't say boo to his jackass of a son.

If I had a gun, all three of them would have been leaking daylight. Right then, I resolved to not speak another word about Grandpa to any of them.

My uncle laid a heavy hand on my arm. "The best thing I've found to help a body deal with grief is hard work. The twins and I mended fences for two straight days when my Kathleen passed on.

Kathleen Jensen was a humorless, raw-boned, bible-thumping woman who I suspected found life on a hard-scrabble Arizona ranch a sight less appealing than walking hand-in-hand with Jesus on them streets of gold. I never did find out what she died of.

As it turned out, I did find out what Grandpa Teddy died of. He killed himself.

THE STRANGE AND darn inconvenient thing about the desert is that it can be skillet hot in the daytime but come night, the desert wind seems like it wants to chill a fella straight into the bone. Grandpa Teddy once explained to me it had to do with clouds. The way he told it was deserts have hardly any rain, so they're lacking when it comes to clouds. With nothing in the sky to hold in the warm, night swallows up all that daytime heat, and within hours of sundown, the temperature drops like a bucket in a well.

Me and Sally hiked along a ridge of the Madrean Mountains. If I followed that ridge south, it would take me into Senora, Mexico. And I figured I might as well keep moving since it was too darn cold to sleep. Not to mention, I needed to put some miles between me and the folks who might be looking for me. I could just picture Dwain and Uncle Norman with their faces all hard and angry. Hell, they'd be out for blood as much for me stealing Sally as putting a dent in Kennedy's thick skull.

Even though my bastard cousin deserved that beating. Yes, sir, he deserved that and a lot more.

THAT MORNING, at Grandpa Teddy's funeral, a man from the hospital told me about Grandpa's suicide and gave me a potato sack full of Grandpa's things. A pad of real store-bought hand tacks, colored pencils, a fountain pen and a bottle of India Ink, two dollars and eleven cents, and a copybook like I'd seen Pa use to write down his sermons.

Uncle Norman and the twins took the money, tacks, pencils, and the pen and ink claiming it would help pay for my board. They would have taken the book, but it was mostly just some scribblings Grandpa'd done. A few maps. Some hand drawings.

"You hold on to that, Willard," Uncle Norman had said all gracious, like he hadn't just robbed me of stuff rightfully mine. "Help you remember your Grandpa,"

I can't believe I thanked the son-of-a-bitch.

A few hours later, it was just me and Kennedy bringing in some strays that had wandered into a long arroyo. When we was taking a break in the shade of some mesquite bushes, I got out the book and was flipping through the pages when Kennedy snatched it from me.

"What kind of nonsense did that crazy old coot have to write about."

I was hot and tired, and on the best of days, I had a baker's dozen of reasons to hate Kennedy Jensen. But the hate that grabbed me then was something brand new. Something that rose up from my heart like lava shooting up out of a volcano. I could feel it burning in my chest. "Give that back, you piece of horse shit."

Kennedy wasn't used to me calling him out. His eyes went all flashing and wild. "What'd you call me?"

I should have backed down, should have just asked nice for the book. Then maybe Kennedy wouldn't have done what he did. Keeping his eyes dead on mine, he ripped out the first page, the page Grandpa had dedicated to me and me alone.

I lunged for the book.

Kennedy backhanded me, and sent me sprawling in the sand.

Easy as you please, my cousin rose to his feet, ripping pages as he did. First one, then a handful.

A red mist clouded my vision. In the brambles of the mesquite, I found a rock. It was Kennedy's own fault he chose that moment to turn his back on me.

I don't even remember getting up from the dirt, but the next moment I was throwing that stone, throwing it hard. It caught Kennedy in the back of the head.

He went down.

That ought to have been enough, but it wasn't. I fell on his back, grabbed his bloody hair, and smashed his face into the hard pack. Blood sprayed all over those pages my cousin somehow still clutched in his greedy mitts.

I pushed off Kennedy. I didn't even check to see if he was breathing. In a wind that seemed to come out of nowhere, the first of the ripped pages went flapping down into the arroyo.

For the next few minutes, I collected my treasure, then I thought of Kennedy. He was still breathing, but the breaths sounded funny, not right somehow, liquid. But even if I could have gotten the bastard across his horse, there was no taking him back. Uncle Norman and Dwain would skin me alive if they didn't kill me outright.

It's strange how a single moment, a decision, divides your life in two pieces. I wasn't going back. I would light out across the Senora Desert, and head into Mexico.

I took Sally, Kennedy's horse, and left him Duchess, the nag that Uncle Norman always had me saddle up. If Kennedy woke, he could ride back on her. If he didn't wake, the Jensens knew where we rode off to that morning. They'd come looking for their precious boy.

I put out of my mind what would happen if coyotes found Kennedy first, came running at the smell of blood.

I packed up food, water, gear, all that I could carry, and with one last look back at my bloody cousin, rode away from that arroyo.

BACK UNDER A STARLIT SKY, I started talking to Sally or maybe just to myself. "Too bad Kennedy didn't have more water or even a blanket." I let my fingers trail into Sally's mane. "As long as I'm wishing, make that two blankets."

I stumbled and almost went headfirst into a patch of prickly pears.

If a fella lives in the Arizona desert long enough, he learns about them cactus pears. There ain't a lot, but some water's growing right there out of the desert sand. I tied off Sally and pulled Kennedy's Barlow knife out of my saddle bag.

"You can have the first drink, old girl. It's only fair." I wrapped my hand in my belt and went to work on them pricklies. After stripping the spines, I squeezed maybe ten drops into my palm. "Ain't ice water at the Morgan Hotel, but at least it's wet."

Like it was the best treat on God's green earth, Sally lapped up those drops and the next ones too. The third sweet drops I drank myself, then went to work on the rest of them pears. By the time I got me and Sally enough juice to call it a proper drink, the sun was creeping up over the mountains. Chewing on the last meat of a pear, I looked around to see where we ended up. I found myself staring up at a big old rock ledge that looked like a kitchen table, right down to rust streaks for the legs.

Then I remembered something.

I pulled out Grandpa's book and went rifling through them pages and there, pretty as you please, was my table rock ledge. Grandpa even wrote about it.

Maker's Altar. Came here as a boy from the Grove. Rite of Passage.

I guess I was paying too much attention to that book because I never heard the sound of riders approaching. What I did hear was the voice of my Uncle Norman.

"He's around here somewhere, boys. I can feel it."

Sally heard them words same as me. Before I could stop her, she went to nickering.

"Up there in the rocks." Cousin Dwain. A shot rang out and glanced off the table rock, sending a rock sliver close to my eye.

I cried out. My hand came away from my face all red with blood.

Sally rose up and bolted. I reached for her reins and came up empty.

"I think I got him Pa." Dwain's voice was a mixture of triumph and something near close to blood lust.

I could see nothing to do but to put that table rock between me and them below. As I skittered around the ledge and climbed, more shots rang out.

"Quit your firing, you dang fool." Territorial Marshall Addis. "Will, you need to come down from there. You got no place to go, son."

I wiped the blood with my sleeve and knew Addis was right. I was on foot, wounded, and if I didn't give myself up, Dwain or Uncle Norman would have an excuse to leave me dead out here in the Senora. I probably would have done just that, but my foot slipped, and the next thing I knew I was falling ass over elbow. My head hit something sharp, and the world went dark.

"WILLARD EARNEST DOWD, time to wake up, son. Might as well open them peepers and greet the day." A voice, gravely but kind, with a just a hint of a chuckle.

I opened one eye and looked up to see a round-faced old man with two side braids of pure white—Indian style—that spilled over his shoulders.

He nodded his approval. "That's better. We have a lot to talk about." He extended a hand, and I took it. I'd been laying on a pallet made up of a thin mattress and an old timey quilt. Grandpa had one just like it, said his mother had made it. The room was small, rough-hewn and smelled of pine.

Surprisingly strong, the old man pulled me to my feet. My hand came to my hair, and I felt bandages. "I hit my head."

"Good thing you have Charlie's thick skull." This time the chuckle was out in the open. I couldn't remember the last time anyone called my grandpa by the name of Charlie—him being Charles Theodore Dowd and all.

I caught the old fella eyeing me with something like a smile, but also the look hid something else, something I couldn't put a name to. "I knew your grandpa when he was just a boy and I got to tell you he saddened and disappointed me. We had a pact, him and me, and he didn't keep up his end. He chose instead to follow his fool son down a rabbit hole."

He waved a gnarled hand as if to brush away his words. "Although you and I would not be having this conversation if he hadn't chased after your father." He took my shoulders in his weathered hands and studied me for a long moment. I could swear he was about to tear up when he released me. He turned away. "Right now, that's neither here nor there. Come, we haven't a lot of time."

I didn't like the sound of that, but I kept my peace. The old man led me out the door and into a forest so thick that try as I might, I couldn't see more than twenty feet in any direction. As far as I knew, nothing like it existed anywhere near where I fell. "Excuse me Sir, is this El Tesoro?"

He sighed then grinned like he personally planted every tree in the grove. "This is indeed El Tesoro. This Grove and the village beyond. I guess you could say I'm also El Tesoro as are the folks that live down below. And before you ask, yes, I am the Old Man."

The Old Man. From the stories, I knew he quickened the ears of the deaf and made the lame walk. In my mind the Old Man could do just about anything from fly as high as a mountain to walking through fire. "If you don't mind my askin' Sir. Are you God?"

My guide chewed on his lower lip like the question might take some figuring. Finally, he shook his head. "I don't think I am, at least not the way them Christians talk about God. I didn't create no heaven and no Earth. And I damn well don't know everything under the sun."

He took off at a pace that made me pretty near run it to keep up. We came to a stream. "These waters are Samuel's Fountain. Funny name since there ain't no fountain and Samuel is long gone."

"Who—"

"Samuel was the first Old Man, back when the world was young. But the name seems all wrong somehow. Shoot, there've been as many Old Women as Old Men."

Funny how some answers only lead to more questions like there might be no end to it all. I decided that I'd save those questions and just keep my ears wide open.

He bent low, scooped some water into his hands, and brought it to my lips. The taste of it filled my mouth like no water I'd ever drank before.

"These waters are the lifeblood of this place and don't show on any map out there in the world you know, not any more than El Tesoro itself does. You and me, we're going to follow the Fountain down into the village so's you can meet some folks before your time is up. More importantly, they need to meet you."

We hadn't even left the trees when we came across a woman. She —all red-cheeked, round, and with child—walked right up 'til she was standing not a foot from me. "I had to see for myself." She cast a disapproving eye on my guide. "There was no telling when you'd bring the lad around."

If the Old Man was offended by the woman's scolding, he didn't show it.

She stood on tiptoe and cocking her head, took to giving me an inspection. "He's Charlie's kin, that's for certain." Her hand, all soft and warm, came to my face. "I was sorry to hear of his passing. But I guess all things happen as the waters want."

"Did you know my grandfather well, ma'am?"

Her eyes filled a little then she gave them a wipe. "Know him, it was Charlie who rescued me, set me to rights. He brought me to live here when I was a girl. Charlie wasn't much more than a boy himself when he gathered me to this place."

The time didn't seem right. Grandpa was ancient when he died, and this woman couldn't have been more than thirty, thirty-five at the most. And pregnant. I looked back at the Old Man to see if it was all right for me to ask more about Grandpa. He nodded.

"How did he come to rescue you, ma'am."

"Call me Cassie." She sighed. "A right proper rescue it was. My father was a drifter and had me whoring by the time I was twelve. I was half starved when Charlie snatched me from my pa's clutches."

"Tell him the rest, Cassie."

The woman reddened. "Of course. Of course. It's been so long I forget. I was blind as a newborn bat."

There it was, an honest-to-goodness El Tesoro miracle like the kind Grandpa had told me about. I turned round to the Old Man. "You healed her."

He shrugged. "You could say that, but it was more this place, these waters, did the healing. Charlie and I took the hurt and pain from her heart, but El Tesoro opened her eyes."

The woman hooked her arm into mine, and all of us set off to walking along that stream. As we came down into the village, a handful of folks met us at the town's edge. There were two obvious Indian folk, I'm thinking Apaches, but I wouldn't swear to it.

Each approached me, and one-by-one, gathered me into a hug. The last, a tall, dark-skinned fella with a beaded buckskin vest, eyed the Old Man.

"I wish you'd change your mind. We could use some new blood, especially..." Now the fella gave the Old Man an accusing glare.

The Old Man returned the glare and shook his head.

"...especially since he's Charlie's kin," The Indian fella finished.

The flash of anger in the Old Man's eyes took another moment to subside. Something had gone unsaid between the two men, and I thought I knew what it was. Again, I chose to keep my peace.

Cassie spoke up to break the awkward silence. "The rules exist for a reason, Lawrence. Trust the wisdom of the waters."

Since I drank them same waters, I'd been feeling different. Thoughts I'd never felt before had been running across my brain. Can't say I liked them all. "I don't get to stay, do I?" I knew the answer, but I had to hear someone say it.

The Old Man shook his head, a tear running down his cheek. "No, son, you can't. You have blood on your hands and have some rescuing of your own to do before you can make your home here."

Back when I was running in the Senora hills, I would have defended what I did, told that Old Fella of all the hurt that the Jensens and especially Kennedy had done to me. But I didn't want to say those words, not anymore. Somehow all that pain and hurt was gone.

"I understand."

The Old Man set to walking again. We had a parade by the time we reached the village. People were gathering in clumps, all watching us as we marched into a square. In the center was a single tree, not more than a sapling.

A gray-haired woman, a mite older than Cassie, was on her knees tending the tree with a watering pail and a trowel. As we approached, she stood wiping at her knees and giving me a big old smile. "I swear boy, you are a sight for these eyes. It's like my Charlie was standing here right before me."

"Are you kin to my grandpa, ma'am?"

She eyed the Old Man, and I could tell she was worried he might say no. But he nodded.

"What you really want to know is if you and me are kin. The answer is yes, Will. Charlie was my son. You, boy, are my great-grandson."

Now I knew things weren't right, and I made to ask what was going on when she spoke up. "Time just ain't the same here, Will."

With so much wonder in the place, I didn't even ask how she knew my name let alone how she came to be calling me by the same version of it that Grandpa used. If a woman—hell, if my great grandma—who was close to a hundred could look so clear-eyed and alive as this one, then sure she could know my name. Nothing could surprise me anymore.

Seems I was wrong.

My great-gran took my hand in hers. "There's someone you have to meet."

She led me to the sapling.

"Say hello to your grandpa."

Forty-five years later

SERGEANT VERNON KILGORE, hat in hand, stepped lightly into Warden Bass's Office. "Old Will is dressed and ready to go, Sir."

Bass stood shakily to his feet. "This is madness. Take me to him."

Will Dowd was the oldest inmate in Florence Prison. The ancient gentleman had been a resident of the place long before Bass had taken over the wardenship. Hell, Will had been one of the original prisoners transferred from the Territorial Prison in Yuma when that relic shut down. Working in the infirmary for the last thirty-five years, some said he knew more about doctoring than most of the medics who came from back east.

Before that, he'd been a legend in the Arizona Territory. A wanted murderer, he'd eluded the territorial Marshalls for all of three years while never leaving the area. In 1878, when he finally turned himself in, he been something of a Robin Hood. He'd been the subject of several newspaper articles and a pulp novel titled, *The Demon Savior of the Southwest,* which chronicled his exploits in liberating countless slaves and abused children, often to great risk to himself.

It was likely his notoriety had been instrumental in his sentence of death by hanging being commuted to forty-five years.

The sergeant himself had spent countless hours listening to Old Will tell of a place called El Tesoro. A place, the old fella claimed, was now the new home of several of the people he'd 'rescued'.

He was half-crazy of course. On more than one occasion, he'd sworn that his grandfather had been reborn as a walnut tree and now resided in that same El Tesoro.

When the warden and the sergeant made their way into the cell block, which had been Will's home for almost four decades, the old man was shaking hands with several of his fellow prisoners.

"I won't lie to you, Dowd." A scar-faced prisoner named Hank Severs—a lifer serving time for hacking up his unfaithful wife and her lover with a machete—was wiping at a moist eye. "I'm going to miss the living shit out of you, you crazy old coot."

Will Dowd pulled the man into an embrace and whispered something into his ear. When the men pulled apart, Severs was nodding. "I'll do that, Will. I give you my word."

"I know you will, my friend." Will turned to look at the Warden and offered him a smile. "Seems my liberators are at hand."

"Where will you go, Will?" The warden asked. "And don't tell me, El Tesoro?"

The old man slowly shook his head. "Then I got no answer for you, warden. But don't worry, I won't be going alone."

The warden frowned at Sergeant Kilgore. "And you're going along with this nonsense?"

"I got some time coming to me, sir, and Will Dowd is more than just some parolee. He's my friend."

FOR THE TWO day's travel from the prison to Table Rock, Will regaled Sergeant Kilgore with what he could remember of El Tesoro and how the place connected to his family. *Just one last painful tale.* "My father was born in El Tesoro, but as my grandfather told it, never really fit in." At the base of the rock shelf, Will pulled up on the reins of his painted pony.

"When he left to rescue a girl down in the Senora, he never came back. My Grandpa went after him only to find that my father had not only met a different girl—a preacher's daughter—he had also found religion."

Vernon Kilgore stared down the old man. "I'm a Christian myself, Will. I'll not have you bad-mouthing my faith."

Will held up his hands surrender-style. "Ain't my place or right to do so. Shoot, there is a Christian Chapel in El Tesoro. The Old Man himself owns a bible and can quote you the entire book of James. 'Show me your faith without works and I will show you mine *by* my works. For Faith without good works is dead.'"

"I thought—"

"You thought El Tesoro was full of heathens, crazy and wild-eyed. Maybe given to dancing naked around bonfires." Will threw back his head and gave out a laugh. "Sorry, my friend, I don't mean to tease. I just wanted you to see that El Tesoro is full of people no different from you and me, but it doesn't force anyone to stay. My father chose a different path and decided to go, although a path that, in the end, he was ill-suited for."

"And your grandfather?"

"My grandfather was a stubborn man. He spent years trying to get my father to change his mind, to come back. The Old Man told him it was a fool's errand, but Grandpa wasted his life trying. In the end, my father died of the Typhoid, and Grandpa's body was too frail, and his mind too far gone to make the journey back to his home."

"And when he died, he came back as a tree?"

Will just laughed. "Not just any tree, ya darn skeptic. My grandfather is the prettiest little black walnut you've ever seen."

He reached out a hand and laid it on Vernon's arm. "Now to the real question at hand. What's to become of you, Sergeant Kilgore?"

"I'll be fine, Will. Don't you worry. I got my work and my faith in the Lord." Last Spring, Vernon's young wife had died in childbirth. The infant lasted only a day longer, then it too passed on. More than likely, being at loose ends the way he was had brought on the decision to accompany Will into the desert.

"And I won't force your hand. Just know this. You are invited. If you ever change your mind, just come right back to this place, and I'll know and be waiting to lead you in." Will climbed down from his pony.

"Maybe someday I'll take you up on it." Vernon wiped awkwardly at a tear.

Will handed him the reins to his pony and climbed the shelf up onto Table Rock. From behind, he could hear the music of El Tesoro —Samuels Fountain, the whisper of the breeze through the grove, and now the Old Man welcoming him home. Turning back to Sergeant Kilgore, he waved goodbye.

HOW FAR IS HEAVEN
JEAN ALFIERI

"Fishy fish. Gotta get some fish."

My Fairy Godmother assured me I'd discover something wonderful today, and I hoped it would fill my empty stomach.

The sidewalk ended at the base of a towering set of stairs tucked into the mountainside. As wide as they were tall, they seemed to stretch to heaven. Each stair was meticulously painted. Vines, leaves, and flowers covered and flowed over each step. The bright riot of colors blended perfectly with the wild forest on either side. The sweet scent of lilacs tickled my nose.

There was no other way to continue my journey, but it felt imposing. Could this be the "wonderful" she'd promised?

Ignoring the jitters, I tested the first step, then the next. Up I went, blending into the stairway's brilliant art. After a while, I paused. There was still no end in sight. Glancing behind, I was pleased to see my progress but doubted I'd ever make it to the top.

"Keep your eyes on the prize," my Fairy Godmother would say.

Good advice. So much good advice through the years. My Fairy Godmother had seen more of the world than I'd likely ever see. She was a sweet, kind old soul, though she hadn't always been treated kindly. I struggled to trust people, but she warned me not to have a cold heart.

"There's good and bad in everyone," she said.

I'd only seen the bad.

A brisk wind swirled leaves through the air, and I noticed the creep of thick gray clouds. A cold dollop of rain pelted my cheek. Thunder rolled low and echoed across the sky, ending in a shuttering rumble that sent me scrambling into the underbrush. I huddled under a giant fern and listened to the huge leaves welcome the water. At the end of a hefty leaf, I caught a mouthful of rain as it trickled off.

My stomach growled. I scanned around but the only food I saw was some sage and parsley.

The wind calmed and whispered more wise words from my Fairy Godmother, "Make the most of what you have."

I collected the herbs as the rain subsided then returned to the stairs. The rain made the paint slippery, slowing my climb. I couldn't help but wonder if I was going the wrong way. Maybe I'd misunderstood my Fairy Godmother.

In all my lives, I'd never traveled this far or been away this long. What was supposed to be an exciting adventure may have been a huge mistake. Who was I to dream there could be something "wonderful" in life waiting for me?

As my energy faded, the questions multiplied. Could I make it wherever I was heading and return the same day? What would I return to anyway? A crowded street - a dark alley. But my alley was familiar, and my neighbors stayed there for exactly that reason.

Long shadows covered the stairs. There was no turning back now. I operated well at night, but so did others. The mere thought of stumbling into someone lurking in the shrubs sent chills up my neck.

I gazed up the stairway and blinked in disbelief. The staircase stretched on, but there was a clearing about a dozen steps up. Could that landing be the destination my Fairy Godmother promised? My heart raced with anticipation. Shaking the rain from my coat, I scurried up.

With a victorious pounce, I made it. Weeds grew tall, bordering one side of the landing, but the other offered a well-traveled trail. Still unsure whether I was excited by what I might discover or afraid of being disappointed, I leaped onto the grassy path. Past a pocket of trees, a hint of smoke got my attention, then the scent of something delicious simmering. I sprinted, rounding a massive oak tree, and stumbled into a small campsite.

He saw me when I spotted the pot of beans over the open fire. Scurrying backward, I thumped into the wide tree trunk. Our eyes met and my heart pounded with fear. I arched my back and hissed. I'd given up on humans long ago. My Fairy Godmother must be slipping. I never met a human that wasn't loud and cruel, yelling: "Get outta here, ya dirty thing!" or "Stay away, ya filthy, flea-bitten..."

But instead of shooing me away, this one smiled. Was it a trick? I lowered my head, suspicious.

"Hey kitty," he soothed.

The flickering fire gave his stubbly face a warm glow. His gaze returned to the long stick where a hotdog dangled. He swished it through the flames. My eyes followed. I wanted so badly to reach out and give it a smack.

My stomach groaned, and I considered my situation. It wasn't fish, but it was food. And my Fairy Godmother would consider it rude if I didn't return a greeting.

"Meow."

Ears back, I snuck forward, keeping low. Then took a cautious sniff of the man's pant leg. How bad could someone be who smelled like hotdogs? I unrolled my tail and offered the herbs.

"This'll be right tasty." He added them to the pot. "Didn't have any spices, but my God Momma always says, 'make do with what ya got.' Thank you, Miss Kitty."

God Momma....he had one too? And he thanked me. How crazy!

"This ain't done cookin', but here's some hotdog."

Mmm. Fish-smish. I munched on the hotdog, savoring each bite. Did I say I'd given up on humans?

Settling next to him, I ate. I didn't even run when he reached to pet me, unable to recall the last time anyone rubbed my ears like that. Inching closer, an alarming rumble startled me. Was another storm approaching?

Oh.

That obnoxious rumbling was from me. I leaned in and purred as he scratched under my chin... and ooh yah, right there on my rump.

My Fairy Godmother was almost right, but this was way beyond wonderful. This was heaven!

PAST POSSIBILITIES

D.J. DAVIS

T homas Bollinger stood in front of the bicycle shop, scratching the vertical scar that bisected his chest. "I fixed your heart," the cardiologist had said. "But you're the only one who can fix the lifestyle that almost killed you." Diet, exercise, retirement. The doctor made it sound so easy.

Leaving the law firm to his partner and moving to the vacation home in Carmen Bluffs, two hundred miles from his Denver offices, was worse than the heart attack. Instead of stressed, he was now bored and lonely.

The low-fat diet was tolerable, but the exercise wasn't. He never enjoyed it, with one exception. When Thomas was a kid, he loved to ride. Maybe that old passion was still there. He went in and strolled the aisles. Race bikes, mountain bikes. Most with more gears than a semi-truck and both brakes on the handlebars. He winced at a puny saddle. He'd never get that miniature seat unjammed from his chunky ass. No relaxing, comfortable ride with an easy coaster brake.

He scooted outside before a salesman could nab him. His Mercedes Benz was parked half a block down in front of a junk shop called *Past Possibilities*. Even its faded sign looked secondhand.

Thomas hadn't been in a thrift store since he was in high school. He bought new and top-of-the-line, one hundred percent all the time. He earned a million-five every year, might as well spend it. Just not on an anal-probing bike that looked more complicated to operate than the Benz.

Thomas pulled the key fob from his pocket. The car's pristine paint reflected the cluttered display window. A familiar fender peeked from the middle of all that crap. He blinked at the reflection, then turned to peer through the glass.

He rushed inside, sending the cowbell over the door into a pealing hysteria. His newly repaired heart stuttered. Jammed among boxes of old canning jars and used shoes stood a dusty Schwinn Phantom. Thomas shoved a pile of ratty suitcases aside that probably hadn't been opened since the Mayflower sailed.

Even through the grime, chrome shone from the fender headlight all the way to the luggage rack. The horn was built into the streamlined tank. Patented spring fork, integrated lock, kickstand, automatic brake light. The balloon-tired cruiser was complete with whitewalls and pinstripes. The red and black paint socked him all the way back to his tenth birthday. Thomas ran his hands over the deluxe leather saddle. A generous seat that a big kid—or a man—could ride all afternoon without feeling like he'd been to the proctologist.

The bike was a dead ringer to the Phantom Thomas had received on that birthday more than sixty years ago.

"Help you, sir?" a woman asked.

"I'll take it."

"These old bicycles are hot on the collectible market right now. And one in this condition is rare. The price—"

"I'll take it." If she asked two mil for it, he'd whip out the checkbook right now.

She swallowed. "Sir, it's five thousand dollars."

"Sold."

As she rang it up, her fumbling teenage employee dragged the sixty-seven-pound Phantom down from the window. Thomas took command as soon as the flat tires were on the floor.

He pushed the Schwinn down to the bike shop. As other pedestrians paused to check out the Phantom, childhood pride swelled in his tired, abused chest. Thomas wheeled the Phantom into the bike shop and let the salesman corner him.

"Hey, man. Great bike. You lookin' to trade it?" He gestured at the array of new rides.

"Not a chance, this one has real class. I want it ready to ride."

"Sure. We can do that."

"Can you deliver it to my house?"

"For a fee."

Thomas nodded. "I'll double it if you can get it done by Friday."

The guy grinned. "No problem. Unless we have to order parts."

"Great." He took Thomas's information and the bike. As he wheeled the Phantom into the back room, Thomas couldn't take his eyes off it. Like the day he dropped his son off for his first day of school. After all these years, he had his bike back. If only he could have his boy back, too.

THE PHANTOM ARRIVED late Friday afternoon, sporting new tires and a new chain. The freshly polished chrome set off the paint like a short skirt set off his ex-wife's long legs. Thomas straddled it and wobbled around the garage. After an hour, he was pedaling smooth and straight—well, mostly straight—up and down his quarter-mile-long driveway.

Over the next week, he wheeled along the lane that passed his house on the way out of town. Beyond a few neighbors, there was only forest and fields. He rolled through leafy tunnels and vast stretches of wildflower studded green, legs and heart pumping in tandem, gaining strength.

The more he rode, the more the boy he had once been beat at his severed breastbone to be let out. Tommy J, who had been left behind in the shadows of his youth. Law school, a wife, a baby. He became a square, and worse: *The Man*. There was no room in that world for

Tommy J with his bicycle and greaser friends and burgers at the diner. 1957 was so far gone it was hard to believe it had ever existed.

Thomas stopped and planted one foot on the ground, the bike's frame cool against his thigh. He traced the streamlined headlight gracing the front fender. Ran his hands over the gleaming chrome and butter-smooth paint on the tank. The Phantom was still here, after half a century. Still here and still rolling—and so was he. Old, tired, and achy, but not ready for the scrap heap yet. There was time.

Time for what?

He still had his money, but his wife was gone. His son was gone.

Just ride, Daddy-O. Tommy J's voice rose from the Phantom, or maybe from his scarred chest. Or maybe Thomas imagined it. Sound advice, whatever the source.

Gravel crunched under the whitewalls in a hypnotic grind of movement and fresh air. He pedaled through the warm scents of pine, flowers, freshly cut hay, cattle. He slowed at the junction where he made his daily turn around to head home.

Just ride.

Why the hell not? No one waited for him at home.

Thomas cruised onto the fork of two dirt roads. His usual way ran straight and wide, making a ten-mile loop back to town. The other was an indistinct two-track with a shaggy green stripe running up the middle. Called *the bypass*, it reduced that ten-mile trip down to six but took hours longer. Or so he'd heard. The only ones who said it was worth the effort were the whitetail hunters, and they only used it if it had been a dry fall.

Thomas Bollinger, Esquire, went straight every time. The safe and familiar route. Tommy J, Beatnik, would lay rubber for the unknown and never look back. Thomas swung left, bouncing over roots and nearly losing his seat. The Phantom wobbled and bucked until he horsed it into the vegetation between the rutted tracks. He found his groove and picked up speed. Weeds thrummed in the spokes like the playing cards every cool cat used to deck out their bikes back in his day. Sunspots and shade flowed over his face and arms in a hot and cold rush.

The burn in his lungs and legs was a welcome throwback to Tommy J as the road steepened. Just before his breaking point, when he'd have to get off and push, Thomas crested the hill. He had a moment of full sunshine to savor the view of farms and forest spread below, and then he went flying down. The wind peeled his thinning hair back and buffeted the T-shirt against his stomach. He let out a whoop and punched a fist in the air. His body's reaction to the exertion felt good, like it had twenty years ago. Not like that last six months, when every random twitch of his cardiac muscle was enough to cause an anxiety attack.

The Phantom slowed as Bollinger reached the bottom and the road leveled out. The timber closed in, and the canopy blocked most of the light. The road twisted through a dark tangle of deadfall and brambles. He rode through the stagnant air, tires whispering over a moldy blanket of decomposing leaves. Ahead was a second fork in the road. Thomas coasted to a halt and studied the two weathered boards nailed to a post.

One pointed right with *CB* painted on it. Carmen Bluffs? Crockett & Bollinger? He rubbed his chest, the scar as bumpy as this road under the thin cotton. Coronary Bypass?

Thomas popped the kickstand down and dismounted. He trailed his finger over the faded letters on the second board. *Alice.*

FOR HIS FIFTIETH BIRTHDAY, the law firm served Thomas cake and champagne. When he got home, Alice served him divorce papers. She said he promised to retire at fifty, to spend some real time with her. They were wealthy enough, and she wanted him full-time. After Allen, she said, she deserved it.

Thomas promised her he would slow down—how she got retirement from that was her problem, not his. And he did slow down, from sixty hours a week to forty. Did she think a townhouse in Denver, the Victorian here in Carmen Bluffs, and the condo in Miami paid for themselves? Thomas prepared for war. He wouldn't take her claim on his assets without a fight. But in the end, all she wanted was a modest stipend and the condo. Thomas got off easy and he knew it. He signed those papers because he was addicted to the prestige and the money and the damn clout his name carried. When all along he should have been addicted to his wife. His beautiful Alice.

He mounted the Phantom and turned left toward Alice, wherever that was. The road twisted between gnarled trunks that stared at him like a jury of ancient mossy trolls. He hunched under their judgmental glares and pedaled faster.

At last, a roofline came into view through the timber. Thomas stopped, arms shaking as he took a water bottle from the rack behind the seat.

Thomas adjusted the gaping waistband on his pants. The fabric must be letting go, no way he lost that much of his gut on a half-day ride. He planted both feet on the ground, the bike leaning in his crotch, and pulled up his shirt. His belly-pooch was there, but it had shrunk.

He wiped the sweat from his forehead and ran a hand through his hair. What the hell? The bald spot was gone. He tugged two fistfuls of hair and laughed when it hurt.

As Thomas walked the bike toward the building, flashes of it became visible through the trees. Slate roof. Dark gray walls. White pillars framing the maroon front door. It couldn't be. He pushed the bike a little farther. Concrete planters filled with pink and purple petunias lined the walkway. Masses of roses hung their fragrant heads over the veranda balustrade. It was the townhouse he and Alice and Allen lived in. Except it was should have been in posh Cherry Hills Village south of Denver—not out here in the sticks several miles from Carmen Bluffs.

The house looked exactly like it did when he was fifty and married and things were still okay. Without Allen, they were far from great, but still okay.

He parked the bike in the shade. The scent of roses, as dark and bloody as the maroon door, filled the air. He mounted the steps and crossed the wide covered porch to pause at the leaded glass window. His reflection stared back from a dozen triangular panes. Thomas touched his face. The deep wrinkles were gone, leaving only the crow's feet around his eyes.

He pulled out his shirt collar. Brown hair just starting to turn white ran up his breastbone—his smooth, pre-heart attack breastbone. He hitched up his sagging pants. Fifty. He was fifty again. *Je-sus Christ.*

THE ANTIQUES, Ethan Allen furniture, Tiffany sconces, and stained glass in the entryway screamed wealth. It meant everything to him once, but now it was meaningless crap. His shoes squeaked on the hardwood floor.

"Is that you, Tom?"

Alice, from the kitchen. He stopped mid-stride.

"Tom?"

"Yeah, it's me." He edged along the wall and peeked through the archway. Alice stood at the sink with her back to him. The green summer dress he liked so much clung to her curves. Her red hair, streaked with silver and still stunning, was pulled into a ponytail. Her feet were bare, and her calves were tan.

She turned, a cucumber in one hand and a peeler in the other. She looked forty-five. No, she was forty-five. How could he have forgotten how attractive she was? Because he'd chosen to, because the memory of it made his soul weep.

"We're having chef salads, out on the veranda."

He nodded, opened his mouth, then swallowed.

"Are you all right?"

Thomas cleared his throat. "Fine. Salad sounds perfect. You make the best." His gaze roamed over the dress. "You look beautiful. Truly gorgeous."

She quirked an eyebrow. "Are you trying to get lucky?"

Could he get lucky with a... hallucination? "Well—"

"Uh-huh." She chopped the cucumber into two big bowls of greens. "Do you want French?"

"What?"

"Dressing? French?

"Oh. Yeah. Sure."

She squirted the orangey-red glop over the salads and took them outside. "Grab that tea, please."

Thomas poured two glasses over ice then sat down opposite her at the wicker table.

She wiped her chin with a napkin. "Did I drip? You're staring."

"Sorry. It's just—"

"What?"

"You, Alice. Always you."

She shook her head. "Wow. You really do want in my pants."

Thomas laughed. "Who doesn't, beautiful?"

"Spare me and eat."

The last thing his crawling stomach wanted was food, but he forked up a slice of hardboiled egg.

She took a bite and eyed him. "Your birthday is next week."

"I guess it is."

"And?" She drummed her fingers on the table.

He remembered that look. The agitation only his career could put on her face, pulling down the corners of her mouth, narrowing her eyes.

"And I'm going to retire. On Monday, I become a silent partner and Crockett will run the show."

"Are you serious?"

"As a heart attack."

Watching the slow smile light up her face was like watching the sun rise over the Rockies.

Except when Monday came, he told his partner he needed to reduce his hours. When push came to shove, he couldn't walk away.

But Alice could shove. She had shoved him right out the door.

Thomas squinted at the tangles of wildflowers gone to seed and the thorny stems of wild roses. The manicured yard was gone. The house was gone. Alice was gone.

THOMAS SURVIVED THE MYOCARDIAL INFARCTION, but the ghost of that awful pain, like someone parked a tank on his chest and then tried to pull his arms off, still lingered in the tissues around his heart. But this... what the hell was happening? Maybe he was having a stroke. Or some mental crisis.

If that was the case, no one would find him out here in the boondocks. Thomas straddled the Phantom. Go home or go on? Return to the bleak future of his solitary retirement or explore the road of past possibilities?

He'd come this far, and he felt fine. Better than fine. Better than he had in years. If he squinted, he could just make out another fork in the dirt track. The sun still rode high in the sky. There was water, trail mix, and a ham sandwich in the canvas bag strapped to the rack. He had nothing to go home to. Besides, a little hallucination never hurt anybody.

Just ride.

"Okay, Tommy J, let's do this." He bumped over roots and stones, swerved in and out of ruts, then flashed through light and shade to the next dilapidated signpost. A board pointed with the same *CB* in peeling paint. He pulled a hank of dead vines off the other: *Allen.*

He feared it would be Allen. He knew it would be Allen. Grief and guilt clawed at him with sharp, dirty talons, infecting his soul and devouring it with spiritual gangrene that had no cure.

What if this was the cure?

Thomas hooked left, to the so-called road narrowing to little more than a path. The trees clumped so tight on either side he couldn't squeeze through them if he lost another sixty pounds. There were only two ways to go, back to his miserable life or into an unknown future. Thomas pedaled ahead. He had to, for Allen.

The path ended in a small clearing. A used car lot took up most of it. Allen leaned on the front bumper of a white 3/4-ton Chevy pickup. Its bed was lined with toolboxes and a generator was mounted behind the cab.

Allen grinned and waved.

Thomas' heart skittered into arrhythmia. His son—eighteen and fresh from graduation—with the world spread out before him like a banquet. With a partnership in the law firm waiting for him, his future was a given. If only he could make the kid understand.

Allen made a *get over here, already* gesture.

Thomas got off the bike. He caught his sagging pants as they slid to mid-thigh. He yanked them up, startled by the sight of his arm. Young skin taut over corded muscles. If the Phantom had somehow transported him to 1991, then he was forty-four. He took a breath and stretched his back, the song of youth music to his body.

Allen met him halfway, throwing an arm around Thomas' shoulders. God, that grin. So perfect. So happy.

"Hey, Dad. You okay?"

"Hey, yourself." The words sounded all right. He licked his lips and tried for more. "I'm good."

Allen yanked him toward the truck. "This is it. Check it." He opened the boxes, pulled out metal drawers on silent bearings, and then popped the hood. "It's perfect, don't you think? And look." He dragged an envelope out of his back pocket. "I got in!"

Technical school. Of course he got in. Any monkey could.

"As I recall, you got into Stanford, too."

The kid made a face. "I don't want to go to law school."

"We talked about this."

"No, Dad. You talked. And talked and talked."

Thomas willed himself to spit out the words he wished he'd said all those years ago—that tech school was a fine choice. But his mouth betrayed him, just like his stupid heart had. "You know I'm right. When the firm becomes Crockett, Bollinger, and Bollinger, you'll have anything you want. Money, cars, boats, prestige. Women."

Allen crossed his arms. "I'll be stuck in a stuffy suit, playing the court jester until I croak."

"You'd rather be a plumber?" He tapped Allen's forehead. "Your skull isn't that thick. Think about it, son. Prestige and wealth, or..." He flung a hand at the truck. "That."

"I like to work with my hands and I'm good at it. Plumbers help people and they make good money, too. Plus, I won't have to spend half my life in college and the other half wiping some judge's ass."

"I'm not buying this piece of junk for your graduation."

"You promised."

"I promised a car. Something that when you drive onto campus, people know you're somebody. Let's go drive the Bugatti. The dealership is holding it for me. The yellow one?"

"I don't want a bug-shit yellow car and I won't go to fucking Stanford."

Thomas clinched his fists. "You'll do both or you'll be cut off. As in, move out tomorrow and don't come back."

"Yeah, right. What's Mom say about it?"

"She agrees." Thomas grimaced. The lie came just as easily now as it did then. "In fact, she's at the department store right now, buying your new clothes for university."

The kid slumped, from his dark brown hair to his shoes. "Fine. You always get what you want."

Thomas gripped his biceps. "Yes, I do. And you will, too. Trust me on this. The world will be yours. That's why you want the clout Stanford will bring, not a pipe-wrench. You can hire anyone you want to fix your toilets. Pay them to crawl around in the shit. You're too good for that. Got it?"

"Sure, Dad." Allen pulled away from him. "Thanks a lot for ruining my life."

"I saved it, Allen. I saved it. Just wait and see."

"But—"

"No *buts*, boy. Not ever."

Allen faded into mist. The truck became a shrub, and the pavement became grass. His boy was gone. Just like Alice was gone. "No, wait!" Thomas ran, strong legs propelling him faster than he'd moved in decades. "Come back! I was wrong." He fought branches and underbrush. Thorns tore his shirt and jerked his pants off his hips. There was no way through, and Allen wasn't in there, anyway. His son was under six feet of earth in Fairmount Cemetery, not far from several Colorado senators, mayors, and judges. Allen should have been among those elite, but not like that.

When Thomas turned back to the Phantom, a ravine split the clearing. The crash of dark floodwaters rose to his ears. He crept to the edge, slipping under the accident scene tape flapping in the gusts. Thunder banged overhead and lightning strobed the churning mud.

The tail end of a brand-new yellow Bugatti jutted from the water. Splintered stumps slammed into it, knocking it farther downstream. It tumbled under a muddy wave of silt and debris. The police report said Allen was going over a hundred and fifty miles per hour when the car hydroplaned in the storm.

He fell to his knees and rolled to his back. "I'm sorry!" he shouted into the storm. "Please, bring him back. Bring my son back."

Thomas wept until he thought he might go into cardiac arrest. He wanted to, anything to make it end. But the deceitful muscle kept beating, kept pushing the blood through his arteries. Little red, bloody bastard kept him alive when everything he had to live for was lost.

The sun pulsed red through his eyelids. Thomas sat up, blinking in the glare. Sweat stung the scratches and punctures on his arms. At the edge of the clearing, the path took up through the forest again. The Phantom waited, leaning on its kickstand. Waited to take him farther into the past.

THOMAS' heart huddled in its pericardial sac like cracked brick— dull, heavy, broken. He reached the bike, holding the handlebars with one hand and gripping his waistband with the other. This self-torture was ludicrous. Time to go home and make an appointment with his doctor. Maybe he was having a reaction to his meds and was dreaming this whole nightmare.

Time to wake up.

Wake up!

Insects buzzed and hummed in the scrub brush. The trees moaned as a breeze stirred their tops. His gaze swept over chrome, red, and black. "Are you magic or a curse?"

The Phantom was as present and solid as he was. If Thomas was meant to find the bike, then he was meant to be here. Which meant he was supposed to go on. The bike had taken him back to the most devastating event of his life. Nothing could be worse than reliving the death of his child. Better to play this thing out to the end. If he didn't, he'd die wondering where the path led. He'd find out and then check himself into the Mayo Clinic.

Thomas threw a leg over the saddle, pumping the pedals with ease. Weight and years melted away like a popsicle from its stick on the Fourth of July.

He sped down the path, the hair lifting from his brow. His shirt buffeted his skin, cooling it. The bright gap ahead grew as he neared the next meadow, drawing him into its glow as helpless as a moth to a candle.

The Phantom delivered Thomas to his father's full-service station. The reek of gasoline and rubber bled into his sinuses. Thomas bumped over the bell hose in front of the pumps and heard the ding from inside the station. His watery reflection ran across the windows —the reflection of a twenty-four-year-old Thomas Bollinger. His neck popped as he whipped his head around to gawk at himself. Had he once been this young, this strong?

Someone lurched into the open doorway. "Look out!"

Thomas veered, his right pedal striking a tire display—three stacked flat and the fourth perched like a giant black donut on top. The Phantom went down. Thomas was on his feet before the bike hit the pavement. He turned, adrenalin spiking into his temples.

His father stood in the door frame, his station attendant's uniform crisp and pressed, the matching cap at a slight angle over his crewcut. "Don't know what you was daydreamin' about, but it sure must have been a doozy." A toothpick bobbed between his teeth.

Thomas opened his mouth, croaked like a dying toad, then worked up enough spit to lube his numb lips. "Papa?"

"Yeah?"

"You, uh... you look great. Really great."

His father raised an eyebrow, as gray and bristly as the wire brush he used to scrub mud off wheels. "You sick, boy?"

"No. I'm just happy to see you."

Papa stepped around the corner, opened the large chest-style pop machine, and pulled out two bottles. "Sit a spell."

"Sure." Thomas sat on the bench below the display window. His father twisted first one bottle, then the other in the built-in cap remover on the side of the machine. The carbonated hiss and rattle of the caps falling into the bin brought his childhood back in a surge.

The curved glass fit his hand, chilling it. The scent of the bubbles popped against his upper lip as he took that first cold, sweet, wonderful sip. Thomas' knee was warming against his father's. He swallowed, then wiped both his eyes and his lips.

"Something wrong?"

Thomas took a longer drink and nodded. "Just a lot of changes, you know?"

"For your mother and me, too." He squeezed Thomas' arm. "We're proud of you."

"I know. Thank you." He gazed at the face he knew so well. Papa was wrinkled and tired before his time, his hair grayer than it should have been for a man only forty-six. "I'll pay my tuition back, every penny. I promise."

"You'll do no such thing. We wanted this for you, more'n you wanted it for yourself. First one in the family to go college. My boy, a Stanford graduate come spring. You did the work, but I had a part in it, too. Don't take that away from me."

"I couldn't have done any of it without you. But I want to help you. Let me make the mortgage payments for a while."

"No, son."

"You work twelve hours a day, seven days a week to keep this place above water. It's going to kill you. Please."

"If you want to pay me back, then go out into the world and show them you're somebody."

"I will. I swear." Thomas drank, the unspoken oath to support his parents going sour on his tongue. Papa died of a stroke before the ink on Thomas' Juris Doctor degree was dry. His mother passed the following winter. A ventricular aneurysm, the doctors said. Bullshit. She died of a broken heart.

"Good enough." His father clinked their bottles together. "Look at that." A hawk rode the thermals above them in ever higher circles. "I wonder what it's like to be so free."

"You would be if it wasn't for me. All that money for college."

"It was worth every penny."

"But—"

"No *buts*, son. Ever. You can't go back."

A feather came spinning down. Thomas tracked its descent into the vacant lot across the street. "I'll get it for your hat." But Papa vanished. Thomas sat in the pokey grass, his empty fingers forming the shape of the old-fashioned bottle.

He jumped up to pick the feather out of the weeds, and then cast his gaze to a bird-less sky. How could the feather be real when nothing else was? He couldn't stay in this meadow another damn minute.

Thomas peeled out of the clearing in a cloud of dust. Stems snapped and rattled in the spokes. He stood on the pedals, pushing for maximum speed, letting his jeans slide off his skinny hips. The next meadow would come soon. It had to. Instead of a meadow, he came to another fork with another sign.

Thomas stopped to read his choices. To the left: *Tommy J, Beatnik*. To the right: *Thomas J. Bollinger, Esquire*.

He could have gotten a two-year business degree and gone to work for his father. Papa would still have a college graduate to brag about and they'd run the station together. His parents would live to dote on Allen.

But no. If Thomas hadn't gone to Stanford, he never would have become a regular at the library where Alice worked. Without Alice, there could be no Allen. On the other hand, if they were fated to be together, to create that beautiful boy, they would meet no matter what. Wouldn't they?

From the left fork, the faint sounds of rockabilly drifted from the drive-in where Tommy J spent Saturday evenings with his friends.

From the right fork, Alice's muffled laughter as she kissed his neck behind the library stacks.

Thomas propped the Phantom against a trunk and took the feather from his back pocket. "I don't know what to do. Help me."

Just ride.

Be somebody.

He was somebody, goddam it. He was a son and a husband and a father. Just because he'd become an attorney, didn't mean Allen had to. He saw that now. Allen could be anything he wanted, and Thomas would back him one hundred percent, just like Papa had done for him. He would buy that pickup and send Allen off to technical school. Then he would cut his hours to three days a week and spend the time with his family that he should have. But what if he had to go further back to make the right changes? Papa's voice on the breeze, *you can't go back*. Then why did the Phantom bring him to his father? "Anybody? Please."

He spun the feather between his thumb and forefinger. The gathering wind rustled through dense branches. When it hit his back, he let the feather go. It danced on the air, and fluttered down to the path leading to Alice.

Thomas rode toward the sultry scent of Alice's perfume. He careened to the end of the path and broke out of the trees into his own backyard. Home! Thomas dropped the bike on the lawn and slammed through the garage door. The Mercedes glimmered like a small fortune. He tripped going up the steps into the laundry room. Through the butler's pantry and into the kitchen. Without Alice's things, the place oozed lonely bachelorhood.

Thomas stumbled into the living room. "Alice? Allen?" The clock ticked on the mantel next to a framed picture of Allen with the yellow Bugatti. "No! No, this can't be. I chose right, I finally chose right. I know what to do now. Let me do it. Give me my family back!"

He wiped his cheeks and ran his hands over his head. His fingers slid over the naked top of his scalp. The button of his pants pinched into his inflated gut. Thomas spun toward the mirror in the entryway. He was old and pallid and fat. He sprinted through the house into the yard, yanked the Phantom onto its wheels, and then followed his track across the grass.

The path was gone, but he still had the Phantom and the feather. His past possibilities had to still be there; he must find them.

His heart, flailing like a frantic bat caught in a net, spasmed its way into fibrillation as he forced the big bicycle into the timber. Sweat tickled down his chest and he scrubbed his shirt over it, the cotton scraping over the long vertical scar. "Allen, I'm coming."

"Just ride." Fifteen-year-old Tommy J, greased ducktail shining in the sun, beckoned from the shadows.

Thomas rode.

THE TRAVEL BUG
BARBARA PRESLIER

I gazed into Selah's eyes as she held me close to her face. "Kittymare, little one, you're officially activated. I've given you a mission to travel the world. You're peculiar looking, that's for sure. Who would have thought to put a cat's head on a horse's body?" Selah sighed. "At least you weren't the creepiest trackable at the sale. That one-eyed green thing was frightening, and the series of glow worms were gross."

I was a Geocaching Travel Bug, or TB. I glanced at myself through the reflection on Selah's eyeglasses. I was orange and tan, made of flat metal, and barely two inches in diameter. There was a tracking code embossed on my tail and a carabiner inserted at the end. Two large green eyes bulged from an innocent face. I looked too young to venture out on my own. I tried unsuccessfully to shake my welded head side-to-side to express my hesitation to her. She stroked my metal ears. "Ah, don't worry, Kittymare. You'll be fine."

Later that day, Selah stuffed me in a clear freezer bag and brought me to my first geocache container, a mini waterproof storage receptacle nestled under a scrub oak bush in eastern Colorado. It was customary for geocaches to be hidden in concealed spaces or remote areas. It made the game more exciting. For them.

"Keep your horse sense about you," said Selah as she dropped me in. "Welcome every adventure. Some humans think geocaching is a silly game. But really, it's genius. It allows people to visit destinations they would never have considered. I always say to my new Trackables, 'Each cache is a new home—it will be what you will. Have a wonderful life.'"

I was quivering like an aspen leaf on a windy October afternoon. Though I knew I was about to embark on a lifelong voyage, I felt forgotten and alone. Huddled in my solitary haven, I groomed my hooves and twirled my whiskers while spiders circled my enclosure, poking at the plastic. I began to question my worthiness as an adventurer. I wanted Selah to come take me back. The sounds of hissing spiders and howling coyotes serenaded me to sleep.

The next morning, I was rescued. What a joyous day! I looked into the soft brown eyes of my savior. He was in a T-shirt, shorts, and hiking shoes. His large hands were in proportion to his tall frame. He had wavy brown hair escaping from under a ball cap and a wide smile.

"Hey, little Travel Bug. What are you doing out here all by yourself? Come along with me. I'm going to hike for a few hours and can use the company." He took a picture of me and clipped me to his belt loop. I took in the views along the trail while he walked, bumping against his muscular thigh. There were juniper and pine trees interspersed with firs. As we went uphill, I could feel drops of his sweat bounce off my head. His breathing became labored as we summited the mountain. My eyes opened wide when I saw the whole world around me. The deep blue sky occupied most of the space. Below, there were a few mountaintops spattered with glaciers. I never wanted to leave this heavenly place.

Brown Eyes drank two bottles of water, ate some raisins and peanuts, and swung his knapsack on his back. He patted me against his jeans. "Sorry I haven't found a large enough cache to deposit you in, Cat-thing. I guess we'll have more travels together." If he could only hear my ecstatic screams.

For the next week, we hiked, kayaked, and bicycled around southern Colorado. I was wet, nauseated, and exhausted from the constant bumping and splashing. Then one day, Brown Eyes unclipped me for the last time. He scraped off dried mud from my left eye and tail. "You'll get a lot more wear and tear as you travel, Cat-thing. Remember, it's not how you look but how you live. And now it's time to send you on your way."

"No," I implored. "Please don't leave me." I tried to press myself into his palm.

"Bye," he said as he dropped me into a large ammo can. I saw him reach for a slick yellow mustang convertible with large eyes for head-lights. Before the lid snapped shut, one of the mustang's eyes winked at me. I felt a push and heard a painful screech. "Watch out!" Then, more voices complained.

"Ouch, you stepped on my tail."

"I hate newcomers."

"What?" I yelled. "Who's here?" As my eyes became accustomed to the dark interior, I noticed shapes. One was a mermaid with floppy arms and a long neon tail. I lifted my hoof. "Sorry."

I saw a miniature red Jeep with brightly painted headlights, providing the only light.

His deep voice echoed. "I'm Jeep 4 x 4. This is Miss Merry the Mermaid. The petite girl in the corner is Birthday Gift. She recently returned from Asia."

"Asia?" I asked. "Is that far?"

The three of them laughed and pointed at me. "TB Newbie, TB Newbie..." they sang. I shrank against the side of the ammo can.

Birthday Gift scooted next to me. "It was my first trip on an airplane. I was petrified. Let me tell you about it."

I could hear groans from Miss Merry the Mermaid and Jeep 4 x 4. He tooted his horn and flashed his lights. "No, please. Not that story again."

"What are you called?" Miss Merry the Mermaid forced herself between Birthday Gift and me, and shuffled a deck of cards with her long, manicured fingers. She tossed back her auburn curls and gave a dazzling smile. "Do you play?"

"I'm Kittymare, and I only know Go Fish." I swung my long legs around, facing her, careful not to repeat the faux pas when I landed on her tail. I freed myself from the sealed baggie. "What do we play?"

"Gin." She dealt out the cards while explaining the rules.

I made many mistakes in those first games, tossing out cards Miss Merry the Mermaid needed, dropping others with my awkward hooves, but I managed to win a few games before we took a break.

Miss Merry the Mermaid handed me the deck. "You've picked up the game well. This will help you make friends. Play again later?" Her lavender eyes fixed on me, daring me to deny her.

I quickly accepted, despite my exhaustion. "I'll be ready. Miss Merry the Mermaid, how long have you been here?"

"Oh, about a month. I came from Texas with four crazy college kids. They drank so much beer, I thought we would end up a statistic on the Interstate. I had to lie in an odoriferous duffle bag for two days. I never realized how stinky human socks could be. I'm comfortable here, but I'm ready to move on." I saw her glance at Jeep 4 x 4 while swishing her tail.

Miss Merry the Mermaid's voice was as sweet as a lullaby. Her yarned red hair bobbed up and down with each note. I should have noticed earlier that she wasn't fabricated from flat metal. She was three-dimensional with a thick, variegated tail, a dark blue bathing suit, and long, delicate hands.

"Your skin looks so soft," I blurted.

"I'm crocheted." Miss Merry the Mermaid giggled. "My designer was an expert with a J-hook. After she finished me, she attached my Trackable identifier." She turned around to show me the metal dog tag attached to her tail. "It's a bit heavy, but I manage."

Jeep 4 x 4 piped up. "I think she's the most beautiful Trackable I've ever seen." He winked at her. "But we don't get too close here. Soon, we'll go our separate ways and never see each other again. We must continue our journeys. My goal is a Travel Bug Hotel in Manitoba, Canada. It's described on the geocaching web page as an exquisite seven-level cupboard-sized wooden structure. Each floor is brightly painted and decorated with tiny furniture and other knickknacks. My activator should retrieve me after I'm logged in, and I guess he'll either create a new mission or retire me."

"I'm to visit all the national parks in the United States." Miss Merry the Mermaid interjected, combing her hair.

I looked at Birthday Gift. "What's your mission?"

The candle-hands sagged against the colorful ribbon. "My activator didn't make a specific goal for me."

Jeep 4 x 4 scoffed at her. "You're always complaining. Your goal lets you travel forever. You've even been to Asia."

Birthday Gift perked up. "You're right. And I've been on an airplane." She turned to me. "Let me tell you all about it," she implored.

Jeep 4 x 4 rolled his lights, "Not now, Birthday Gift."

Miss Merry the Mermaid and I giggled.

I asked Jeep 4 x 4, "How long have you been here?"

He turned his lights on me. "Two long weeks. It usually takes longer in winter to get picked up. The weather conditions keep the geocachers away from the mountains. This container is solid, though. If we need to stay until spring, then I guess I'm okay sharing it with you three." He let out an unconvincing honk.

Miss Merry the Mermaid snarked. "Well, that certainly makes my scales tingle."

I muttered. "Well, I'm just glad to have friends."

Birthday Gift remained quiet as Miss Merry the Mermaid shrank away from Jeep 4x4's strong headlights. No one spoke for hours. I braided and unbraided my long whiskers as I contemplated my fate. These TB's were comfortable here, but I didn't belong. As I begged for Selah to rescue me, a few tears rolled down my face. I remembered what she said. "It will be what you will."

A few weeks later, after countless airplane tales and annoying jeep flashes, we played our final gin game. The ammo can was lifted. I barely sealed the baggie around me when the top flew open.

"Well, looky here. Four TBs, guys. Who wants one?" A thin girl dumped out the contents of our temporary home.

My friends and I were cast on the ground.

I slid under the plush Miss Merry the Mermaid so she would be chosen.

"I'll take the mermaid," said the skinny girl.

"I've got the jeep," spoke a middle-aged man.

"I guess I'll take the cat thing." I was immediately picked up by a woman wearing army fatigues, a thick tan vest, and heavy hiking boots. She snapped a selfie with me. "Yep, you'll do. Let's get rid of the ones we brought."

I could hear Birthday Gift swearing as new TB's fell into the ammo can with her. I called out a quick farewell to my new friends. I would miss them, but I was on my way to carrying out my mission to travel the world. A few minutes later, I nestled into the warm satchel of my new companion. I fell asleep on a red bandana, with the rhythm of her boots stomping on the dirt trail.

I woke up on a window ledge overlooking a forested area. I watched outside and enjoyed the birds that came to nibble on the grain left in the small wooden house attached to a tree. I spotted foxes, rabbits, and even a bear. It was peaceful, but I was antsy to move on.

As if Army Pants read my mind, I was grabbed by my tail and tossed next to a computer and a book in a zipped bag. I could barely see out through the metal teeth of the zipper. The taxi driver's sharp turns made me spit furballs all over myself. When we stopped, the bag I was in went through a tunnel. I felt painful and penetrating stabs along my body. Was I being melted down? Had my journey ended so soon? Had I failed in my mission?

The light returned, and Army Pants lifted the bag to her shoulder. Soon, we entered a portal to a giant metal machine. I wondered if this was my next interim shelter. I was placed on a dirty carpet with two feet pushing my face against the computer cover. There were loud noises and horrible vibrations. The sounds made me flashback to my birth day. That very first time I had opened my eyes to screeching metal and the pain from a hammer against my tail.

Army Pants shoved me aside and removed the book, leaving the zipper open next to a cold, oblong window. I glanced out to see gray skies filled with white clouds. With no visible ground, I knew I was in an airplane. After having endured hundreds of Birthday Gift's stories of flying, I finally understood her exhilaration. I enjoyed the constant humming and occasional dips, fantasizing that I was a foxy fashionable feline among archaic mundane trackables.

A few days later, my brash human courier lifted me out of my confinement. I could see green grass everywhere, dotted with white rocks. No, those rocks were moving. They were sheep. They had a blob of pink or blue color painted on their butts. Army Pants took a farewell photo with me, and then placed me in a small can tied to a fence. I fell back and settled in. Through small holes in the can, I could watch the sheep graze. After a few minutes, I heard a gruff voice that exhibited a thick strange accent.

"You've been here five minutes and don't say hello. Where'd you learn your manners? I'm Captain Sharp from London, England."

I stared at a large metal man with a sword and a pirate hat. His rough scarred face appeared to have been through many battles."

"I'm from Colorado, USA. My name is Kittymare."

"You're a what? A kitty and a mare? Ha! Do you bite?"

I frowned and pawed at my whiskers. "Of course not. I'm really nice."

"Well, you're in Ireland now, Kittymare. Do you play cards?"

Hoping to make him a friend, I said to the ostentatious man. "Of course. Gin."

"Do you know how to shuffle? Watch this." Captain Sharp was a magician with the cards. I learned many tricks from observing him.

As Captain Sharp won yet another game, he said, "Ha, beat you again."

I kept thinking about Selah's words, "It will be what you will." I became determined to master the technique. Later, while he snored, I practiced. My delicate paws soon lifted each card like a conductor her baton.

I was extricated the next day by a charming older couple who smiled at everything and anyone. They left Captain Sharp behind and chose me as their travel companion. I can't say I missed him. I grinned like a Cheshire cat with the knowledge that I sacrificed my card game victories for the pleasure of watching him gloat. If only he knew.

We drove to the Blarney Stone near Cork, where Mr. Toothy Smile placed my face to the famous rock for a kiss and took a bunch of photographs. When I glanced down, I was surprised to find that I wasn't afraid of falling.

I spent my next few days in Dublin, Ireland, clipped to Mrs. Red Lipstick's purse. The three of us hit a few pubs before leaving. We sang, ate and drank a lot. Well, I only sang, but the shepherd's pie and Guinness ale looked scrumptious. Then we were off on another airplane. This time, I had no fear. I was fascinated to learn how this thing worked. To me, it was magical. *Like me with a deck of cards.* I smiled with satisfaction.

We spent two glorious days enjoying the sights in Munich, Germany and doing a bit of geocaching. Most of their "finds" were micros—very small containers about the size of pill bottles. Since I was too big to fit in those, they documented my visits with photographs of me at each location. I had a great view from the purse strap as Mrs. Red Lipstick walked around. She settled herself on a bench in front of an enormous clock set in the top of a tall building. When the world-famous Glockenspiel rang out, I counted along.

The third morning was as gray as Mrs. Red Lipstick's hair. She kissed me, leaving a faint smudge on my back hooves, put me in her pocket, grabbed an umbrella, and ventured out. We stopped at a small bistro, where she had a schnitzel. As we walked back to the hotel, she slipped on the wet cobblestones and fell. Two men lifted her and made sure she was unhurt. They helped gather her dropped belongings. As she limped away, only one thing was left behind.

"Wait! I'm down here! Please don't leave me!" My squealing reached nobody's ears. I was left behind like trash, swimming in a murky puddle.

I spent the night freezing. The plastic baggie kept the muddy water out, but not the cold. As the day progressed, humans walked over, around, and so close to me that I could nearly touch their rain boots. Yet no one saw me. I spent the next two nights in tears. I dreamt of my old friends. Did they meet a similar fate, or were they fulfilling their missions? If I wanted to get out of here, I needed to keep my wits about me. I kept repeating, "It will be what you will."

I can't remember if it was days or weeks, but the rain subsided, and the puddles dried up. I no longer looked like a piece of trash. My metal grabbed the sunlight and created a small rainbow.

"Look, Mama. What's this?"

My tired body was lifted by a little girl with blond curls that touched her waist. She wore a clean blue dress with white stockings and black shoes. Her gentle hands warmed my soul. "It's so pretty. Like a horsey and a kitty cat." She handed me to her mother.

"Hmm. It says it's a geocache TB. Your Uncle Wilhelm knows about that. We'll ask him, Lara." Mama put me in her purse, where I immediately sank into a clean handkerchief and closed my eyes.

"Mama, can I keep it? Please?" I heard the adorable child ask as I fell asleep.

I awoke to Lara removing me from my baggie and grabbing my waist. She had me gallop on her floor, her desk, and finally, her bed. She cuddled with me until there was a knock at the door. She shoved me under her pillow.

A man called out. "Lara, it's Uncle Wilhelm."

I heard Lara say. "You can't take her. I found her. She's mine."

I heard Lara sob as Mama and Uncle Wilhelm burst into the room.

"May I see the item?" Uncle Wilhelm had a stern, monotone voice.

Lara retrieved me and lifted me by my carabiner.

"Ah, yes. This is a Trackable. It needs to be taken to a cache container. Sorry, Lara, you may not keep this. I'll move it along." He reached for me, but she clenched her hand. When the skirmish was over, I was minus two whiskers and warped in one leg. Uncle Wilhelm had won, of course. I was overjoyed when he placed me in a new, clean, double-zip plastic bag.

I was traveling again, this time with the lanky, pragmatic Wilhelm. We took a train to Salzburg, Austria, the birthplace of Mozart. Willy had a three-hour meeting in a nearby office building. I napped in his jacket pocket while a dozen humans discussed ways to improve profits. Later, in the hotel room, I watched the clouds march in front of the moon, which reminded me that my next wonderful adventure was on the horizon.

The next morning, we took a ski lift to the top of a mountain. Since it was the end of summer, there was a vast green meadow with a backdrop of the Alps. The deep blue sky was cloudless, and the faraway mountains had a spot or two of snow at their peaks. Willy walked to a stand of trees and lifted me out of his shirt pocket. He snapped a photo of me with the Alps. I noticed dozens of people opening their arms and making a circle, singing "The Hills are Alive."

Willy brought me in close to his face. "Tourists. They come to Salzburg so they can 'Climb Every Mountain' and pretend they're in *The Sound of Music.* He shook his head and when he looked into my eyes, a rare smile appeared.

"Farewell, enchanting Kittymare, on with your travels."

He dropped me into a large metal box. I crashed to the bottom and heard voices complain.

"Hey, watch it. That's my head."

"Ow, you're on my horns."

"Who the heck are you?"

I answered the voices. "I'm Kittymare. Who are you?"

"Well, we're not Julie Andrews," a girl's voice spoke as everyone laughed.

I became acquainted with my new roommates and settled into a warm, cozy spot in the center. I peeled back my protective baggie. My whiskers had grown long since I stopped pulling them. I was content in my new surroundings. I knew it wouldn't be long before I was chosen again for my next extraordinary adventure. I had finally understood Selah's words. "It will be what you will."

One of my new friends came over. "You play cards?"

"Of course." I answered, pulling out my deck and performing a one-handed shuffle. "Gin."

BOUND HOUNDS
BOWEN GILLINGS

"You just had to kiss her, didn't you?" Rom grumbled, white-knuckling his sheathed sword as he ducked under a rough-hewn beam.

Drood came up behind, shoulders slumped and fiddling with his bowstring.

"You try saying no to a goddess," he said.

"I did say no," snapped Rom through clenched teeth.

The pair crept along a torchlit mineshaft. Flickering flames cast dancing shadows. Chill, smokey air whispered past like a soft breath, as if the whole mountain lay in wait to see what happened next.

"How many times I gotta apologize?" asked Drood, trying to see past his large friend to what lay beyond the next pool of light. "I'm sorry, okay? Sorry I kissed a lust goddess. Sorry that, in a moment of, well, less than stellar judgement, I thought with something other than my brain."

"As you are wont to do. Frequently," Rom replied.

"Doesn't matter now, does it? I'm bewitched." Drood pointed to his lips, still ruby red from the days-old enchanting kiss. "If we don't get back Kandissa's harp and slay the thief, I'll spend eternity in a state of...hardened, perpetual longing."

Rom glanced down at his companion who was, for the hundredth time, trying unsuccessfully to adjust his trousers. The big swordsman sighed. Willpower had never been Drood's strong suit.

The contents of Drood's many pouches jingled as he twisted and shifted. The sound rang frighteningly loud in the echoey stone confines. He stopped messing with his pants and quieted his accoutrements.

"Sorry. Again."

Rom prepared another cutting remark then stopped short at shouts from far ahead—men's shouts—that sounded damn angry.

"Here we go," Rom said, moving into the center of the tunnel to gain fighting room.

Drood crouched in the shadows and pulled a half-dozen arrows from the quiver on his back. He set them in easy reach. "I'll thin them out first."

"Fine." Rom tested the uneven ground. "Don't feel a need to save any for me."

Curses and racing footfalls echoed up the tunnel, growing louder with each heartbeat.

Rom drew his sword and swung it in lazy circles, loosening muscles gone tight with a day's trek and growing irritation. He gave his friend one more glowering glance.

"You know," said Drood, nocking an arrow, "my pappy always said worrying about what you can't fix makes as much sense as fixing what ain't broke."

"Logical man, your pappy." Rom took up his stance, blade low.

Drood raised his voice to be heard over the resounding battle yells. "I'm just saying you getting riled at me doesn't change what can't be changed."

"You promise to do better next time?" said Rom.

"I promise," called Drood.

A wall of men charged into view. Drawn weapons and hateful eyes flashed amber in the wavering pools of torchlight. Their roars blared bugle loud in the mineshaft.

Drood took aim at one in front: a broad, bald man, brass rings in his beard. He slowed his breath to loose his arrow then noticed the bald man wore a smith's apron, not armor or battle leathers. The others, too, were dressed in homespun and cowhide breaches. Rushing at him was a mob of laborers and artisans, simple men.

"Crap," muttered Drood, and let fly.

The arrow took the smith in the knee, and he went down cursing. Drood drew again.

"It's a bunch of yokels," he shouted, piercing a second man in the shoulder joint. "Bet someone's been using the harp."

The wounded man's knees buckled, and the others trampled him in their headlong rush.

Drood winced.

"Meant to just twist him sideways," he said, and nocked a third arrow.

Rom blew out his lips. "Alright. So, no killing?"

Drood dropped a third, then a fourth with crippling shots.

Rom took his friend's silence for a yes and prepared to go to work with the flat of his blade.

The assault was down seven men when Drood groped the floor for another arrow and found none.

"Hells," he spluttered, as the diminished mob crashed into them.

Drood ducked a maul swung to turn his head into jelly. It smashed with a resounding *crack* into the solid rock wall instead. He kicked the legs out from under the man wielding it, then hit him in the throat as he dropped. Maul-less Man flopped to the ground just as another leapt over him. This brawny fellow had arms hairy enough to be a fur shirt. He struck out with a woodsman's axe as if Drood were a prize oak.

"For Anna!" yelled Hairy Arms.

"Who?" asked Drood, parrying the axe with his bow stave and looking for Rom to step in quick.

Rom was busy with three attackers of his own. He dodged a thrusting hay fork, deflected a cut from a broad iron cleaver, then caught the gnarled shaft of a reaping scythe in his big hand and tore it free of the wielder's grip.

The disarmed reaper gawped, blinking in confusion at his empty hands.

Before the man's wits returned, Rom struck. His sword pommel clunked against the side of the fellow's head, knocking him unconscious against the one with the hayfork. Both were small and wiry, with the leathery skin of a life tending fields. They tumbled to the ground and Rom kicked Hayfork in the teeth.

Neither man got up.

The one swinging the cleaver was big as Rom, with an ale barrel gut and a mustache to be proud of. He cut at the swordsman high and low and high again.

"Die!" shouted the mustached man.

Rom caught Mustache's blade with the scythe handle then kneed him where it counts, only that big gut took the blow not the sensitive bits stowed beneath.

Mustache snarled.

Rom growled.

"You'll not hurt my daughter," swore Mustache and punched Rom in the face with his melon-sized fist.

Rom rolled with the blow, letting go the scythe. He staggered but kept his feet.

"I don't *want* to hurt your daughter," said Rom, "whoever she is."

He feinted left, then returned Mustache's clumsy punch with a hard, skilled one of his own. The sound of crunching bone crackled about the tunnel.

Mustache's head snapped back. His eyes went crossed and blood welled from his flattened nose. Rom disarmed him with a flick of his sword then gave that barrel belly a shoving kick. Mustache whooshed air and sprawled hard on his back.

Drood couldn't wait for Rom's help.

Hairy Arms was fast with that axe. Swing after swing Drood had to duck and dodge, darting in with bow limb jabs to Hairy's stomach and ribs. All these did so far was piss off his attacker.

Red-faced, Hairy Arms spluttered, "You stay away from Anna. I won't let you hurt my daughter."

He chopped down but overreached and chunked his axe into the tunnel floor.

Drood sprung, stepping on the axe head to pop the weapon free of the man's grip, then poked him in the eye with his bow.

Hairy Arms roared, cupping his face with one hand, flailing at Drood with the other. The archer slipped around and chopped him hard at the base of the skull with the blade of his hand.

Hairy crumpled like a sack of grain.

Drood checked his friend. The big swordsman stood amidst downed foes, sword held loose, torchlight glinting off its clean blade.

"You good?" asked Drood.

Rom huffed out a breath and rubbed his jaw. "Yeah. I'm good."

He stepped past the unconscious attackers to the only one still writhing around. It was the man in the smith's apron Drood first shot. The smith clutched at his knee, breath hissing through what few teeth he had.

Rom crouched down. "Are we going to have any more trouble out of you?"

The man spat. "You'll not hurt my daughter. I'll kill you for Anna."

Growling like a cornered dog the smith seized Rom's leg.

"Who's this Anna—Ow! Hey, no biting!" Rom jerked his leg back, but the smith clung fast. "I just wanna—. Enough already. Get off." Rom thumped the smith's skull with his sword pommel. The man groaned and collapsed, out cold.

"Well," said Drood, coming up and adjusting his pouches, "That was an odd bit of work, smiths and field hands charging into swords and arrows."

Rom stood and sheathed his sword, brows furrowed as he looked down at the smith.

"Sounds like a girl named Anna is up ahead," continued Drood. "Her father put up quite a fight back there. Thought I was a log needed splitting."

"You mean fathers," said Rom.

Drood open and closed his mouth, head cocked sideways.

"The big one over there with the mustache," said Rom, pointing back up the tunnel, "said he was fighting for his daughter, Anna. So did this fellow." Rom prodded the unconscious smith with his boot.

A breeze blew past, sending the torch flames jumping and shadows raking across the men's faces.

"I really don't like this," said Rom, hands on hips as he looked down the tunnel.

"Neither do I. Not that I have any choice in the matter." Drood adjusted his strained trousers then pulled a length of cord from a pouch. "Best truss these guys up in case they come to still looking to kill us."

The pair set to work scattering weapons and binding limbs before trudging once more down the tunnel.

"Bunch of men claiming one girl as their own? Maybe it's not the harp's power, but a commune or coven deal like that temple back in Sandh," said Drood. "Calling each other brother and sister, that sort of thing."

Rom thumbed the pommel of his sword. "Maybe. Somehow, I doubt it."

Drood clicked his tongue. "Yeah, me too."

The pair rounded a half-dozen corners when Rom held up a hand.

"You hear that?" he asked in a tight whisper.

Drood gave a tense nod.

A woman's lithe, sweet humming rippled up the tunnel.

Rom's jaw slackened and his eyes went winsome. He rubbed at his neck.

"My mum used to hum that tune when I was sick," he said. "And when she darned our mittens."

"That's cute," said Drood, jaw clenched. "Remember why we're here."

Ahead, the dank tunnel's sporadic, flickering torches gave way to a steady glow. The air warmed, teased with scents that tickled Rom and Drood in very different ways.

"Smells like applewood and pan biscuits," whispered Rom. "Melting butter, blueberry jam—no, blackberry."

"How you figure?" replied Drood from the corner of his mouth. "Stinks like a new grave beside an old tannery." He lifted his bow, arrow nocked.

Both had been creeping, cat quiet, ready for another wave of men. But now Rom stood upright, rocking on his toes and grinning like a farm boy when the dinner bell rang.

"Hey," snapped Drood, tapping his friend's elbow. "Focus."

Rom blinked, shaking his head. "Right. Sorry."

The hummed tune repeated clear and strong as the pair slipped closer. They kept low, peering around a jutting bit of tunnel wall.

Opening before them was a high-ceilinged chamber that had once been a tunnel junction. Now, the other shafts were closed off with rubble and this room converted into a hodgepodge lounge of sorts. A threadbare patchwork of once-fine silk rugs carpeted the floor. Mismatched furniture lay scattered about, upholstery as tattered as the carpeting. Melted tallow of various hues coated flaking, gilt candle stands in the corners and black, oily smoke twisted up from the misshapen blobs burning atop each. A low fire glowed in an iron brazier at the room's center.

Rom grinned the grin of one enjoying a long-awaited homecoming.

Drood scowled like a priest entering a bawdy house.

A single soul occupied the room: a girl in her early teens, reclining on a divan beyond the brazier. She wore a white linen dress that drooped from one shoulder. Her small feet were bare, her raven hair plaited and pinned atop her head in the noble fashion. Eyes closed, lips pursed in a soft pout, she worked a hand in the air, fingers dancing to the tune she hummed.

"There be the daughter," whispered Rom.

Drood sucked his teeth. He fixated on the softly glowing, cherub and nymph covered platinum form of Kandissa's harp resting in the girl's lap.

"Anna," he said, voice tight and lifeless. "Thief." He drew the nocked arrow to his cheek.

Rom caught the movement.

"No!" he barked, slapping at his friend's weapon.

Drood cursed. His bowstring thrummed. The arrow flew wide.

The girl stopped humming.

Rom dragged Drood upright.

"She's just a child," he said, scanning the blank face of his long-time companion. "We don't kill children."

Drood worked his mouth, bright red lips crinkling, and returned his friend's gaze with a questioning one of his own. "I-I know we don't. I didn't want to. Just...Just suddenly—."

"You were compelled." The girl's voice flowed past both men like a singing brook.

They turned, Rom still gripping Drood's arm.

"Are you Anna?" asked Rom.

She tipped her head, watching them with languid eyes. Sitting up, she pulled the harp close, her dancing hand drifting to her lap.

"He *was* compelled," continued Rom, voice soft. "He's under a geas to return that harp to its owner." The swordsman left the curse's other stipulation unsaid. "So, if you'd kindly hand it over, we'll be on our way."

She laughed, a gay chuckle too knowing for one so young. "Let me guess. A kiss? Oh, Kandissa. Still sending hounds to do her bidding. Funny, but I don't feel *compelled* to give up her toy just yet."

Drood tensed in Rom's grip, shoulder muscles bunching, knees dipping as if ready to spring. Then his breath caught, he cleared his throat, and he straightened again. A bead of sweat trickled behind his ear.

"Y-you must," said Drood, free hand twitching. "The goddess wants it b-back."

"Anna, please," urged Rom, "give it to us and we'll leave you alone."

Anna smiled at the big swordsman, caressing her harp.

"What's your name?" she asked.

"Rom," he said, blushing.

"I like you, Rom." She licked her fingertips. "I think I'll keep you."

Drood's eyes went wide. "Stop!" he shouted, but too late.

Anna plucked a note.

And sung.

Rom had argued their entire journey here over the supposed

power of Kandissa's harp. Drood had no doubts, since he was here because of an enchantment from the very goddess that claimed it.

The song Anna struck was childish and off key. Drood cringed and snarled, squinting one eye against it. Rom's grin broadened. His eyes grew vacant. His grip on Drood fell slack.

"Mum's tune," mumbled the big swordsman. "Fried fritters and mulled cider."

Drood yanked free of Rom's hold, feet stomping, one hand fighting the other for control of his bow.

"Gah! No!" he sputtered, chest heaving like a dog on a hot day. "I w-won't..."

Little Anna kept playing, making no shift in her leisure save a slow tilt of the head as she watched what unfurled.

"This is home," said Rom, unblinking. He raised his sword and turned to Drood. "I will protect Anna."

Drood stared wide-eyed at his friend's transformation. His own twitchy perturbations ceasing at this new predicament.

"Rom," he said clearly. "What are you—? Aw hells."

He dove sideways as Rom chopped down. Air whistled with the force of a blow that would have split Drood's skull.

"Rom! Get a grip on yourself." Drood scrambled, backpedaling and tumbling behind rickety chairs and broken tables.

Anna licked her lips and played on.

"Okay, okay, I see what's happening here," sputtered Drood to the girl as he dodged behind a chipped marble pedestal. "Having a little fun, are we?"

Anna flashed pearly teeth. "Just a little."

Rom charged in.

"You'll not hurt her," he bellowed. "You won't hurt my daughter!"

His sword chinked off the cut stone as Drood dodged aside, jumping behind a chair. Rom hacked at him again. Wood crunched and cracked.

"Knock this off, will ya?" shouted Drood, sheltering behind a rickety set of freestanding shelves. "My pappy once said enemies stab you in the back, but friends do it to your face. Never thought he was being literal." He jumped over a mahogany bench as Rom roared behind him.

The big swordsman seized a busted chair with one hand and hurled it at Drood.

"You'll not hurt her!"

Drood squeaked and ducked. The chair remnant exploded in fragments against the wall. He kicked an accent table at Rom then rushed for the entrance.

Anna lay on her divan, playing, singing, and smiling, adding a musical giggle as Drood sprinted by.

Drood reached the mouth of the chamber and skidded to a stop as if an unseen hand had him by the belt. He gripped his bow tight and stood stiff.

"I'm s-sorry, Rom," he muttered. "Kandissa will not be denied."

He pulled an arrow from his quiver and turned. Sweat ran freely down his cheeks.

Rom stumbled over Drood's kicked table then lifted his chin, knees trembling, sword shaking in his hand.

"Go ahead," he said. "I-If you don't...I...I...."

Anna glared at her hesitating champion and changed the tune. "He's not your friend," she hummed. "He wants me dead. Only you can stop him."

Rom's own cheeks were wet. His lips quivered. When he spoke again, his voice was wooden.

"I will stop him," said Rom.

And he leapt forward.

"I'm sorry," Drood muttered, tears mingling with sweat.

He loosed his arrow.

Rom blinked half-way through his leap. The vacant glaze slipped from his eyes and his mind screamed to look out. He dropped his sword a heartbeat before barreling into his friend.

The pair crashed to the floor in a heap of groans and curses.

They lay there for a moment in a tangled pile, breathing hard, not moving.

Rom rubbed his head and got off his friend.

"What the hells happened?" he asked.

Drood let out a thin, wheezy whine and rolled to his side, hands cupping his crotch. He squealed, "My sausage and taters, you big ox. You mashed em' both."

"Sorry," said Rom. "Wasn't exactly—oh, gods."

Color left the swordsman's face as he looked wide-eyed at little Anna. She stood behind the brazier, harp abandoned on her divan. She was red-cheeked, and her lips twitched. Six inches of arrow shaft stuck straight out of her chest.

"You shot her," mumbled Rom.

Drood's wheezing ceased, and his voice dropped back to its normal pitch.

"Had to," he breathed. "It was her or you."

Anna looked down at the impaling arrow. A dark stain grew from the wound. Not a red stain, a black one, black as an empty cave. When she spoke, the words came out in a throaty gurgle of bottomless malice.

"Now that wasn't very nice."

Rom popped to his feet, pulling Drood up with him.

"Easy," said the archer, wincing.

Anna toyed with the arrow in her chest as if it were a piece of jewelry she disapproved of.

"That shot would have dropped a bear," grunted Drood, adjusting his trousers and taking up his bow.

"Boys," said Anna, wrapping both hands around the shaft. "Do I look like a bear to you?"

"I don't know what in the hells you are," said Rom, color returning to his face.

The girl's expression hardened, eyes narrowing to steely slits. Her lips curled back in a snarl of rage.

"Kandissa can have the hells," she crowed. With a swift tug she jerked the shaft from her chest, the length dripping shiny black as it came free.

Drood swallowed the lump in his throat at the sight of that ichor-coated arrow.

"Is this better or worse?" asked Rom, leaning over his friend.

"I'll let you know." Drood grabbed another arrow. He only had three left.

The room echoed with a wooden crack as Anna snapped her arrow in two with one hand. "The harp stays with me. As do you, in my belly."

Anna's green eyes went iron black, and she wailed.

Both men clapped their hands to their ears against the pain of that cry. But their gazes stayed fixed on the horror before them.

Anna grew into something...terrible.

Her arms and legs stretched to lanky, sinewy limbs. Knobby-knuckled, iron-clawed hands brushed the floor. Her dress burst to expose black veined, mottled flesh stretching and sagging over her growing form like wet leather. The plaited hair shredded into lank lake grass that circled a bald, bulbous pate. The child's face contorted, twisted, snapped, and popped. Jaw and nose became a vicious, needle-toothed maw. And her ears melted away, leaving only oozing holes in her skull.

The saggy, naked abomination that had been Anna, cackled and pointed with a dagger claw at the two men. Gone was the babbling lilt of a young girl, now she spoke with the burble of a paint pot bubbling up, and the acrid reek of sulfur came with it.

"I shall feast on you tonight then play Kandissa's harp to ease my digestion."

"This is worse," muttered Drood, nearly dropping his arrow as his hands shook. "She's no Anna, she's Anna M-Midnight—bog demon, devourer of the forlorn—a hag, a true gods-damned hag."

"That may be, but now we know what to do," said Rom, retrieving his sword. "What we do best. Go for her eyes!"

Rom charged.

Anna Midnight met him with a cackle and a swing of her tree limb arm. Hooked talons clawed the air, eager to rend him apart.

Rom ducked her attack, countering with a sword stroke at her wrist that sent a spray of black across her abandoned divan, and Kandissa's precious harp.

Anna howled in rage.

"Ha-ha!" Rom shouted. But his celebration came too early.

Anna's backswing caught him full in the chest and sent the twenty stone man flying. He crashed through a knick-knack laden bookcase and a decorative floor vase before crunching against the cave wall.

He slid to the floor with a groan, eyes closed.

"Shit," said Drood. Anna Midnight stood side-on to him after knocking Rom away. Drood sunk an arrow high up between her ribs.

She howled, again. Leaving the unmoving Rom, she thundered for Drood.

"I will tear off your limbs," she chortled, spittle dripping from her lipless maw, "and drink the lifeblood from your still beating heart."

Drood skittered aside to put some obstacles between him and the hag. He shot for her eye, but Anna got her left hand up and took the shaft in the twisted flesh of the same forearm Rom had cut.

Her clawed hand hung limp. Rom had severed the sinews.

Side-stepping, Drood scanned the tight battlefield. Chairs were upended or demolished. Settees and divans thrown aside. Only one piece of furnishing remained unmoved, glowing warmly as it had been when he and Rom first arrived. A sly grin grew across Drood's face as he maneuvered and nocked his last arrow.

Rom didn't move.

Anna yanked the arrow from her side and ripped the other from her arm with a gurgling cry.

"I've a better idea," she said, spittle flying. "I think instead I shall bind you and start by eating your feet, then work my way up, bit by tasty bit."

Drood circled then stopped when there were a good ten paces between him and the hag. Sweat caught in his eyebrows, edging the hag with a blurry sheen. He shifted his bow to his right hand, then reached into a pouch.

"My feet?" he quipped. "What, raw? That's no good. Everyone knows a sautéed foot is best, with a little rosemary and garlic."

"Now I'm really hungry," cackled Anna, flexing her good hand, talons rasping together. "Let's finish this."

Drood glanced at Rom. His eyes were open and Anna Midnight had her back to him.

The swordsman didn't move but met Drood's eye.

The archer nodded, then spat at Anna.

"Yes," he said. "Let's."

The hag lunged, reaching over the lone, crackling, smoking obstacle to bury her claws in the archer's chest.

Drood shot, aiming again for her eye, not looking to see it hit. He dove headlong beneath her clutching hand. Coming up on a knee, he hurled the open vial of oil he'd drawn from his pouch, aiming at the hag's distended, mottled gut. Then he threw himself bodily at the flaming brazier.

His arrow had missed, but it forced Anna to shield her face, allowing every drop of Drood's oil to splash across her leathery torso.

Drood hit the brazier and knocked its contents flying at the hag. Sparks flew. Red-hot embers landed to sear into her and set the oil alight. Cave air filled with the foul reek of burning flesh.

Anna Midnight reared and wheeled.

"The pain!" she cried. "The pain!"

Flinging her arms, she spun in a wild dance to escape the biting flames. Furnishings were battered aside, scattered like ninepins. The fire caught on frayed upholstery and torn rugs. Smoke choked the chamber.

Drood covered his nose with a sleeve and fought to ignore the hag's piteous cries. He crouched against the cave wall and looked for Rom. The swordsman had lain not a stone's toss from where Drood now hid, but he was no longer there.

"Please, gods," whispered Drood, blinking against the smoke.

The hag's scream grew louder. She spun and stumbled right at Drood. Her right eye had melted and now dribbled down her monstrous face. Her hair was aflame, her chest charred black, skin split and oozing.

Drood grabbed for an arrow that wasn't there.

"Oh, crap." He dug under his belt for a knife.

"Tear you apart!" cried Anna, both arms out, good claw clutching for Drood. Iron talons glistened despite the smoke.

Then her terrible, taloned hands dropped from her arms to

crunch on the cave room floor. They rocked and writhed like spiders dying on their backs.

"Gah!" cried Drood as cold, black liquid stung his face. He swept his eyes clean and saw a tall silhouette slide into the smoke between him and the hag.

"Your day is done, Anna," called Rom.

The hag reeled back, arms thrown to the sky, ichor squirting from the stumps of her wrists.

"Devour...YOU!" she roared, needle teeth clashing.

The hag threw herself at Rom, great maw open to swallow him whole.

Drood reached for his friend.

"No!"

Over the crackling flames and wailing hag came a sound like wind cutting silk and then a sickening, sucking chop. Anna Midnight's enraged cry ended in a wet wheeze and a heavy thud.

A boulder big as a strong box rolled straight for Drood. He scurried back. It stopped two feet away, rocking to a halt—Anna's head, lone good eye staring upward.

"Holy hells," he breathed, one quavering hand pointing his knife at the hag head, the other pressed to his heaving chest.

Rom loomed up out of the smoke. Black goo was splattered across his chest. More clung to his sword blade and boots.

"We should go," he said, offering his friend a hand.

Drood took it, grinning.

"I thought you were a goner," he said.

"I've heard that before," replied Rom, rubbing the back of his head. "Damn thing was wicked strong."

"Let's get out of here," said Drood patting his friend on the shoulder as he brushed past.

The nimble archer zigzagged through the fire, flames lowering as what remained to burn burned up. He scooped up Kandissa's harp. Despite the flames and flying hag blood, the instrument lay unsoiled. The rug beneath in perfect, if a bit worn, condition.

Rom waited for Drood at the chamber's entrance.

"After you," he coughed, mouth covered by a surprisingly clean handkerchief.

"My thanks, Good Sir," quipped Drood and the pair sped away, freeing Anna's no longer bewitched men, then leaving before anything else went wrong.

THE ALLEYWAY LEADING to The Pig and Pie tavern was unchanged from when Rom and Drood had left it three days ago. If anything, it had acquired more rubbish and a stronger stench of repurposed ale. To the pair of smokey, singed, and battered adventurers, it could not have been more inviting.

"Never thought I'd be happy to see this place again," said Drood. He brushed the dust from his clothes and adjusted his tented trousers. He spat in his palm and smoothed down his hair.

"What are you doing?" asked Rom, taking no pains to alter his road-weary appearance.

Drood stopped his grooming. "Well, we are about to see a goddess after all."

"The same thrice-cursed lust goddess that put us through the wringer just to get her toy back." Rom held up the sack containing Kandissa's harp.

Drood shrugged and grinned at his friend. "Still a goddess." He gave his hair another once over, settled his pouches and quiver, and strode for the door.

"You go for a kiss, and I'll knock you flat," called Rom, stomping after his friend.

"If kissing appears imminent, you are welcome to do so," said Drood.

The inside of The Pig and Pie was much like the outside. Instead of piled human waste scattered about an alley, wasted humans were scattered about a low room, leaning heavily on cracked and gouged tables. And while the smells of piss and ale lingered, they were tempered by man sweat, leather, and bad mutton left too long over a greasy fire.

In a far corner, lit by three sooty lanterns and a sultry radiance all her own, sat Kandissa. She reclined on a cushioned bench, a half-dozen empty wine bottles on the table beside her. Today, she dressed the part of a voluptuous pirate captain, complete with golden chalice in one perfect hand and a sleek pipe producing curls of fragrant smoke in the other. She propped her booted feet on a stool, their leather tops leading to tight, thigh-hugging leggings of creamy calf-skin. Her red coat with rolled cuffs and gold accents lay splayed open over a lace-bodice shirt lacking any laces, exposing plenty of bodice. Her brown curls spilled past her shoulders, framing a sleek face with high cheeks, watchful eyes, heavy lashes, and full, ruby-red—and very kissable—lips.

"Here come my heroes." Kandissa gave a wicked smile, pulled on her pipe, and puffed out three heart-shaped smoke rings. "A sweet tingle down low tells me you've brought me good news. And a present."

She didn't offer them a chair. Nor did she sit up to see what they'd brought her. She merely eyed Drood like a leopard spying a wounded fawn and took a swig from her chalice.

"Dear Kandissa," said Drood with a smooth, sly grin to match hers. "We have traveled far and endured many trials to fulfill your wish. We return successful." He took the sack from Rom and held it up. "I have here your very—hey!"

Rom snatched the bag back and tossed it on the table. Wine bottles tumbled to clink, clatter, and shatter on the floor.

The swordsman thumbed the pommel of his sheathed blade. "We did your dirty work. Now free him from your damn spell."

Kandissa shifted her gaze from Drood to Rom. She pulled the pipe from her lips but stayed put.

Drood gasped and stepped forward. "My lady, I do apologize for —mph!"

Rom slapped his free hand over his friend's mouth, keeping his eyes locked with the temptress.

Kandissa uncrossed her legs to thump her boots softly on the floor. She set down chalice and pipe and tugged at the string binding the sack shut. She did all that without surrendering her gaze from Rom.

Reaching into the sack, she touched its contents, and a wave of ecstasy swept her face. She closed her eyes and smiled, then caught Rom's eye again as she drew forth her harp.

Drood gasped.

Rom growled, "You'd best leave that in the bag until we're long gone." He gripped his sword tighter, corded muscles in his forearm emphasizing his point. "Get rid of the spell, now."

Kandissa gave Rom an appraising look, eyes roving over every inch of him.

Then she licked her lips.

Rom's eyes went wide. The lump of his throat slid up and down. He let go his sword. His cheeks twitched, and he stiffened.

Drood watched the exchange and paled behind Rom's smothering hand.

The goddess shrugged, withdrawing her hand from the sack to take up pipe and cup once more.

In a voice of velvet by firelight she said, "He was free the moment I touched the harp."

And he was. Drood felt a distinct *relaxation* in his trousers.

"Though truth told," said Kandissa, "there is another service you two could help me with." She leaned back, leaving her feet on the ground and legs splayed open. "The pickings around here are...less than desirable, and you both deserve a reward for your hard work."

She played the stem of her pipe between those lush, hungry lips.

Drood cocked an eyebrow. A thin whine escaped his stifled mouth.

The swordsman's hand shook in front of Drood's face. His whole muscly arm quavered. He smacked his lips.

"A r-reward?" mumbled Rom, gawping.

"Why yes," hissed the Goddess of Lust, tracing her pipestem down the curve of her neck to tap at the top of her swelling bosom. "You've earned it."

A shaky, cockeyed grin grew on Rom's face. He looked down at Drood and released his friend.

Drood huffed and sucked in a breath, eyes darting between his longtime pal and the personification of prurience before him.

Then, together, he and Rom laughed.

They laughed until their jollity filled the dank breadbox that was The Pig and Pie. The big swordsman slapped his thigh, tipping his head back and howling. Drood laughed himself out of breath, doubling over in a tight wheeze only to rise back up, face red as the goddess' coat, blinking away tears.

When both had wind enough for words, they took one look at Kandissa—with her sour, puckered lips, her narrowed, dagger eyes, and her white-knuckled grip on her wine cup—and broke down laughing yet again. The goddess turned aside, feigning interest in a few words of profanity carved in her tabletop, as the drunks around the bar laughed along, not wanting to be left out of whatever joke had just been told.

When the rollicking wave subsided, Kandissa cleared her throat and straightened in her seat.

"Finished, are we?" she asked.

Drood whistled. "Yeah, just about. Oh, but that was a good one. The three of us? Oh..." He dabbed the corners of his eyes with a knuckle.

"Lady—er, goddess, madame—you've had your fun," said Rom, "And it's been a while since we've shared such a laugh. So, our thanks for that." He tapped his chest as if quieting a racing heart, then dropped his hand to rest once more on his sword pommel. "But you're crazy if you think either of us is getting within arm's reach of you ever again."

"Yes, our thanks," said Drood, adjusting his loose, comfortable, flat-front trousers. "But my pappy always said, 'A friend is someone you should share everything with, except a lover and a debt.' And Rom and I have been friends a *long* time."

Both men turned for the door. Rom looked back from the threshold, glancing around at the bleary patrons, all of whom now gave Kandissa their full attention.

"Besides," he said with a smirk, "Looks like you have plenty to entertain you."

Rom and Drood left The Pig and Pie, chuckling their way down the alley.

After the door banged closed behind them, Kandissa pulled her harp from its sack. She smiled as she set it in her lap.

"Barkeep!" snapped the goddess as assorted barflies left their stools to swagger her way. She licked her lips. "Another round for these lads. And I believe some music is in order."

SOMETHING ABOUT MARY
BILL BUSH

"My name is GRIT."

The pretty young woman ignored my introduction and continued down the empty sidewalk.

"Mary, I said my name is GRIT."

She quickened her pace, but I had no trouble keeping up.

Twenty-two, physically fit, wavy dark hair, and in the middle of a master's program in biological research. And stubborn.

"Mary Samantha Yoder."

She spun, zapped me with a taser, and ran. They always run.

I followed at a distance and remained out of sight. She was obviously going home, and it would be easier to wait until she quit running.

She effortlessly darted up the three flights of stairs to her apartment and slammed the door.

When I entered her apartment, Mary sprinted from her bedroom, screamed, and swung an aluminum bat.

"I wish you wouldn't do that."

The veins distended in her neck; her forehead, arms, and legs dripped with sweat.

She swung again, and I caught the bat with my hand. Mary gaped, abandoned the bat, and locked herself in her bedroom.

"Please hurry," she cried into the phone when I appeared before her.

"Hello? Hello?"

She threw her phone, and it crashed against the wall where I had been standing when she let it go.

She shook her head and backed up to the wall. "Please! Don't!"

They always assume *I'm* the bad guy. It hurt.

"If you calm down, I can explain my presence."

I hated the look of fear that washed over Mary's flawless face. The last thing I wanted was to cause her anguish. I simply wanted to know her before...while there was still time.

I shouldn't have exposed myself, but I couldn't resist. I loved her.

"What are you doing here?" she demanded.

"I wanted to approach you weeks ago, but I'm not allowed to interfere," I explained.

"How do you know me? Have we met?"

"No, we haven't met, but I've been following you for weeks."

"What?" she slunk to the floor, shaking.

"It isn't what you think. Stalking people is part of my job."

That didn't help. She sobbed, and when I tried to console her, she pulled away.

The doorbell rang, followed by loud pounding. Mary tried to scream but instead coughed and clutched her chest.

"The neighbors can't help you," I said, moving aside so she'd have a direct path to the door.

She didn't make a move to escape; I'm sure from a lack of strength. Mary only had a few minutes left.

"What, what do you want with me?" she sputtered between breaths.

I sat beside her on the floor. "I'm just doing my job."

"You're here to kill me?"

"No, I'm not allowed to interfere."

"What do you mean?"

"GRIT stands for Grim Reaper in Training."

She gasped.

"Actually, I'm GRIT 66783. You're about to experience a pulmonary embolism."

"A blood clot in my lungs?"

"Any minute now," I said grimly.

She looked up. "You did this to me?"

"No. My job isn't to cause death; just to collect your soul."

Her red eyes dropped another tear. "You mean..."

"I'm afraid so."

"Shouldn't you be happy?"

Sirens roared outside as the doorbell buzzed again.

"I'm not very good at my job."

She stood but fell against the window sill for balance. "What does that mean?"

"You better lie down."

She nodded, and I helped her to the bed.

She lay staring at me. I'm sure she was trying to decide whether or not to believe me.

"I like people. I get attached. I didn't need to watch you before today, but I read your bio and I had to know you."

The doorbell rang insistently, followed by pounding.

She stared at me for the longest time. I didn't know how to read her quietness, but it made me uncomfortable.

"If you love me, can't you stop it?"

I gently brushed the hair from her face. "Like I said, I'm not allowed to interfere."

She violently coughed again and blood splattered from her mouth. I grabbed two towels from her bathroom—one to clean up blood and the other to wipe the sweat from her face.

She glowed like an angel. Watching her suffer tormented me. I wanted to reach inside and remove the clot to save her, or squeeze her heart to end her suffering.

Why her?

Finally, a crash, shouts, and footsteps.

Mary's eyes shot wide for a brief moment before they shut, and she went limp.

The door burst open, and two police officers stormed in. One began CPR while the second radioed for an ambulance.

I LOOKED DOWN AT MARY, lying in white. After all she had been through, she looked content and peaceful. Beautiful.

Her surgeon was scribbling in her chart when the two police officers tapped on the open door and entered.

They introduced themselves and asked how Mary was doing.

"That was a close one, but she should pull through." The surgeon shook his head. "A few moments later...you two saved her life."

Hours later, in the dark hospital room Mary opened her eyes. She coughed and winced.

"Are you here for me?"

"Yes."

Her face fell.

"I-I mean no," I quickly stuttered. "I'm just visiting."

I smiled.

She reached out, so I took her hand.

"I'm not dead?"

"The doctor said you will be fine."

"But..."

She closed her eyes. I thought she'd faded back to sleep, but when I stood, she squeezed my hand. "You saved my life. If you hadn't chased me, I wouldn't have called the police and no one would have been there when I..."

I shrugged.

"I thought you aren't allowed to interfere?"

"I may have arrived a little too early," I admitted. "But like I said, I'm not very good at my job."

SEAFROG

JOHN ARTHUR NEAL

"Sit ye not in the seat of the scornful," said the sailor to his beer. Erik's mouth cut into his beard like a slash across a glacier, as bitter as the drink he downed. Slowly, he rippled the tattooed dragon across the dark wooden muscles of his forearm.

"What you on about, matey?" Sven, a ship's cook, sat on a stool at the scarred mahogany bar to his right, so drunk he dribbled ale on his shirt.

There was a time Erik had no patience for slobs like Sven. But they'd served together on numerous ships—fishers, shrimpers, whalers —him up in the masts and out on the nets, and Sven below decks in the galley. No, he would not bash that bleary imbecility battered by bosses and booze and too, too many boats. Sure, Sven was soft and slow, but he was one of the few men Erik might count as a friend.

"Me." The sailor took a sip of his lager. "*I* am the scornful."

"Aye, you have thorns. So does a plum tree." Sven belched. "You canna be what you are not. What is more, the world needs plums."

"You're as full of shit as a sperm whale."

Sven shrugged.

Erik snorted and looked around the basement tavern. Pipe smoke curled among the rough-hewn rafters, the stuffed fish on the walls, crewmen and townsmen throwing darts and laughing raucously. Still no Jude. She sure was taking a long time with her last customer. Or maybe she'd quit for the night, already bedded down in the tall, wooden inn above the tavern. He hoped not, for Lady Lust stirred deep in his bilges.

Jude was a paid piece of ass, but at least she was fair. She had her rules and she had her prices, and she never discriminated on account of race, creed, color, or what flag your ship flew. Jude was his favorite lady in all the towns where he'd docked. She looked at him as though he mattered, as though he was worth more than the bills he left for her. She was getting older—as they all were—but she was still a beautiful woman with a tender soul.

Erik spat tobacco juice at the can surrounded by peanut shells. He never missed the spittoon. To do so would be yet another failure, another sign that he was as stupid and weak as his father always said— before his pa went to the fair—forever. His mother claimed he must have been mugged. His uncles wondered about wanderlust. All Erik knew was that his father's voice haunted him still. "Perfection is the only goal."

"FIRE!" someone shouted.

Erik could smell the wood smoke, as though the word alone had conjured it up.

Sven stumbled off his stool and lurched against the bar. His eyes casting frantically about, pleading for deliverance. Like a feral dog Erik had harpooned once for barking in the night, Sven's eyes begged for mercy from a merciless man. Erik knew who would die in a tie for survival. It wouldn't be him. And it wouldn't be Sven dying there that night, either.

Erik grabbed Sven's shirt and dragged him across the room. Five long strides took the sailor to the stairs, with Sven trailing like a dinghy behind a schooner. Another five steps took them up to the door and the cobblestone street outside.

A crowd gathered and gawked.

Erik walked away from the building and turned back to see. The tinderbox inn above the basement saloon was ablaze. Flames engulfed the first floor and flickers could be seen through the second-floor windows. The third story was dark, as was the widow's walk, the railed porch around the uppermost garret, where wives paced day after day to watch for their husbands' ships to come home from the sea. To the women left behind, the ocean was a whore who'd stolen their men's hearts and sucked out their blood, leaving only rum and forgotten birthdays. And all too often, the briny deep spawned storms that dragged their men to watery graves.

"Cor," said Sven as he stared at the blaze.

With a crash, the first floor fell to the ginmill below. To quell his pity for the poor souls he heard screaming, Erik spat at a lamppost. He never missed.

Nothing to do but join the bucket brigade. It wasn't his battle—he wasn't a townsman—but Erik fought it anyway. He took the front line and dashed into the fiery inferno to splash where it would do the most good. He grinned against the heat at the challenge, for work was too easy these days, what with the bloody unions and the all-day card games. A man of action, Erik loved the feel of sweat soaking through his shirt and the need for speed and efficiency.

He was relentless in his demands for more, more, *more* water from the line of volunteers. Many of them were feeble, most of them were tired, and all of them were afraid to stop swinging bucket after bucket after leaden bucket. The dozens—nay, hundreds—of heavy pails of seawater scooped from the bay would tax the strength of giants, let alone mere mortals like these townsfolk. Nevertheless, Erik urged them to keep going, to stop the raging fire from spreading to neighbors and roaring through their little burg.

The second floor buckled, and a wall fell away with the *whoomph* of a mainsail collapsing. Ribbons of fire curled out from the flower boxes on the third story. The wooden gargoyles under the eaves hissed and snickered.

The buckets stopped coming. Erik swore at the midshipman, who only looked puzzled.

Then he noticed people pointing upward.

Behind the rails of the widow's walk, above the old oaken beams now lit with an eerie golden glow, something moved. Or rather, waved. From side to side. Something white, like a sheet.

Over the roar of the house-sized stove, a wee woman's voice. Jude's voice, Erik knew, as she called out once more.

Her kinfolk came running with blankets. Would Jude jump into one? Could she?

Something told him no. Erik had heard her voice too many times —laughing at the bar, giggling in his ear, whispering to him as he left her bed. And he'd heard pure panic before, too. He knew Jude wouldn't jump, even to safety.

Erik couldn't let her die.

He growled at the brigade to keep the water coming and tramped over to the side of the building. Perhaps he could go up on the roof of the store next door and climb across the abyss to rescue her. Ha! An opium pipe dream. He stuck out his neck for no one. He wasn't a coward, he told himself, but neither was he a chump.

Nevertheless, something in him knew he *could* do it. Or rather, that it *might* be possible. And there was something in Jude's voice that sounded so sad and lost and lonely—the way whales sigh when they know they're going to die—that he had to try. Losing Jude would leave a hole in his heart too big to fill.

He ran to the wharf and untied a hemp rope from a mooring. He reached for the coil, and froze. But only for a moment. He didn't allow himself to think, for in *thinking*, Jude was dead and so might he be, too. He would only *act*, the sooner the better.

He kicked in the door to the store and ran past the stacks to the stairs in the back. Two at a time he took the steps—one flight, two flights—until at last, he found the attic hatch. He pulled a string, and the ladder fell with a clatter.

Erik climbed into the deep darkness and paused. He was all alone, and it was quiet. The shouting and sputtering came thinly through the walls. He felt removed from the scene outside. No one knew where he was or why. He wasn't a hero, had no medals of honor. No one would know if he failed. Well, except for himself. He'd know.

He spat. At what, it was too dark to see.

Why should he care if some slut boiled in her own piss? Do the world a favor—stop venereal disease. But he did care. He cared more than he ever imagined he could before her life was in peril.

Aye, but would he do it? Risk life and limb on a senseless gamble? An idiot's errand? Sven said we cannot be what we are not, and he was definitely not a fool. Erik sighed. He'd figure out *why* later. Right now, he had to figure out *how*.

Dimly he saw where light from the fire fought through a paint-caked window. Erik grunted and crawled over. He felt for the latch and found it. The window was hinged at the top and opened out from the bottom, but only as far as a brass chain allowed. He closed the window and then, with a sharp jab, snapped it back out. The chain didn't break—it pulled loose from the dry-rotted wood.

The window was a wee bit wider than his shoulders. If he laid on his back and wriggled out under the window pane, he might be able to reach the rain gutter with his fingertips. Would he fall backward and land on his head, six fathoms below? Would a rickety rain gutter hold his weight? He'd seen the condition of the wood. And he had no idea how the roof was fixed for handholds. He stalled.

He was brought out of his doldrums by the sound of singing. No, it was praying he heard. Sobs and Hail-Marys and I'm-sorrys all mixed up in a tuneless croon. He hadn't realized he was that close. He could look right across at the flaming flower boxes, and the voice he heard wasn't far removed. And if he didn't do something about that voice, it would haunt him for the rest of his life—and then some, maybe.

So, looping the itchy rope over his shoulders, Erik rolled over on his back and inched out over the concrete sidewalk far below. He was top-heavy, for he tolerated no paunch, and the rope was an albatross around his throat. The window kept falling on his face, so he had to hold it as well as himself. He managed to reach up and grasp the rim of the rain gutter as his rear end left the window ledge. He had no choice but to trust that the builders had used enough nails as he wriggled the rest of the way out.

Standing tiptoe on the window ledge, he chinned himself on the rain gutter and looked around. The roof was steep and scaly, with splintered shingles and loose leaves.

A pipe poked up from the debris about ten feet away. To get to it, he'd have to let go of his toe-hold on the window ledge and dangling, edge sideways on the rain gutter. That he could do it, he did not doubt. Why, he'd once hung on a broken yardarm in a storm for over two hours. That the molding would hold, he did doubt. But like that yardarm, he had no choice. It was do or die trying, because if you didn't try, you'd die for sure. And the moans from above reminded him it wasn't his fate alone that dangled there that night.

As he grip-slid sideways along the rusty gutter, he scraped his hands a number of times. Once he missed a hold and pried off a fingernail. Youch! But hell, he'd lost bigger chunks of meat before, all in a day's work. He finally wrapped his bloody palm around the pipe.

Gritting his teeth, Erik hauled himself up and hooked his armpit around the pipe. Now he was stable enough to swing a leg up to the side and catch his ankle on the gutter. Slowly, like a burly boa constrictor, he coiled his torso over the edge and, at last, lay on the slip-shod shingles.

The smoke was thicker and blacker now as flames lapped up the roofing tar on the inn.

Across the gap, about six yards over, Jude's whimpers turned into coughs.

Carefully, the sailor got to his feet. Cupping his hands, he yelled, "Yo, Jude! Listen 'ere! Catch this rope and tie it to the rail!"

"Erik?"

The crowd buzzed, and people pointed and waved. He heard Sven explain who he was.

Erik repeated his instructions to Jude, who called back, "I'll try."

He had no harpoon but figured the weight of the rope itself would carry it far enough.

His first toss slithered down the opposite wall. So did his second. And third. But Erik wasn't about to give up. He threw the rope again.

Jude waited with arms outstretched though she couldn't possibly see through the soot.

Finally, it seemed she felt the sting of the stringy hemp as it slapped against her neck. By reflex alone, it appeared, she snagged it. Jude wasn't a knots man, but she could whip up a batch of half-hitches, the simplest knot—loop the rope and pull through, loop and pull, loop and pull.

The sailor tied his end of the rope to the pipe and tested the tension. It would have to do. Gingerly, he extended his body along the rope and swayed above the crowd far below, grateful for his rope climbing skill.

He got to the top, climbed over the banister, and found Jude had passed out cold. He knew it was only minutes—if that—before she died from the fumes. He stripped off his belt and cinched it around her waist, then knotted the loose end of the belt around the rope so he could slide her over to the store. He eased her over the rail, climbed after, and wrapped his legs around her ribs. Her head nestled against his chest as they began their descent. Jude was as limp as cold flounder, and he dreaded finding out she was indeed dead.

Halfway down, he heard an ominous creaking. The railing behind his head was giving away. If a rope could rattle, that's what it did. He took a deep breath, relaxed his grip, and slid. The momentum of two bodies gave him rope burns he knew would leave scars he'd always see. Just as the rail behind them broke free, they reached the lower end of the rope, banged against the store's panels, and wobbled to a stop.

The sailor blinked unbidden tears from his eyes. Damn, his palms smarted!

He looked down at the piece of broken rail, which twitched as it swung. The rope was far too short to reach the ground. And his tortured hands wanted nothing more to do with climbing.

His charge came coughing to life and tried to breathe deep into lungs bound tight by the belt. Jude clawed at him, and her feet blindly battered the siding planks.

Erik swore at her and clamped her with his legs so hard she had to listen. "Hold the rope while I get up on the roof, then I'll hoist you up like a catch of mackerel."

She settled down and gripped the scratchy cord with all her might.

He gingerly disentangled and clambered up.

Although he could wedge one foot behind the pipe, the other had little traction, and he almost lost his footing. To get Jude past the rain gutter, he had to lean out over the long drop.

The townsfolk below were quiet, watching his every move.

Thanks to the belt, Jude could hang onto the rope with only one hand and her legs. She grasped the pipe with her other hand just as

Erik was about to topple over. He knelt down and helped her over the rain gutter. Panting, they planted their asses safely on the roof, with their heels propped in the gutter to keep from sliding.

As they sat clinging to each other, the sailor felt something in his guts come unsprung. When he feared she was dead on the slide down the rope, he'd locked her away in a cold mental coffin, next to his old mare of a mother, his whiskey-drinking uncles, and his long-lost pet falcon. Now that Jude was alive beside him, he realized he would have missed her far worse.

Who would miss him, were he never to come back from an ocean away? Not his captains, for he took no guff, though he did what he was told. Not the barkeepers around the world, for he'd broken too many bottles and bloodied too many decks. Certainly not his crewmates, who never laughed much at his rough games.

But maybe here, in this little port town, they'd remember that crazy sailorman swinging from the rooftops with a trollop 'tween his trousered knees. Maybe those town folk down below, holding blankets to catch the two of them, could accept a man as mean as he.

He let Jude loose to remove his shirt, for her nightie was next to nothing. He wrapped it around her and helped her arms into the sleeves. As he buttoned it up, he wondered if this soft warmth in his tummy was what mothers felt. But it seemed even deeper, for Jude was no child. She was a full-grown woman, both kind and caring. A friend, a lover—more.

For the first time in his life, the sailor said, "I love you." It sounded funny and she didn't hear him, so he repeated it. "Judith, I love you," he croaked, a frog struggling for princehood.

She melted then, or so it seemed, and her tears trickled down his chest. She clung to his stomach as though to a buoy. Clumsily, he patted her.

After a while, he got antsy and she got chilly, so they carefully stood. He lodged his foot behind the pipe for balance and held her close. The crowd cheered.

He lifted her up, cradling her in his singed and sooty arms, and told her he'd throw her on the third swing.

He hurled her out on the second swing, of course, for he wanted no last-second grabbing.

When he saw her safely enfolded and the blankets again ready, he pointed to the one he'd aim for, and people rushed over to help hold it.

Then he himself jumped and let himself fall, and fall, his fate out of his hands.

As he lay there floating in the woolen water, he smiled at the faces around him, for they had caught him, hands lined up knuckles to thumbs, some puffy and some knobby, some too old or too young to help much. But lined up like that, fifty fists in a big square ring, they'd caught him as he fell, helpless in the empty air, no going back.

As they set him down carefully, he bumped gently to the ground.

He stood and someone handed him a beer, which he chugged. Then he spat at a lamppost, and missed, and didn't mind at all.

ALICE
STEVEN ANDERSON

The light from Dad's study drew me across the living room like a phototactic creature. That's how he would have described my behavior, and I smiled at the big word in my head. I floated into the room pretending my arms were wings until I wrapped them around him to better see what he was working on.

"What's up?" I asked.

"You are, apparently. It's past your bedtime."

"I'm a mallee moth. We're nocturnal." I moved my head to peer at his screen. "Are those the advisor assignments for your graduate students?"

"They are."

"You were supposed to be done days ago. You moaned about it to Mom all through dinner on Wednesday. I liked it better before you were in charge of the Geology Department. You didn't moan as much."

"Go to bed, Alice. Or we'll both be in trouble."

I didn't move, and after a moment, I knew I'd won the silent battle over my unreasonably early bedtime. I hooked my chin over his shoulder. "Where's the problem?"

"The University of Palma Sola's geology program accepted too many students again. It's my job to balance the load. Each instructor has classes to teach, research to do, papers to publish, and now this. For example." He slid his finger across the display, and the photo of an earnest-looking boy appeared above his academic record. "Blake Herrington wants to be a geochemist. I should put him with Katrina, but she's full up."

"Put him with Professor Conley."

"Conley's a paleontologist."

"So is Blake. He just doesn't know it yet."

Dad twisted around to look me eye to eye. "What are you seeing, Alice?"

I reached my arms over his shoulders and zoomed in on Blake's transcript. "Look at his grades. He's an OK chemist, but he slams at biology, and you always say paleontology is just the biology of dead things. Put him with Professor Conley. Blake will love it."

"I should talk to him first."

"No, just do it. He doesn't know what he wants. Trust me. He'll be happier looking at fossils."

Dad chuckled. "That's your mission in life now? Bestowing happiness?"

I smiled, feeling an epiphany coming on. "It's what we mallee moths do. Let's fix all the other students tonight. I'll bet most of them don't know what they want to be either, not really."

Mom found us hard at work sometime after midnight, and we were both in trouble.

But that didn't stop me. Dad delegated the whole roster, and I set up a spreadsheet to track my successes and failures during the semester. It was disappointing. Blake took the hint and gave up a life of petrochemicals when he discovered a passion for shiny little foraminifera, but others were too dense to accept my control over their lives.

I needed more— more tools, more ways to nudge or block and keep everyone where I wanted them. When Dad gave me access to the class registration system for the first time it was like striking the mother lode. I took over the undergrads for the next three years and controlled which classes they could take. Sorry, Ms. Albrecht, mineralogy is already full. You'll have to take geomorphology this semester. Trust me, you're going to love it.

It was always for their own good, of course. I had the data to prove it. Detailed mind maps complete with pictures replaced my primitive spreadsheets. I set up a long-term campaign for every student and my success rate improved.

I started my own freshman year at seventeen and declared myself a geology major. That was mostly to make Dad happy. Geology was his passion. I made it mine so he'd give me access to the summer field session assignments. I didn't tell him that, of course. But I knew he'd do it anyway. *Quid pro quo.*

But something was still missing. Not every student reacted to my manipulations in healthy ways. Some resisted. Some even left the department. It made me feel like I'd failed them.

I went to my first We-Made-It-To-Friday party a couple of weeks into the semester. Dad recommended it. He and Mom had raised me, educated me, and turned me loose on the world. He didn't say it aloud, but I'm sure he thought I'd never developed any social skills. What he did say was I should meet the people whose lives I'd changed through my manipulations.

I loved it. It was like being in a 3D simulation of a world I'd created. Susan Albrecht sat on a barstool in the kitchen talking to a friend about karst topography, and Jason Pence wouldn't shut up about the stratigraphy of the trans-island exposure. They were exactly where my plans for them said they were supposed to be. They didn't know I'd altered their lives by selecting which classes I'd allow them to attend and which paths were forever closed. They were happy. It literally brought tears to my eyes.

My drink was supposed to be rum and some kind of fruit juice. I never touched it though. I was already drunk on what I'd accomplished and new dreams to expand this skill to other parts of my life.

Sadly, Dad was right about my lack of social skills. I had found a place to sit and watch the other students so I could make notes about them on my display pad. Apparently, that's not how parties work. It attracted attention.

A boy who was drunk on something other than accomplishments

and dreams put his hand on the wall behind me and leaned into my space. I kept typing, trusting my peripheral vision to warn me if he got too close.

"Hey," he slurred. "Don't ya know there's a party? Do you want to..." He tipped his chin, inviting me to, I don't know what. Dance with him? Have a drink? Go somewhere private? I looked up into his blurry, watery eyes.

Seeing my face, he took a step back, the palms of his hands toward me. "Oh, hey. It's OK. I'll find someone else."

He turned and staggered back to his friends. He hadn't said anything about the way I look, but it hurt anyway.

I'm not hideous, but I think God must have run out of curves the day before he built me. I'm all straight lines and flat planes from high cheekbones to skinny legs. My blue eyes go squinty when I smile or laugh, and that doesn't help. I wear my hair long so I can hide behind it when I need to.

Mom and Dad had raised me in a sort of bubble where none of that mattered. I was me, and they loved me no matter what. That party at the University of Palma Sola wasn't the first time others had judged me before I even opened my mouth, but it was the first time I ached for acceptance.

I tipped my display pad up to capture the boy's face when he next turned to stare. His mind map filled the screen and I judged him without him needing to say another word to me.

I went to a lot of We-Made-It-To-Friday parties after that.

It didn't take long for my identity to become known. I suspect the leak came from Dad's staff. The daughter of the Department Chair deserved respect, or kindness, or to be left alone, depending on the student's personality. I used how they treated me as a data point, one I couldn't get from a transcript or an advisor's assessment. And it revealed so much. I'd never allow a brown-nosing sycophant to advance any more than someone who insulted me. Paths closed for some, opened for others.

Late in the fall, a rumor oozed through the students that I controlled class access and advisor assignments. I denied it, of course, and silently wondered how Dad could have let that bit of knowledge escape. With Dad, nothing is ever an accident. I could have asked him straight out, but I knew he'd be disappointed if I couldn't solve it on my own. I'd just have to weather the storm.

One Friday evening at the start of the Spring semester, Brigeda Hutchins asked me straight out if it was true. I'd kept her away from geophysics because she'd never mastered the math despite her father being a mining engineer. She switched to structural, probably because of his pressure. I blocked her again and gave her classes in environmental geology. She was doing great. How could she not be happy?

"You," she demanded, a plastic cup of beer in each hand. "Princess Alice, are you the one ruining my life?"

I blinked back at her, aware of other voices in the room falling silent. I should have told her I had no idea what she was talking about. But, again, poor social skills. "I would never do that, Brigeda. You should love environmental. You get to be outside, and the mapping, and species surveys and–"

"You scheming little bitch!"

I stopped talking. Cold beer running down your face will do that. I responded with the only thing that came into my head. I grabbed the other cup and dumped it on her.

We stood in mirror image, arms apart, beer in our hair and dripping from our noses. I knew I was about to die. She was more than capable of killing me, and I doubted anyone would stop her. I mourned in that moment for a world without Alice Vandermeer in it.

Her mind map flashed before my eyes in my remaining seconds of life. Logic would be useless on her or else I'd still be dry. Argument? No time. Her advisor had noted a quirky, irreverent sense of humor. My only hope.

"Damn it, Brigeda," I shouted. "Stop wasting the beer."

The image of my impending dismemberment faded from her eyes. She didn't laugh, but I got a tipped head and a grin full of sharp teeth. "You're still a scheming little bitch, Alice."

"Maybe," I conceded. The sound of conversation in the room picked up now that the chance to witness a murder had passed. I lowered my voice. "Do you like environmental or not?"

She rubbed beer from her face and flicked it on the floor. "Yeah, I do. Surprisingly. That's not the point though, is it. What gives you the right–"

"Screw your dad."

"What?"

"Screw him if he's trying to control you. Do what you love."

The grin returned and I imagined a snarl coming from her chest to go with it. "Sure. Screw him. It's not like he can be more disappointed in me than he already is." She started to turn away.

"Who told you what I'm doing?"

She shrugged and looked over her shoulder at me. "Everyone knows. Stop while you're ahead, Alice. Before someone beats the crap out of you."

I smiled my best innocent smile and let her go.

It seemed wise to lay low until after spring break, but boredom got the better of me, and I needed to decide who would be allowed to take classes over the summer. I'd already blocked a couple of students who'd applied for the three-month practical petrology course. They were wasting their time, that was obvious. Still, it felt like I needed the nuanced data only available from personal interaction. I wasn't sure why, but I wanted it.

I got a couple of furtive glances when I arrived, but most of the students ignored me. I found an old sofa next to a tray of sliced cheese and pieces of apple, and settled in to observe and take notes.

Philip Rensburg plopped down at the other end of the couch. I recognized him by his eyes. He'd stared straight at the camera for the student ID picture that was now part of his mind map. He had deep brown eyes, warm and full of mystery. And he was one of the students I'd blocked from summer petrology.

He smiled at me and the corners of his eyes crinkled. "OK if I sit here?"

I nodded, cautious and alert for how he'd try to play me.

He raised his cup of beer. "Happy Friday, Alice. It's been a week, but we survived it."

Good. No pretending he didn't know me. I didn't have a cup of anything yet, so I awkwardly waved an apple slice at him and gave the traditional reply. "May Monday never come, Philip." He drank. I chewed.

"Would you like something to drink?"

I shook my head. Maybe he planned to get me drunk, but there was nothing mocking in his voice, and his eyes never left mine. I stared back, unsure what to say or do. A voice in the back of my head chided me. *Really, Alice? You've attended thirty-six of these parties and your social skills are still at zero? What's wrong with you?*

I slid the plate of snacks closer to him and almost knocked it off the table because I didn't look away from his face. "Hungry?"

He rescued the tray and moved closer to me. "Did you see the email from the department this morning? It said class assignments are based on an objective, fair, and transparent assessment of each student's goals, accomplishments, and the needs of the university."

"That's right," I assured him. Word of my altercation with Brigeda must have reached Dad and he'd intervened without talking to me. He'd signed the statement with his own name, which would just confirm the rumor of my role. Alice Vandermeer, spoiled, scheming brat of a daughter who did the objective and fair assessment of each student's goals, accomplishments, and the needs of the University. And the transparency part? A blatant lie, and it was going to lead to someone beating the crap out of poor Alice. Maybe Philip would be the first to do it, but I didn't think so. His eyes were still locked with mine. I swallowed hard and failed to look away.

"Alice? What kind of algorithm are you using?"

Not the question I expected. I lowered my voice so only Philip could hear me. I might be able to outrun him, at least long enough to make it out the door, but probably not a whole mob. "It's, um, one that's objective and fair."

Philip leaned closer. "Bullshit. Why not automate it?"

I dropped into a whisper, his face so near that I worried about the sharp taste of cheddar on my breath. "There are subtleties. I've tried to get rid of them, but people are complicated. Being at these Friday parties helps. I can watch and learn more about someone."

He laughed at me. "But you don't participate, Alice."

His laugh broke the spell, and I could again see and hear the party going on around us. I told him a truth, and it shocked me to hear the words coming from my soul. "I don't know how. I can't talk to people I don't know and I can't get to know them without talking." I shrugged and fell back into the deep brown of his eyes. "Trapped."

"You're talking to me."

"Well, you're my first real conversation. Other than Brigeda. You're not planning on throwing beer on me, are you?"

His laugh matched the warmth of his eyes. "Not today. I think I can help you."

"To talk to people?"

"Maybe, but I mean automating your decisions."

"I'm not sure I want to do that."

"You're planning to do this the rest of your life?"

I chuckled. "No."

"You have someone in mind to pass it to?"

"No, not that either."

He shrugged, his hands in the air. It made me laugh. I looked down and let blonde hair fall across my face. His hand touched my cheek as he pulled my hair back. I looked up.

"Don't do that," he told me. "I want to see you laugh."

I studied his face, looking for the lie. Didn't find one. "OK," I told him.

"Let me tell you the subtleties of why I need petrology this summer."

A cynical chill tingled the hairs on the back of my neck. No one else had approached me this way, but he was talking to me because he wanted something only I could provide. So obvious. "Sure. Go ahead."

He tried to regain eye contact. I resisted by pretending I needed a slice of apple. I reached for where he'd shoved the tray, and my bare arm touched his. I looked up at his face and forgot about the apple.

He spoke so softly I had to move closer to hear him. "I'm working with a couple of friends. Katie Laval's a computer science major. She writes code so beautiful the angels sing when it executes. Johnson is a business major headed to law school in a couple of years. Together, we're trying to build and market a model to better predict where to find and exploit mineral resources. I'm the geologist, or I'm supposed to be. I know I screwed up in chemistry last semester."

"Big time," I told him. "Boom. Smoking hole." My arm was still pressed against his, and neither of us seemed ready to pull back. I felt him tense. "Sorry," I mumbled.

"No, you're right. I'm working hard to make up for it this semester and I'll be ready for the summer session. Let me prove myself. Please. I'll introduce you to Katie. She'll love what you're doing with the class roster and she'll think it's funny that you blocked me. She can help you convert what you're doing into code. If I screw up again, which I won't, you can bust me all the way down to liberal arts. What do you say?"

Temptation filled me. I'd gone about as far with mind maps as I could. *This is why you come to these parties, Alice,* my inner voice told me. *Factors that can't be found any other way. Subtleties.*

No, I answered the voice. *I already have a plan for Philip Rensburg.*

Actually, my plan for Philip ended with this block. He'd leave the department, and I didn't care where he went next.

But...

I visualized Philip's mind map. What would happen if I allowed him to take petrology over the summer? I watched his future fracture into hundreds of opportunities, some scholastic, some not. And I had full control of which might become real. The thought thrilled me. Goosebumps rose on my arms.

Philip noticed. "Are you all right, Alice?"

I opened my eyes with no memory of having closed them and executed step one of my updated Philip campaign. "Yeah. Fine. I need to think about it." Keeping him off balance and interested by delaying my answer a few days definitely came first. I could see the next couple of steps, but I really did need to think about what came later and how to maneuver Philip into the exact slot where I wanted him.

I glanced at my watch. "I need to leave." I stood, then bent to snag a slice of cheese and again feel the touch of his arm against mine.

He stood, a polite gesture, maybe, or to show that he was 30 centimeters taller than me. He looked down into my eyes and I decided it was both.

"So, I won't see you until next Friday?"

I smiled and nodded while I waited one heartbeat for him to ask me out. It was adorable how he went right where I wanted him.

"There's a new Alarie film opening tomorrow. Do you want to go? Katie and Johnson will be there."

Alarie's films are my favorite, but I shrugged as though I didn't care. "Sure. Johnson doesn't have a first name?"

Philip laughed. "He's ex-military. Having no first name is part of the terms of enlistment."

He might think it funny, but I needed to make mind maps of both his friends before I met them and there were probably a dozen Johnsons in the business school. More work for poor Alice.

"What time?" I asked.

"Time?" The remnants of his laugh lingered in the deep brown of his eyes. It felt wrong not to stare back into them.

"The film. Tomorrow."

"Right. I'll pick you up. At six."

"Six. You know where I live?" That seemed to snap him out of our mutual trance. He blinked.

"Sure. Everyone knows where Professor Vandermeer lives. The sandstone blocks of your front porch are full of fossils. Every first-year geology student has to touch them. It's kind of a tradition."

I laughed and didn't hide it behind my hair. "I hate that tradition. Some of them do it at two in the morning."

"That was me," he confessed. "Sorry."

"OK, but remember. Pick me up at six tomorrow. Not two."

"Got it. Pick you up at two."

I gave him the roll of my eyes he was fishing for and walked out the front door without looking back.

THE FLOOR behind me creaked at two the next morning. Dad had tried to fix that board years ago, but I always pried it up a little when he wasn't looking. I like the warning it provides.

I kept typing. I had Johnson's mind map spread across my three displays, color-coded and almost complete. Ex-military didn't begin to describe him. And Katie, still open on another tab, had a background almost as bizarre. They'd both seen the tail end of the last war before enrolling at the University of Palma Sola. Exactly where they'd served, what they'd done, and how they'd met Philip remained a mystery. But I'd solve it. Talking to them in person would help, not that I'd ask them anything directly. That's not how I work.

Dad placed his hands on my shoulders. "What's up?"

"You are, apparently," I answered. "Isn't it past your bedtime?"

He ignored the question. "Who are you working on?"

"Friends of someone I met tonight. I planned to merge all their maps together, but there's too much. I can't hold enough in my head to see the connections between the connections."

Dad used his gentle voice, the one that always has a challenge buried in each word. "How will you solve it?"

I parsed his question. Keyword *you*, followed by *solve* and *how*. I changed to Katie's tab. "Katie Laval. I've reached the limit of how many steps in a campaign I can see without help. She'll help me go all the way."

He leaned close and feigned surprise. "Ah. A former Department of Cultural Intelligence programmer. How interesting. What's your new campaign?"

I laughed at Dad probing with such a direct question and gave him a squinty-eyed smile. "Bestowing happiness."

He gave my shoulders a final squeeze. "I should get to bed."

I let him reach the door before stopping him. "Dad?"

He turned. "Humm?"

"Thanks. He's perfect. I couldn't ask for a better one."

He chuckled and shook his head, equal parts amused and disappointed in me. "Get some sleep, Alice. You get all muddled and sentimental when you're tired."

"Love ya, Dad."

The floorboard creaked as he walked away down the hall.

HEARTACHE

JEFF SCHMOYER

A young woman dressed in scrubs stood in the doorway of my hospital room. I set my book on the bed, and she came in. "Do you need anything?" She looked sad, her eyes red.

"I'm good, though maybe you can tell me why I'm still here." I had come in much earlier for a solution to my disheartening chronic fatigue.

"You're supposed to stay overnight for observation."

"They must be really sneaky about it—I haven't seen anyone observe me yet."

She gave me half a smile. "That's what the machines are for."

I glanced at the numerous wires running to me as I fiddled with the call button, careful not to press it.

"Will you be around to observe me later?" I asked.

"My shift ended hours ago. I'm going home." She looked away. "I...lost my best friend tonight."

I may have been the first person she had said those words to. "I'm very sorry for that."

"I don't mean to burden you with it. I need to go." Tears overflowed her eyes.

"Of course. And it's no burden. Visit me again if you like." I hoped she had someone at home to comfort her.

She squeezed my hand and left me.

I tried to reach for my book, but my arm seized. My chest screamed, and the machines next to me formed a chorus. I smashed the call button as hard as I could. I heard running footsteps and excited voices.

I SAT on a bench in a park. It was a warm spring afternoon, and flowers bloomed everywhere. Birds stood on low clouds watching me. The woman in scrubs sat next to me. Rain streaked her face, though no cloud admitted to the act.

"You're young and fit," she said, without looking at me. "Why are you in my park?"

"I think I might be here for you—it's hard to lose someone. My heart aches like yours."

The pain in my chest grew. Unfamiliar voices pulled me away from her.

I HEARD ODD WORDS—DONOR, retraction, suction. I saw masked people above me, horrified looks in their eyes.

"Riley, fix this," a man said.

I couldn't make my lips say that I wasn't Riley.

I WAS BACK on the park bench. This time the young woman was kneeling in the flowers.

She joined me on the bench. "My friend would like you to have this."

It was the strangest flower I had ever seen. "What kind is it?"

"It's a heart valve," she answered.

"Thank you. And please thank your friend."

"I cannot do that." She looked very sad.

"Then I will thank your friend myself." I started to get up from the bench.

"Please, you mustn't go to him," she cried.

"I will stay with you."

She kissed my cheek.

I OPENED MY EYES, and she was sitting beside my hospital bed.

"You're still here," I said.

"Someone needed to keep an eye on you, so I volunteered. There was a small problem with your anesthesia."

"Riley."

"Yes, Dr. Riley. How could you know?"

"I'm okay, now. You've had a very difficult day. You should go home." My eyes fell shut.

SHE LAY at my side in our bed at home, her skin warm against mine. Her head was on my shoulder, and she was crying quietly—not for me, but for her lost friend.

THERE WAS a new voice in my hospital room. I looked at the male nurse and tried to speak but could only croak.

"I'll get some warm tea for your throat," he said. "Your surgeon will be along shortly to check on you. And your family will be here in the morning."

The surgeon and tea arrived at the same time. I took the tea from the nurse and had a soothing sip.

"How do you feel?" the surgeon asked.

"I don't feel very much."

"That's good," he said. "We want to keep you as pain-free as possible from the heart valve replacement. You were lucky we had a donor so close by."

"My friend?" I asked.

"You knew Mr. Lopez?" He sounded surprised.

I shook my head slowly.

The surgeon looked at the nurse, "Well, that's a HIPPA violation."

"He won't remember. He's still pretty out of it from the anesthesia."

I heard other words—cardiac event, genetically predisposed—as I drifted off.

SHE WOULD BE HERE SOON with our children—we must have children.

MY EYES FLICKERED OPEN to the bright, late morning sun.

My mother held my hand and called out to my dozing father, "Eli, he's awake!"

I was not only awake, but sharp for the first time in I didn't know how many hours. I remembered Edna and Eli Sloaks, parents of Leonard Sloaks, 28, single, no children. I was hungry. I felt renewed—like I could finally live my life.

My mother said, "I thought we had lost you. When the hospital called..." She let out a sob of relief.

My father, always the lawyer, said, "When you're up to it, we need to talk about that anesthesia problem."

A young woman appeared at the doorway, the woman of my dreams.

"Mr. and Mrs. Sloaks," she said, "may I show you where the coffee is? I know you've had a long morning."

My parents shuffled off with the woman, who thankfully returned forthwith.

"It's you," I said.

"You remember me?"

"I could never forget you. Thank you, and I thank your friend as well."

"How did you...?" She looked at the floor.

"Your friend must have been a very generous person."

"He was an amazing man. Parts of him will live on in many people." Her eyes went to my chest.

"I would like to see you again," I said.

She laughed. "That's good because I'm your physical therapist, Celia. I'll be back a little later to get you on your feet, Mr. Sloaks."

"Please, call me Lenny. I can't wait."

THE COMET'S DANCE
CS SIMPSON

Through cold vast darkness she flies alone—dust, ice, and
    stone; streamlined.
On and on she sails through scattered heavenly bodies.
    Resigned
to circle over and over on an orbital path, blind,
past asteroids, near planets, and beyond—her lover again to
    find.

Searching for this long-lost dance partner, a blazing stellar
    mass,
she waits for his familiar attraction—a pull to surpass.
Oh, to be near his powerful being, drawn by gravitas,
close to his burning sphere of radiance, as he waits for her to
    pass.

Then, sensing his proximity, a mighty magnetic strain,
she approaches, accelerates, eager to see him again.
Feeling his solar wind reach for her, that far-flung hurricane,
it blows back the dust, her comet tail unfurls, a vaporous
    weather vane.

Advancing now in earnest, she rushes into his control.
Temperatures rise and the shadowy ice-tail lengthens. A toll
he takes—a loss of her essence. She gives him part of her soul
a little each time they meet, caught deep in his gravity bowl.

She slides beside, yet too fast to touch—celestial spheres align.
They dance together, aware of no other—spirits combine.
Alas, the ballet is brief—all nature allows by design.
To embrace for only a moment, 'tis a tragedy—'tis divine.

For the power which once pulled them close now slingshots
        her around.
Far behind he slips, though sensing him still—eternally
        bound.
Her vapor tail vanishes, yet she's left delicately crowned
in a fine crystal dust. Despite the brevity, it feels so profound.

Sadly now, she must retrace the long elliptical flight through
lonely stretches of naught but space-clouds and cosmic
        residue.
Across cold emptiness she sails, the dance again to pursue,
awaiting the feel of his blazing closeness to ignite her anew.

Both knowing the moment could not last, 'twas nonetheless
        sublime.
They shall be content with each fleeting chance—their short
        pantomime.
Every sweet encounter must be enough until the next time,
and the chance to be near the other—a tantalizing paradigm.

THE GIRL AND THE SNAKE
KK QUINN

The first bell echoed across the bone-dry crater, the distant hum rattling Kazra's insides. The sacrifice to Niobbu, the Great Snake, had begun.

Cheers rang out from across the Eight Tribes that circled the crater. The smells of roasting pig and spiced fruits filled the warm morning air, and musicians beat a steady joyful rhythm on their drums.

A heavy weight of dread settled within Kazra. Despite what she was raised to believe, this was not a cheerful day. The God, Niobbu, required seven sacrifices to satiate his hunger for the next year. One sacrifice for every month that the crater was flooded.

Long ago, when the eight witches cast the curse that imprisoned the Snake God, they each vowed to send a member of their own tribe to pay the price. But there would always be one survivor, so the witches decided to make a sport out of it. The sole survivor would be celebrated for the next year and granted seven wishes by the elders of the tribes.

It was barbaric and cruel and Kazra's heart ached for the trapped God. She knew what it felt like to be bound to a life of misery, to want to explore the wild world, but be confined to one place.

Kazra stood in the sacrifice's tent, cornered by people on all sides. Her parents stood behind her, blocking her escape. Others from the tribe stood to her left and right, and in front stood Azeer, their tribe's chosen sacrifice.

Azeer had asked for her, specifically, to watch the entire gruesome event from his tent. Refusing wasn't an option when her father was the headman of the tribe, his influence and power second to that of the elders. She could not flee to the comfort of the forest, to the comfort of Niobbu's tiny kin that Kazra preferred to her fellow tribesmen.

"Time to say your goodbyes, Azeer," the priestess of the tribe said, waving her arms through the air as she spoke. The beaded tassels along her brown robe chimed, the sound far too calming for the day's event.

Azeer straightened his broad shoulders and grinned. It was an honor to be selected as a sacrifice. Azeer had spoken of nothing else since he'd been chosen half a year ago.

And Azeer *was* the best choice for their tribe. At only seventeen, he was already one of the strongest men, and like many others, he'd spent most of his childhood toning his body and building his endurance for the chance to be chosen.

Kazra crossed her arms and kept her face neutral as Azeer put on a little show of saying goodbye to his admirers in the tent. Once he'd finished, Azeer hugged his parents before turning to Kazra, his grin widening in a sickening way as he approached. Kazra's feet twitched with the urge to run, but she dug her toes into the warm desert sand.

"I feel that Tileah has already chosen me as this year's champion," Azeer said, his voice booming.

Kazra tried not to grimace at the mention of Tileah, one of the eight witches that were worshiped among the tribes as Gods. If Tileah had cared about the tribesmen, she wouldn't have chosen a God's power over their lives. Kazra was one of the few among the tribes that would rather see Niobbu freed than watch as more men were eaten.

Azeer placed a roughened hand on Kazra's cheek, and she barely managed not to flinch. "Once I reach the Spire and am crowned as champion, I will ask for your hand in marriage as my first wish and we will be together until the end of our days."

Kazra swallowed bile and stared over his shoulder. The Spire, a spiral-shaped tower marking the center of the crater, shone in the distance. Built of stone blocks set with glittering gemstones, it stretched high into the sky.

It was a magnificent structure that represented a terrible fate.

Azeer had no real desire to be with Kazra. What he desired was to marry the daughter of the headman–the daughter that talked to snakes and ran barefoot through the forest. He wanted nothing more than to be the one to tame Kazra's wild side.

"May Tileah be with you today," was all she could say, though her voice was quiet and laced with bitterness. Her only comfort was knowing that Tileah did not listen to her prayers.

She would have no choice but to marry Azeer should he wish for it, to provide him with heirs, to cook and clean and forge weapons for him. She would not be given the chance to train as a priestess, to learn about the secret magic of the tribes, and eventually become an elder. She'd never be allowed to leave the borders of the tribal lands to explore the wilderness.

Azeer grinned, leaned forward, and planted a wet kiss on Kazra's mouth. She resisted the urge to shove him away. There were too many eyes on them—the priestess, Azeer's parents, Kazra's parents, and nearly everyone from her tribe that had come to watch.

"Come, Azeer," the priestess said, suddenly beside the two of them. She placed her thin hand on Azeer's broad shoulder to pull him away. Her golden eyes flicked toward Kazra but she did not scowl at her as so many others did.

If Kazra was like the other girls in the tribe, she would be worried for him and maybe a little excited, too. But she wasn't like the other girls. He stood every chance of making it to the Spire, of surviving this year's sacrifice, and it filled her with dread.

And if he was the champion, Kazra's life would be over. Azeer– and many others within the tribe–did not want the snake girl to gain power. They didn't trust her.

At the crater's edge, the priestess began her yearly speech. "The elders have been sequestered in the Spire for seventeen days now, praying to the Eight Goddesses for a bountiful new year and preparing to welcome the next champion into the shrine."

She paused and raised Azeer's arm into the air. Everyone in the tribe—except Kazra—cheered.

"And now," the priestess continued, her voice booming, "on this day, the longest of the year, the eight sacrifices will enter the crater. Seven will come face to face with the trapped God, Niobbu the Snake, and will serve the tribes by satiating his hunger for the next year. The eighth, and final sacrifice will climb the Spire and enter the shrine at the top to be greeted with glory and honor and a long life of comfort."

The tribe cheered again, but movement near the crater's edge pulled Kazra's focus from the speech. One of Niobbu's kin had slithered close to Azeer's heels. Kazra's eyes narrowed on the little black snake, and she felt a spark of hope bloom in her chest.

Please, do not let Azeer survive, she prayed. *Take him swiftly, so that I might truly live.*

The snake tilted its head in her direction and appeared to nod.

Kazra sucked in a sharp breath a moment before the snake lunged, striking Azeer's legs over and over.

Azeer screamed and crumpled to the ground. Several other screams broke out among the rest of the tribe. Azeer's parents rushed to his side as the priestess tried to calm Azeer's thrashing movements.

Kazra's gaze remained on the snake as it left Azeer's side and glided in her direction.

"What have you done?" a quiet voice said on Kazra's right. Kazra flinched and looked into the terrified eyes of her mother. Her mother's vibrant green eyes—the only feature she shared with Kazra—were striking in contrast to her dark skin. Her mother grabbed Kazra's wrist and asked again, "What have you done?"

"I didn't mean to," Kazra whispered, numb. The snake that had attacked Azeer sidled up to Kazra's bare feet and curled around her ankle as if in a hug before it continued on its way.

"K-Kazra," another voice croaked, breaking through her reverie.

She snapped her head up and found Azeer sitting up, in the arms of his parents, the priestess by his head, as they all stared at Kazra in horror. Azeer, the color of his skin gone from a golden brown to a deathly gray in a few heartbeats, thrust an accusing finger at her.

"She did this," he said, gasping for breath. "Send her... in my place. Send her... to be eaten... by the God she so clearly worships." Spittle flew from his mouth with every word.

Kazra's father appeared on her other side. He placed a warm hand on her shoulder and gave her a worried smile. Kazra's heart fluttered. Her father would protect her.

They didn't have time to form a response before Azeer took his last, rattling breath and went rigid from the snake's poison. His mother wailed. His father sat back on his feet and stared at the body of his only son. The priestess closed her eyes and her shoulders slumped.

The second bell thundered from the top of the Spire.

Kazra flinched as the priestess's eyes snapped open and bore into her.

"We send the girl," the priestess said.

"What?" Kazra said.

"No," her father said at the same time.

Kazra's insides turned to liquid, and her knees weakened.

"We do not send women as sacrifices," Kazra's father argued, and his hand tightened on her shoulder.

Her mother, however, let go of Kazra and stepped away. Tears burned the back of Kazra's throat, but she was not surprised. Her mother had always seen Kazra as a curse.

The priestess rose and stalked towards Kazra, the beaded tassels chiming with urgency this time. "It is incredibly rare, but it has happened in the past. We have no time to prepare a proper replacement, and we must honor the final wish of the dead."

The priestess snatched Kazra's wrist and pulled her closer to the crater's rim. Kazra dug her feet into the ground and reached back with her free hand to grab her father's arm.

"No, please," Kazra begged. "I didn't mean for anything to happen. You can't send me down there."

Kazra's father gripped her hand. "Please, Yara," he begged, using the priestess's true name. "I'm the headman. Don't take my child away from me."

"I am sorry, Raz, but I outrank you while the elders are at the Spire," the priestess replied. "Or would you like to explain to them why we sent no sacrifice this year? Why our entire tribe will suffer because of you? Or better yet, why don't you turn around and explain to your fellow tribesmen right now why we will likely starve and suffer disease for the next year?"

Raz's face crumpled and his grip on Kazra's hand loosened.

"No, father, please. No!" Kazra's voice rose. She desperately yanked her arm away from the priestess, but the priestess's grip was like iron. The jeweled necklace around her neck glowed a deep, blood-red from the magic held within. Magic that gave the priestess extra strength, among many other gifts. Magic that Kazra had never craved more than in this moment.

"I'm sorry, my little jewel," her father said, his voice empty of all emotion. "I am so sorry." Tears pooled in his golden-brown eyes. He moved with her as the priestess pulled her closer to her fate. "I can't stop this. Yara is right. We have no time. You are light and agile. Maybe you can reach the Spire first. Maybe... Maybe Niobbu will spare you."

The edge was only a few steps away now. Kazra sobbed and gripped her father's hand with all her strength. He was right. Neither the priestess, nor the tribe, would let her get out of this after the way Azeer had died. She couldn't stop this, but maybe she could talk to Niobbu. Maybe she could beg him to spare her life and in return she would vow to free him.

The priestess pulled Kazra to the crater's edge, then gave her a firm shove.

Kazra, her grip still tight on her father's hand, hovered over the edge as her feet desperately clung to the crumbling stone. Over her shoulder, the bottom of the crater loomed far below her, and her vision blurred and dimmed.

"Try, Kazra," her father pleaded. "You must try."

He kissed the back of her hand. Kazra stared into his eyes, nodded, and let go.

Time slowed as Kazra fell backward.

Down, down, down.

Her father's voice echoed in her mind.

Try, try, try.

She landed on her back with a painful thud, sprawled on a crescent moon shaped ledge that jutted from the wall several feet below the rim. The force of the impact left her breathless and she gasped for air.

Kazra had been on this ledge many times before. Nearly every member of her tribe had at some point in their lives. It was where the water level usually sat, seven out of the eight months of the year, and was a popular place to get away from the adults.

As it did every year, the water had begun to recede seventeen days before the sacrifice, carried away by the magic infused in the crater until it was all gone. For one day, the crater would remain dry before the water would trickle back in.

Kazra opened her eyes and saw the priestess's head hovering over the crater's edge. In her hands, she gripped that blood-red gemstone. Kazra was not yet old enough to study the gemstones, but she had no doubt that whatever magic was locked inside the one the priestess held would send her flying off the ledge. The priestess's job on this day was to ensure their tribe's sacrifice made it to the bottom of the crater.

Kazra could see that the journey to the bottom was treacherous, but not impossible. The water that normally filled the crater had worn the stone down in uneven patterns, creating the perfect hand and foot holds. Kazra's real worry was whether or not she had the strength to make the climb without slipping.

But she had to at least try.

She crawled to the corner of the ledge and swung her legs over. With a deep breath, she dug her fingers into the uneven stone and pulled herself off the edge.

Down she went one small bit at a time. The sun burned hotter as the day progressed and her tunic became drenched in sweat. Her lips dried and cracked, and her mouth was void of moisture. Her limbs had numbed at some point. They shook with every step down she took, but the aching had long ago subsided.

She had no idea how much time had passed when she looked over her shoulder and saw the sandy floor of the crater within jumping distance. She freed the tension in her fingers and fell. As soon as her bare feet touched the sand, she sank to her knees and sobbed. She had made it. She was still alive.

The third bell tolled.

Kazra's sobs cut off in an instant. Her eyes searched the crater floor, desperate to locate the God. The third bell was the signal that He had surfaced.

The ground shook. To the right of the Spire, Niobbu, the Great Snake, exploded from the sand.

Kazra gasped. She'd seen the God from above before, but from this angle, his size left her breathless. He had to be as long as the Spire was tall and three times as thick as the largest man in her tribe. His scales were nearly black, with a hint of colorful shimmer.

He was magnificent.

And utterly terrifying.

Niobbu had emerged directly in the path of the sacrifice from the Mazren tribe, the tribe two over from Kazra's own. The sacrifice, which Kazra could only spot due to his height, froze mid-sprint and tumbled to the ground near the base of Niobbu's tail.

The God tilted his massive head toward the boy, flicked his tongue once, then seemed to grin. The boy scrambled to his feet and took off at a sprint again, choosing to run in the opposite direction of Kazra. The Great Snake did not hesitate to go after him.

"No," Kazra croaked. Her parched throat ached at her pitiful attempt at a shout.

Niobbu continued after the boy, towards the opposite side of the crater.

Kazra rose to her feet and her legs trembled. She took one hesitant step, and her bare feet sunk into the soft, damp sand.

The crater had only dried on the surface. Below the cracked top layer, the ground was still moist. With every step Kazra took, her energy drained with the effort it took to free her feet from the softened ground.

To either side of her, she caught glimpses of other sacrifices running. These were young men that had trained for this. Their bodies had been molded to withstand the immense effort it took.

Kazra would never make it to the Spire before them, but maybe she would cross paths with Niobbu next. She had to speak with him. She had to try.

All around her, hundreds of years of debris lay embedded in the sandy muck. Her feet scraped against broken bits of wood, and she had to skirt around clusters of strange shells and algae. A few steps ahead, a wrecked boat blocked her path.

She collapsed against its hull, the rotted wood creaking under her weight. Her legs burned, she couldn't suck in enough air, and her mouth was beyond parched. The sun had risen, marking midday, and her skin burned under its heat. The tunic she wore had no sleeves to protect her arms from the damaging sun.

She glanced over her shoulder. She'd made it over halfway between the edge of the crater and the Spire. Her body ached and throbbed. The thought of continuing made her want to cry, but while her eyes burned, there was no moisture left to form tears.

Try, try, try.

Her father's last words were the only thing that pushed her off the boat and forced her legs to continue forward. She made it five more steps before her legs gave out beneath her and her knees crashed into the earth.

A sharp cry escaped her. Her knee had collided with something much more solid–and sharp–than the sand. She burrowed her fingers into the ground until they wrapped around the object and pulled it free.

It was a stunning necklace, made of gold hoops looped together to form a chain. Hanging from the end of the chain was the biggest gemstone Kazra had ever seen. A vibrant orange with traces of blood-red color dispersed throughout, it was nearly the size of her palm. How had one of the gems from the Spire ended up buried in the crater's ground?

She brushed a finger against the stone's surface and gasped. A surge of energy flowed through her, washing away the aching and throbbing, replacing it with a strength she'd never known. A strength that was forbidden to any but a priestess or an elder.

But it was a strength that might save her life. She draped the chain around her neck and settled the gemstone above her racing heart. As magic pulsed through her veins, she lurched back to her feet, her legs more stable than ever.

And then she ran.

Her vision narrowed on the glittering Spire in front of her, the gemstones nestled throughout more vibrant than moments before. Her sturdy legs beat against the damp sand, carrying her the distance of several steps with each leap.

Perhaps Tileah was with her on this day. Or perhaps this was a gift from Niobbu Himself.

Kazra didn't care if it meant she would live.

The Spire appeared larger the closer she got to it. As far as she could tell, none of the other sacrifices had yet begun their climb. To her left, there was a boy nearing the base. Kazra pushed her legs to carry her faster, willing the magic to push her body beyond its limits.

The boy reached the Spire and leapt onto the first jutting stone a heartbeat before Kazra did the same. The boy locked eyes with Kazra and they both froze. He was young, far younger than Kazra herself. He couldn't have seen more than thirteen years.

A shiver ran through Kazra's body. Over the boy's shoulder, a dark shadow rose from the sand. Kazra opened her mouth to warn the boy, but it was too late.

An ear-piercing shriek came from the boy as he was torn away from the tower, the Snake God's thick tail wrapped around his leg. Kazra's grip on the tower loosened, and she fell back onto the sandy earth, her mouth open in awe as she took in the full glory of Niobbu.

His dark scales shimmered as his body coiled around the young boy. His head towered over the boy, slowly swaying from side to side on a neck as thick as the thickest tree in the forest.

Kazra had seen many snakes in her lifetime, but none so beautiful as the God before her.

And as with the other snakes, she knew this pose, knew that Niobbu was preparing to devour his meal.

"Stop!" Kazra shouted.

To her surprise, the God went eerily still. Then His head turned and His slitted, yellow eyes landed on Kazra.

She gulped. Would the curse compel him to eat her? Why had she thought she could reason with a creature of unimaginable power that had been bewitched by dark magic?

You...

The gravelly voice boomed through Kazra's mind. She stumbled backwards and fell onto her butt. She wrapped her hands around the gemstone at her neck for comfort.

I have seen you.

Niobbu dropped his head closer to her. Kazra couldn't stop the whimper that escaped her mouth. She clamped her eyes shut as she waited for her death.

A gust of hot air enveloped her. This was it. She was about to be swallowed whole.

Instead, she heard the voice again, but this time, it was no longer in her mind.

"What... What is your name?" Niobbu said.

Kazra stilled. Her heart thundered against her chest.

She opened her eyes and gasped. Standing where the Great Snake had been was a beautiful young man. His black skin glowed in the sunlight, shimmering with color like His scales had. His long black hair floated in the breeze and His yellow, slitted eyes were fixed on her.

The young boy that Kazra had saved from death sat on the sand behind Niobbu, his mouth open and eyes wide. He trembled but did not move or make a sound.

"What is your name?" Niobbu asked again. His voice was like silk now. Soft and smooth and she had never heard anything so lovely.

Her voice shook as she murmured her name. "K-Kazra."

Niobbu stepped forward and fell to His knees as if he hadn't yet learned to walk. Kazra's eyes widened, mirroring His own as they studied each other.

"Kazra," He whispered. His voice sent shivers down her spine. "Nine hundred and forty-seven years I have waited for you." He held his hand out to her.

"I—" Kazra's voice cracked. She swallowed and tried again. "I don't understand."

He dropped His hand. His yellow eyes, so much like the little snakes that roamed the wilderness around the tribes, danced with ancient rage. "Nine hundred and forty-seven years these lands have siphoned away my magic. Nine hundred and forty-seven years I have waited for someone to break this curse." He dropped his head into his hands and made a sound that might have been either a sob or a laugh.

Kazra untangled her hand from the gemstone necklace and Niobbu's yellow eyes narrowed on it.

Niobbu said, "Each gemstone taken from this crater holds a piece of me, a piece of my magic. When I am trapped in the sand, my power is channeled into the gemstones. Only one day a year am I freed to replenish my strength, to keep feeding the witches' never-ending curse."

His eyes met hers again. "But every curse can be broken. Only a descendant of one of those witches can free me. A descendant with an affinity for snakes. I have seen you through the eyes of my kin. You are the one I have been waiting for."

He held His hand out to her again. "Kazra, will you free me? Will you be my Queen?"

Kazra trembled. This was all too much to comprehend.

How could she possibly be his Queen? She was a powerless mortal.

"Kazra," Niobbu said, crawling across the sand toward her. "I am not a cruel God, but I am a powerful one. Become my Queen, share my power, and I will treat you with all the respect a true Goddess deserves. I will worship you."

Kazra could hardly breathe. "I... I don't even know you."

Niobbu's head tilted, so much like the snakes Kazra had met throughout her life.

"Are you sure?" He asked. "Because I have known you since you were small. I have known you since the first time you were lost in the forest, when one of my kin found you, brought you food, and guided you back home."

Kazra sucked in a breath. She remembered that day and others.

When she'd been teased, when her mother had been cruel, when she'd felt so alone, the snakes had always been there for her.

She searched Niobbu's eyes but found no signs of deceit, no sign of cruelty.

"I will not harm you if you refuse, but what kind of life will you return to if you go back up there?" He pointed to the edges of the crater, from where the tribes were watching them.

The tribes, full of people that did not understand her. Full of people that wanted to chain her to a life of misery.

She had never felt accepted by them, but the snakes were different. They had become her friends. They had protected her. They had saved her from a horrible fate of becoming Azeer's bride.

They had guided her to a fate she could never have imagined. A fate she now wanted more than anything.

Kazra eyed Niobbu's hand. Her gaze trailed up his arm, shoulder and neck and met his eyes again.

She had known those eyes and their comfort all her life.

"What will become of the Eight Tribes?" Kazra asked. The Tribes relied on Niobbu's magic for so many things.

Niobbu did not take his gaze away from hers. "They will need to learn new ways, but there is enough magic left in the land for them to survive."

"And where will we go?"

Niobbu smiled. "Anywhere. Everywhere. I do not know what has become of these lands during my imprisonment. I would like to see the entirety of this world and when we bore of that, we can explore other worlds."

"Other worlds?" Kazra asked, leaning forward.

The God nodded once. "There is so much more beyond the forests surrounding this crater. I can show it all to you, if you choose to be my Queen."

Kazra's gaze trailed back down to his hand. She let go of the gemstone necklace and slipped her hand into his. His skin was smooth and cool, his grip strong as he clasped her hand.

"I will be your Queen," Kazra said, her voice breathless.

Niobbu smiled and rose to his feet, pulling her up with Him. His free hand cupped her cheek, then he pressed his lips against hers. The ground shook, and thunder sparked through every cell in Kazra's body.

The Spire began to disintegrate as the gemstones shattered, releasing bursts of blood-red magic into the air. The magic swirled around the Snake God and His future Queen.

The bell at the top of the Spire rang once more, for the last time.

ALIEN EARTH
WENDY OLIVER

Earth, 2115

I angled the thrusters on our landing approach to compensate for the uneven ground. This was our last opportunity to gather supplies before returning to Mars. The biologists back home had assigned us these mountains in their quest to acquire wild plants adaptable to our greenhouse conditions. They sent an elaborate catalog of items to obtain.

Rocky Mountains
Mushrooms (as many species as available).
Any and all berries (maybe mountain varieties would survive).
Lichen (for experiments outside the domes).
Pinon cones (for later). (If we have a later).
Soil (ideally teeming with life).

Our cargo hold already contained grains and legumes, and fruit seeds. We'd collected small canopy plants from the rainforest to expand the hydroponics lab. Now we hunted drought tolerant and cold hardy mountain plants.

As I pitched *Ceres* upright, flashes from the view screen nearly blinded me. I squinted. A lake beside the clearing rippled. In space, changes in light occurred slowly, giving the view screen time to adjust. Of course, in space there was only the one light source. The lake reflected the sunlight into thousands of tiny sun shards. I'd never seen anything like it. In fact, the only familiar sight was the dust now swirling around the ship.

A touch on the yoke spun *Ceres* away from the distracting sparkle. I eased back and we slowed to a soft touchdown.

Rutton, our chief scientist, unclipped his harness with one hand and jabbed at the console with the other. "What's the air like? Is it safe?"

I pushed his hand off the screen. "You know the protocol. Wait for the ship's methane to clear. Give it a couple minutes, just like at the three prior locations."

He flipped off his harness and stood.

Narda, our horticulturist, shifted her seatback. "I swear every time we land, I get heavier."

I scrolled through the exterior camera images. Towering peaks fenced us in. Green trees carpeted the surrounding slopes. I switched to the near-infrared sensors. There was too much biomass to differentiate useful plants from the luxury of thousands of trees.

Narda stretched and flipped on the auxiliary screen. She rewound the image and paused it. "Did we fly in over a town?"

I glanced at her screen. "Looks like it. I don't know if anyone saw us, or if they'd react even if they did."

"Do you think they'd be friendly, like the Siberian farmers, or more like the hostile Australians?"

I shrugged.

"How far away is it?" Rutton asked.

"About fifteen kilometers."

"Then we'd better work fast," Rutton said. "Commander, are we clear to disembark?"

Without waiting for an answer, Narda pushed to her feet. She opened several lockers on the walls and snatched out her sample kits and gear.

I scrolled to the atmospheric sensors. "Most of the methane has dissipated. Readings show excess carbon dioxide, sulfur dioxide, and general chemical contamination similar to data we gathered on the other continents."

Rutton stripped off his shorts and tee shirt to pull on his heavyweight coveralls. "Breathable. But I wouldn't want to live here."

He and Narda took the elevator to the lower hatch and exited down the ramp. I shut down the flight systems and reported our position to Mars Base. Seven minutes later, they responded to my "all nominal" with the automated "All's well. Carry on." I read their written message, surprised that mission control hadn't answered directly. Were the radios failing? Or was influenza disrupting the work schedule? Nothing I could do from sixty million kilometers away.

I headed outside to check the methane synthesizers. Our next launch would propel us to high Earth orbit, where our nuclear thermal engines would ignite for the return home.

The summer air felt cooler than at our last stop in the Amazonian rainforest and more lightly perfumed. A bit of dirt. A bit of something sweet. Pleasant, although still quite alien. The early Mars colonists wrote impassioned odes to all smells left behind, as if the scent of Earth's air was some magical elixir.

Eh. It was OK.

Narda and Rutton periodically checked in while I managed the routine chores around *Ceres*, preparing for our return voyage. At their current rate, the methane synthesizers would fill the tanks within six hours. I shuffled some of the cargo around to keep the ship balanced when the scientists brought in the new samples. When all was shipshape, I grabbed a pack loaded with sample kits and headed out to hunt plants.

The sparkling lake drew me. I'd never before seen such a huge basin of standing water. More water filled this valley than was contained in all the habitat domes combined. Could I bathe in it? I waded in until the water lapped my boots. I bent over and plunged my hands into the liquid.

Ouch! I yanked my hands out and jumped back, hunting for whatever bit me. Not seeing anything alive, I swished one hand through a second time. That water was cold! My fingers cramped. Forget the bath. Submerging in that frigid lake would be agonizing.

I shook off my hand and dried it with a cloth from my pack. Following the shoreline to some dense bushes, the water lost clarity. I pulled out several containers and filled them with murky, scum-filled samples. Our biologists would enjoy identifying the microorganisms.

The warm sun and soothing breeze lured me away from my duties. I spotted a protruding rock and sat on it. Tall trees wrapped around the far end of the lake. Closer, the bushes concealed a gurgling stream, cheeping birds and other mysterious sounds.

The rippling water half hypnotized me.

Movement on the far shore roused me. I squinted, trying to identify the shape as it moved between trees. It looked like an extra tall animal. A giraffe? No, not in the Rocky Mountains.

I snatched up the pack and samples and raced to *Ceres*. Scrambled up the ramp and inside. The flip of a switch turned on the viewscreen. I pivoted the side camera and zoomed in.

The image showed something I'd only ever seen in books. Six people were riding creatures. Horses?

I scrambled for the radio. "Rutton. *Ceres*. Urgent."

"*Ceres*. Rutton here. What's up?"

"There are people coming. They're riding horses!"

"Copy. We'll return to the ship."

I checked all the readouts and activated the pre-start protocols on the engines in case we needed a rapid exit.

Rutton and Narda returned, dragging the hand cart. Together, we hauled it up the ramp and stowed the sample cases in the hold.

"How'd we do?" I asked.

Rutton shook his head.

Narda said, "Less than a quarter of our list. And some of that is low quality. We really need another full day out there."

Rutton glanced over from lashing down a box. "Ideally, we'd stay for half a day after that to prepare the mushrooms and collect the spores. We can do it on board, but the process is messy."

I took a deep breath and faced them. "What's the minimum time we need to gather the critical supplies here?"

"Noon tomorrow." He unlatched the cart handle and stowed it flat between a pair of crates.

Rutton picked up our portable table. Narda raced to the galley for our left-over cookies.

We exited *Ceres*. I paused on the ramp to close the hatch. Historically, Earth culture required offerings of gifts or food when meeting for the first time. I only hoped the cookies were adequate. We had nothing else to spare.

Four of the riders were close enough for me to see the size of the horses. They could crush us. The riders wore short-sleeved shirts exposing bare arms bulky enough to wrestle the horses. We would never win if this turned into a physical fight.

They stopped in front of us.

Rutton held his empty hands out at his sides and tried a friendly greeting. "Hello. We're the crew of *Ceres*. From Mars."

A reddish horse tossed its head. The humans were silent.

Rutton tried again. "Thank you for welcoming us. We're here gathering samples to return to Mars. The terraforming efforts require more plant species."

The biggest man glowered. His horse took two steps toward us. I braced my knees to keep from backing away. He said, "You are not welcome."

Narda raised the plate. "We brought you cookies."

He stared until she lowered her arms and looked down.

I breathed the lake scent, filling my lungs. "Hello. I'm Commander Tiana. This is Rutton and Narda. We're not here to cause trouble. We're here gathering materials for the colonization efforts on Mars."

In a voice as cold as the lake, the man said, "Your grandparents stole resources that could have saved Earth. They ran away to live in luxury."

His anger startled me.

He continued. "Did you people screw up? Was it a disaster from the start?"

"Our grandparents adapted and built a functional civilization. But there weren't enough supplies. Shipping more was too expensive." I fought with my own temper.

"You obviously survived."

"Barely. And that is why we are here. We're not looking to take gold or diamonds. We need a better variety of nutrients."

One of the women rested her hand on her horse's neck. "Are your people getting sick?"

"Yes. And dying early. No one expected the deficiencies, like scurvy.

The angry man glared at her and then at me. "You abandoned us. You squandered our resources."

My guts roiled. He frightened me, yet his facts were utterly wrong. "If used carefully, our money and resources might have saved a thousand people. Nothing on our ships had the capacity to slow the temperature spikes, the rising seas, or the diseases. That's why our grandparents sacrificed their lives here and immigrated to a freezing rock. No one knew if humanity would survive on Earth. The Mars colony is a second chance."

His horse pranced in place. I shuffled away from those sharp hooves.

The last two members of his party arrived. His horse tossed its head and snorted. I prepared to run but paused to admire one of the new horse's white and black coat, like a work of art. The rider stared at me. I realized she was a young girl. *They let their children ride these four-legged monsters?*

"Ali. Stay back." From the concern in his tone, the man on the red horse was probably her father. "These people are dangerous. We don't know why they're here. They might be planning to kidnap you for slave labor."

I squared my shoulders and faced off with his horse. "We are here as representatives of the Martian Colony to collect new plant samples for the terra-forming efforts on Mars. Few of the original plant species survived. We must increase our biodiversity."

"What makes you think you can just swoop in here and steal our plants?"

Narda pointed to the far hillside. "Obviously, you're not using them."

"But we are. We're using every green thing on this planet. There are far fewer now." He flicked his head toward Ali. "You can't just raid Earth."

He pulled a strange tool off his belt. It took me a moment to identify the shape as an old-fashioned gun.

I swayed in shock. No one else moved.

The wind whispered through the wild plants. A horse shook, rattling its equipment. The nearby bushes shivered.

One of the women pointed toward our ship. "Please go."

"We need two days." I struggled to force the words through a throat as dry as the Martian plains.

"Two minutes."

What would convince them? Our people would perish without these supplies. I couldn't fail.

A dark animal charged out from the bushes. It rushed toward us and reared on its hind legs. Horses bolted in all directions. The grey spun and hit Narda in its panic.

The bear huffed in our direction and then loped along the lakeshore and out of sight.

I darted toward Narda, panting on the ground, and dropped to my knees. One of the Earth women joined me. Narda sprawled in the dirt, gripping her right hand.

"Are you OK? Where are you hurt?" My hands reached for her, but I waited for her answer.

"My leg. It stomped on me."

Blood oozed between her fingers. I turned to her legs. She shifted her left leg and pointed to the right. As gently as possible, I brushed my hand down her injured leg. She gasped when I reached her calf.

"Rutton. Get the med kit."

He dashed toward *Ceres*.

I inspected Narda's ankle-high carboplastic boot and scowled. "I'm sorry. It has to come off now, before your leg swells."

She nodded, willing to accept the pain now rather than risking our cutting it off later. I braced one hand on her calf and grasped the heel with the other. A quick yank and her foot slipped out

She shrieked. The Earth woman squatted at Narda's shoulder and caught her good hand. "Why didn't you wait for the pain killers? You hurt her."

"The boots insulate too much for ice to be effective. It had to come off."

"Ice? Why didn't you wait for your med kit?" She gestured toward Rutton scrambling down the hill toward us.

I met her eyes. "There's nothing in the med kit for pain. We have methods to knock someone out completely for surgeries and such. But this isn't that serious." As I talked, I gently rolled up Narda's pant leg and wriggled off her sock. My heart sank. An odd lump marred the bone above her ankle. I involuntarily grimaced.

She panted. "What?"

"It's broken. The horse must have pinned your foot as it knocked you over." I fought to produce a tiny smile. "I hereby relieve you of duty until we reach microgravity."

She closed her eyes while still cradling her hand. Rutton returned carrying the red box.

Gently sliding my fingers beneath her hand, I said, "Let's see it."

The deep red half-oval matched the marks on her foot. "That brute trampled your hand, too. Can you move it?"

Narda held her breath while wiggling all five fingers. We both nodded. Rutton murmured, "That's good."

I released her hand. The Earth woman carefully supported it. "What are you going to do?"

"Splint both the hand and leg and then ice them." I glanced around. "Actually, let's move her to the lake. It's cold enough to numb."

"Do you need help moving her?"

The leader's deep voice startled me. I glanced around. All the Earthlings surrounded us. The horses grazed on a grassy patch below *Ceres*.

The woman on her knees half smiled. "I'm Pauline. I teach and am on the town council."

"Pleased to meet you." I rummaged in the med kit, pulling out a metal brace and strips of fabric. "Sorry, Nards. We'll soak you up for a bit, then straighten that bone."

Ali's father grunted. I spotted his gun holstered on his hip. "That's crazy. Give her something for pain."

Fed up, I snapped. "Like what? We don't have anything. All the meds they brought were either used up decades ago or degraded. No one's opened a pharmaceutical company up there."

He exhaled. "Wait," he said and then marched off toward the horses.

I pulled out an alcohol swab and dabbed the antiseptic on Narda's hand. She gulped and gripped Pauline's hand even tighter. All I could do was repeat, "Sorry."

Rutton returned to the ship to fetch a chair. I wrapped Narda's leg and hand with waterproof material to keep scum like I'd sampled earlier out of her abrasions. Ali's father returned. He knelt and gave Narda a shot. She instantly relaxed. Next, he and Pauline helped her sit up and swallow a couple of pills.

"Lucky for you," he said, "we do still manufacture drugs on Earth."

Rutton brought a crate and set it in the water. We lifted Narda, carried her into the lake, and gently seated her. She gasped when her foot hit the ice water.

Pauline returned to the shore and sat on dry ground. "It sounds like Mars is awful. Why don't y'all come home?"

Ali's father growled.

She waved at him. "Ross. Stop."

"There are five hundred and four people living on Mars. That," I pointed at *Ceres*, "is our only space vehicle."

Ali found one of the greenish cookies on the ground. "What's this?"

I glanced over. "A cookie."

She blew off the dust, sniffed it then nibbled the edge. Her face tightened, and she spit it out. "That's a cookie? It tastes like horse food."

Narda drew a shaky breath. "I baked those special to celebrate landing."

"That's what you eat?" Ali sounded shocked. "That's gross."

I asked, "What do you mean? They're a specialty at home. We can't usually afford the sugar."

Ali, oblivious to the mood, asked, "Did you fight space pirates on your way here?"

Confusion laced Rutton's face as he looked at her. "Pirates?"

"Of course. Pirates. *Ahoy ye scurvy dogs of Mars. Heave to, or we'll blast yer airlock.*" She saw our blank faces and continued. "You know. Captain Smythe and the Planetoid Pirates."

Her father glanced at her. "It's a video series."

Rutton shrugged. "We don't get Earth programs. They did at first, but the receiver broke."

"You sound so pathetic." Ross laid his hand on his gun. "You stole the best of everything - sugar, technology. Hope. And you want more? You don't deserve anything."

"We're not thieves. How many resources do you imagine we're 'stealing?' Look at our ship. Three-quarters of our space goes to the methane refinery, fuel storage, and engines. We can't even take a full-grown tree!"

Narda whispered, "Although we'd sure like to."

Despite my fear of his weapon, I had to make them understand. "We need seeds and soil and fungi and Earth bacteria. The Mars colony will fail without them. We have five years at most."

"Why should we care? You loaded up all our resources and blasted off."

"Fourteen shipments. Fourteen. How many resources do you really think they crammed onto fourteen rockets?"

"All the good ones." He crossed his arms.

"They took ordinary ones." I softened my voice. "Potatoes, which developed blight. The rice failed without micronutrients. Turnips and rye are the only foods doing well."

"Well, it looks like we're doing better than you. Serves you right."

"We're human, just like you. We've lost friends and family, just like you. Without increasing our biodiversity, the entire project will fail. They're counting on us to collect a few plants and some soil."

Ali cocked her head. "Soil? You mean you want to take dirt?"

"Not dirt," I explained. "Soil. Mars has plenty of dirt. But it's sterile. Plants in plain Mars dirt aren't very healthy. They're lacking too many nutrients that come from bacteria breaking down dead things to make soil."

"Dad, they came all the way here just to get dirt." She took his hand.

He smiled at her and turned to face the other Earth natives. One by one, they nodded. He sighed. "You want two days. And then you'll leave?"

"Please. Once we leave, I promise you'll never see us again."

"You mean you'll avoid our territory?"

"Mars lacks the resources for another visit for a very long time. If ever."

He nodded. "We grant you two days. Be gone before sunset, day after tomorrow."

"Thank you," I whispered.

Ali studied the cookie and then looked at Narda sitting with her foot immersed in icy lake water. "It doesn't sound very fun there. Why would you go back?"

I shrugged. "It's home."

OPAL UNDER THE SKY
KELLEY J.P. LINDBERG

As if I don't have anything better to do—like, say, finding my worthless brother—here I am, sitting in Professor Dark-thread's Advanced Silicate Manipulation class, listening to him talk about the sky. Not the ceiling, mind you, which is directly over our heads and has a vein of quartz in the corner that we all agree looks like Professor Tabor's nose. And not, you know, silicates.

No, the sky.

"I know some of you don't think this is important," Professor D says like we didn't hear him the first dozen times this week, "but being under the open sky can be very disorienting. Dizzying, even."

I've seen the sky.

Like everyone else in Telos, I've watched a thousand out-world movies and videos, so I've seen the sky a thousand times on my screens. I've read about it in hundreds of books. Big deal.

Personally, I think out-worlders are obsessed with the sky to an unhealthy degree. They see their sky every day, so you'd think they'd be bored with it. That they'd ignore it.

Like ceilings. You hardly ever pick up a murder mystery and the narrator's going on about the ceiling—unless Michelangelo painted it or something, I guess. But you know there's a ceiling in every room the narrator walks through. They just never bother to mention it. There's no need.

But somehow, every out-worlder who's ever written a book or filmed a movie has made some mention of the sky—clouds, stars, sunshine, blue firmament, dome of heaven, sunsets, moonrises, whatever.

Seriously. Can't they find something else to talk about?

It's just a really tall ceiling made of air, for dirt's sake.

"It can even make you experience nausea or vomiting," Professor D continues. "It happens to a lot of people who get selected for Extrusion, especially in their first few days. It's nothing to be ashamed of."

Extrusion. Being sent to the out-world to see how the other half—well, the other 99.99 percent—lives. Extruders are sent outside to experience and learn everything they can, then bring that first-hand knowledge back here, to Telos.

As if any of us in this class will get picked for Extrusion. Or, as we usually call it when the professors aren't around, "skying," as in "walking around under the sky." See? Even we get obsessed with the word sky. And we don't even have to look at it all day.

You don't get sent to Professor D's class if you're at the top of anyone's list. Certainly not top of the list of candidates for Extrusion tours of duty.

But here we are, in our final year of First University, preparing ourselves for thrilling work prospects like mail sorting or sanitation. And learning about skying, "just in case."

Just in case of what, exactly? In case all fifty of this year's skying candidates come down with the plague, and we bottom-dwellers have to step up to the chore?

Not bloody likely. Especially not for the likes of me, whose older brother managed to destroy any chance I had at leveling up when he disappeared out there.

Most people think Anton became a sky-runner: someone who pulls a disappearing act because they decide they'd rather spend the rest of their life in the out-world than inside our mountain. But I know Mom and Dad still cling to the hope that he's out there some-where, hurt, maybe, or caught in a situation he can't escape. They believe the rumors. That out there, out beyond the mountain we live within, there are people trying to find us.

Catch us.

Study us.

The darker rumors say they're killing us, dissecting us, or running vicious, torturous experiments on us.

But those are just rumors. Nobody's ever found any evidence. They're just scare tactics to keep us safe and happy inside Telos.

Mom and Dad want to believe Anton would never run. I just want to find out the truth and drag my parents out of their broken hearts.

And frankly, I would have liked the chance to become a skyer myself.

Because he chose the out-world over our home here in Telos, Anton was probably the last skyer our family will ever be allowed to have.

Thanks, Anton.

Out-world lover.

Sky-runner.

Jerk.

I hope wherever you are in the out-world, the sky is making you vomit.

"Opal! Aren't you ready?" Shae asks, standing in front of my family's door. She's eyeing my threadbare pajamas with something close to horror.

I shake my head. "Thesis," I say. I just got a new round of edits back from my advisor, Professor Sparks. I'd added some new calculations to support one of my shakier theories, and I couldn't wait to see what she thought. I'd already made myself a nice cup of tea.

"Seriously? Come on. You can take one night off."

Apparently, I don't say no fast enough, which makes Shae think she's getting through to me.

"How often does Jet get permission to perform in the Finishing

Chamber? His voice is gonna sound incredible. You know what the harmonics of those Blues do. And who knows? They say if you're stuck on a problem, think about something totally unrelated for a while." She gives me a downright evil grin. "Thinking about Jet instead of math for one night might just be what your tired brain needs. Honestly. I'm only thinking of your mental health."

Temptation finds a tiny crack in my resolve. I still have three weeks left before I have to publish and defend my thesis. I could probably spare a couple of hours to go see Jet's concert. And getting out of the apartment tonight has a certain appeal to it. Mom's in one of her sad moods, and Dad's hiding in his office. Like he has ever since Anton left.

I have to admit, the silence in our home lately has been awfully numbing.

Shae's right. Jet's voice in that room of occluded sapphires would be worth it. Jet's voice, his smile, his eyes, and all the rest of him—all worth it.

Even if he's with that pile of arsenic flakes, Bette. Jet and Bette. I'm positive he's only dating her because their names rhyme.

A girl can dream, right? And dreams sound better in a room full of blue sapphires.

"Fine," I say, huffing a little like I'm making a big sacrifice. "I'll go."

Shae grins. She knows why I caved.

I'm as transparent as liquid quartz.

But what Shae doesn't know is that what I'm craving right now, more than the flash of Jet's smile, is the chance to feel something. Those moments are few and far between for me, these days. My fault, I know. If I'd just get out of the house and go hang out more often with Shae and our other friends, maybe I'd feel more like... me. But it's so easy to crawl into my research project and hide.

My brother's absence erodes my bedrock like a trickle of water through sandstone, a few grains at a time. The only way I can think of to stop it is to keep working on my project—to keep developing the algorithms that might someday help me find Anton.

And to let Shae drag me to a concert.

BECAUSE I HAD to ditch my pajamas and run a comb through my hair, we're nearly late. We have to settle for standing at the back of the Finishing Chamber. It's nearly full tonight, with at least fifty people crowding in the spaces between the sapphires. Most, like Shae and I, are wearing blue in deference to the crystals surrounding us. The walls are pocked with niches, all of them full of cut Blues this season, waiting for their final polishing. Some of the niches hold bowls of smaller gems. Larger alcoves cradle free-standing clusters of raw sapphire crystals. A few monolithic sapphiric stones frame the small stage.

This chamber is one of my favorite places in Telos. Its main purpose isn't for concerts, of course, but what the maturing crystals do to music in this room is beyond belief.

And sapphires? I don't think there's a word for what blue sapphires do. I mean, all crystals have an amazing effect on sound. Every type of stone hums at a different frequency, every color or shade produces a unique resonance, and the size and shape of occlusions in the stones can scatter, focus, echo, or dampen sounds in a million different ways.

But the Blues? Those beauties do to music what Jet's eyes do to my stupid heart.

I can barely see Jet between all the heads and shoulders blocking my view of the small stage.

Being the shortest person in the room is highly inconvenient.

Shae squeezes against the person next to her, opening up a tiny space for me. At least now I can see a sliver of the stage.

"Thanks," I say.

Shae grins back. She's been feeding my Jet obsession shamelessly for months. Not that it's doing any good.

Then the overhead lights dim, and tiny lights directed at the clusters of raw sapphires cast the entire room in blue.

The music begins.

Jet's not alone. Two other musicians are with him on stage: a flute player and a guitarist. The two instruments start out slowly, picking out individual notes, sounding more like harmonic sighs than music. Ordinarily, just hearing the guitar and flute tones blending together would be enough to justify squandering an evening I should have spent working on my paper.

But then Jet begins flowing his voice into the music, filling in the space like water pouring into a well of marbles. The closest of the sapphires echoes his voice with a faint ring.

His voice lifts, and more sapphires begin to hum in resonance. Soon, every crystal in the blue-washed chamber is singing.

As the music weaves between stones and people, stage lights shift along the color spectrum, easing into monochromatic swells and valleys, plunging into waves of fast-flowing colors, then fading back again to cool washes of blue.

The vibrations are already finding me, filling my nerves and bones with energy. With life. With joy. I haven't felt those sensations since... well, since the last time Jet did a concert and Shae dragged me along.

Jet begins a new song, and the lights burst in a kaleidoscope pattern, scattering blue and shadow across the faces around me. Shae's hair starts to wave like she's floating in water. I feel my own hair rising, my arms going weightless.

By the third song, we're all—all fifty of us in the audience— suspended in the air between the sapphires.

We start to spin.

Slowly at first, then faster. And faster.

And people begin winking in and out of view.

No one leaves this plane for more than a second or two. As kids, we all learn how to use our bodies' personal vibration frequencies to phase in and out of that sparkling, swirling, pure-energy plane that exists—although "existing" is probably an inadequate word—between physical locations. The Creation Zone, our ancestors called it when they used it to travel between stars. No one can stay in that zone for long. Just a moment or two to recharge is all most of us are capable of. With extra training, those who are tapped for leadership roles or Extrusion duty, like Anton, can modulate their personal vibration frequencies to travel through the Creative Zone from one place to another. But only within a twenty-mile radius. Not between stars like we used to.

I struggle to control the energy coursing through me. I don't want to let myself start winking. That's a lie, I know, because I really do want to give in to that joyous feeling. But Anton was the first person who brought me to a concert in this chamber, and I can't help feeling guilty. I should be home, working on the math that might help me find him.

I fight the energy again, but then I hear Shae laughing as she winks back into the room beside me. "You need this!" she yells into my ear. She's probably right, but...

Then Jet hits a note that sears right through me, and I let go with a thousand shivers of blue-tinged breath that tastes like hope and death and children's toys.

With a sense of desperation, I fling myself into the sound, the light, the vibrations. I dance in the air, arms reaching up and away, hands flexing, fingers tingling, like I can shape the song into crystals no one's ever seen before. And I'm gone.

Then back.

Then gone again.

Every time I let myself blink out of this plane, I'm gone only an instant. In that instant, I'm not dancing *through* energy—I *am* energy, dancing. Chaotic, electric, phantasmagoric, euphoric. Then I'm back, full of more colors, more hums, more songs than even Jet can sing.

I am dancing.

We are all dancing.

This is what happens when Jet sings and the Blues listen.

WHEN JET'S VOICE, the flute, the guitar, and the deepest indigo sapphires finally fade into silence, we're all once more on the ground.

The silence is thick for a heartbeat. Two heartbeats.

Then everyone laughs, which is the only way to celebrate a concert like that.

The Blues ring the laughter back to us as we slowly file out of the chamber.

I'd like to stay. To hang back by the stage. To say something to Jet about how his music hums into me like no other performer's. Something witty and meaningful and intense... but not too intense, of course. Something about how listening to him helps soften the sting of Anton's betrayal and helps me keep looking for him no matter how much it hurts. But no one wants to hear about that.

It doesn't matter anyway, because Bette has already wrapped herself around him, and they're smiling at each other like they might still be listening to the Blues in some personal little cocoon.

I let Shae drag me out of the Finishing Chamber.

And smack into my advisor, Professor Sparks.

"Opal," she says, "we need to have a word with you."

"Um. Okay?"

She turns and starts walking through the crowd. I guess I'm supposed to follow. I take a few steps, then realize Shae hasn't moved. I reach back, clutch her by the elbow, and drag her along. No way am I doing this alone, whatever it is.

Eventually we reach the Parliament offices, which is not at all what I was expecting. Walking right past the reception area, Professor Sparks opens the door to a waiting room. Shae and I hesitate outside the door. Professor Sparks ushers me into the room, holding Shae back, then shuts the door behind me. My parents are the only other people in this room, and they're looking as confused as I feel.

This does not bode well.

TWO HOURS LATER, I'm still in the waiting room with my parents.

Mom and Dad are sitting closer together than I've seen them sit in eons. They're even holding hands. That doesn't mean they're talking, though.

When I tried to ask them what was going on, they both shook their heads and said we'd have to wait for someone to tell us.

Waiting. I was anxious at first, but after two hours, I'm more bored than anything. It's already past eleven o'clock. I have a 7:15 class tomorrow morning and a feeling I'm not going to get much sleep before then.

I've identified the scientific name and chemical makeup of every visible vein of mineral and crystal in the walls by the time the door finally slides open.

Without a word, the man who opened it waves to show we're supposed to follow him. So we do.

Dad wraps his arm around my shoulders and hugs me to him, but in a distracted way that tells me he's more nervous than affectionate right now.

That's okay. I'll still take it because I'm suddenly back to being pretty damned nervous, too.

When the man ushers us into the Obsidian Chamber, my knees go all wobbly. The Obsidian Chamber? The office of the Chief Guide herself?

I did not wear the right shoes for this. Come to think of it, my blue mini probably isn't appropriate attire, either.

My heart beats against my ribs like a miscalibrated sonic drill. I step closer to Dad, hoping he'll put his arm around me again.

He doesn't notice.

The Chief Guide stands up and walks around her carved amethyst desk until she's standing in front of us. Despite the fact that it's almost midnight, she looks perfectly official and imposing, every line of her dress and strand of her hair in place. I'm sure I smell sweaty from all the dancing, and my hair is a rumpled mess.

The Chief Guide bows slightly in greeting.

We all return the bow, but lower. I have never executed such an awkward bow in my life.

When she gestures to the three chairs arranged in front of the desk, we sit. The curved black walls of the famous dome-shaped office seem distressingly grim. They don't look this terrifyingly black in photos. And the room is bigger than I expected, with the domed ceiling overhead disappearing into the shadows. Oh, look at me, noticing the ceiling! I shove the irreverent thought away.

Instead of sitting down behind her desk, the Chief Guide leans against it. She's right in front of us. Intimate. All friendly-like. This is either going to be really good news or really terrible news. I hold my breath and stare at the pendant she's wearing so I don't have to meet her eyes.

"We've been tracking your son, and we think we have a lead," she says. Then our leader breaks into the broadest, most genuine smile I've ever seen.

Mom gasps and claps her hands to her mouth. Dad lurches like he's just been shocked.

And I leap out of my chair, then freeze. Did I hear her wrong?

My mom chokes out the one word we're all trying to form: "Anton?"

The Chief Guide nods, then immediately tries to soften her grin to a more official-looking serene smile, like she just remembered the head of Telos can't seem overly excited or happy or, you know, ordinary.

"I need for you to understand," she says to my parents before any of us can ask a question, "you need to manage your expectations. We have information indicating—possibly—that Anton may still be alive. We can't confirm that yet," she says, putting up her hands like she's trying to tamp down our excitement, "but I've got a team working on it."

"And is he..." my mom starts to say, then can't quite finish. "Is he...?" she tries again.

The Chief Guide gives a tiny shrug. "The signal we're tracking, if it's really him, shows that he's alive, apparently in northern Montana, but we can't ascertain his condition. We've sent an extraction team to the area. However, we're still trying to narrow down the precise location. As soon as we can locate him and transport him here, we'll have our best medical team evaluate him."

My mom starts to cry, quietly. Her shoulders slump, like she's been holding herself together for the last couple of hours, but she just can't anymore.

My Dad asks, "Northern Montana?" His voice is deeper, raspier than usual.

The Chief Guide shakes her head. "We don't know for sure where he's been held all this time, but that's where he—or at least the signal we think might be him—is at this moment. For now, we're focused on getting him back safely."

"Been held?" My dad's voice hardens. "What do you mean, 'where he's been held'?"

She shakes her head again. "Apologies, that was a slip. A rumor. Again, we don't have details, and I shouldn't be speculating at all."

The next ten minutes consist of my dad trying to get more information out of the Chief Guide and her apologizing for not knowing anything yet.

But I'm hung up on the word "signal." They've found a signal that may be Anton? Are they tracking my brother somehow?

My senior research thesis is on personal vibrations and how to potentially isolate them in a crowd. As part of my research, I surveyed all the current literature on personal vibrations, and I investigated different technologies we already use to identify them. The problem is, those technologies only work within a limited range—like within a small room. The best devices have a seventy-five percent success rate at identifying a particular person in a fifteen-cubic-meter space with up to ten people inside. But that's the limit.

Personal vibrations (which maybe isn't the best term for what our energies do, but we've been using it for so many eons that we're sort of stuck with it) are kind of like fingerprints. Everyone has a unique vibration, but it can be hard to isolate, even under lab conditions. It's especially hard because people can modulate their vibrations at different frequencies to shift between planes. I postulated a technique that could, in theory, be used to isolate and identify them across long distances. My basic hypothesis involves using some tricky nonlinear plane mathematics to home in on frequency clusters, regardless of interference.

Ever since Anton disappeared, this has been my research focus. But it's early days yet. I haven't built a prototype of a device to interpret frequency clusters, and I probably won't have the capability to do that until I'm enrolled in Second University. In fact, that's exactly what I've been planning for my 2U research project. But right now, it's all theoretical.

Did the administration somehow make my idea work?

It's more likely that someone in the Science agency has beaten me to it. There goes my whole thesis project.

I raise my hand.

The Chief Guide blinks at me once. "Yes, Opal?"

"Can you tell me what you mean by 'signal'?"

A smile quirks the corners of her lips.

"Ah, yes. I was getting around to that." She sits back in her desk chair. "It seems your research project has caught the attention of some of our lead scientists."

"Um." I try to stomp on a little tremor of nerves. "In a good way?"

The Chief Guide's smile grows wider.

"Yes. Very."

A little thrill of excitement competes for attention with my nerves.

"Professor Sparks brought your research to our agency's attention a few months ago. They found merit in your idea, and they've been building and testing prototypes."

"Without me?" I manage to squeak.

Her smile seems a little patronizing. "Yes, Opal. They didn't want to interfere with your thesis project. They instructed Professor Sparks to monitor your work but not to unduly influence it. Your education is important."

Yeah, so is finding my brother, I think. But wisely, I keep that to myself.

"Last week," the Chief Guide continues, "they began field-testing the prototype. We thought it safest to try it with subjects suspected of hiding..." She hesitates for a moment, looking apologetically at my parents. "Your brother was one of the three subjects they tried to locate in the first round. And they got a 'ping,' as they say. Really quite surprising, I have to be honest."

Personal vibrational frequency is registered in everyone's health records at birth. It's essential to everyone's healthcare, after all. Usually, it's protected information, but if anyone is assumed to be dead or in hiding after a skying mission, their health records can be opened up for investigations—and research. That's how I got access to some of my data for my work. I was limited to people who were confirmed dead, though. Not missing, like Anton.

If Anton is a sky-runner, how is he going to react when the Chief Guide's team catches up to him?

Now the tremors and thrills in my gut are joined by a wave of nausea.

"Our scientists tell me they're 73% certain it's Anton's frequency. But they might achieve higher confidence in their results if they have a control to use as a comparison. So... they'd like to do some testing with his sibling."

I blink. "Uh, sure. Okay. Of course."

Mom and Dad look at me with worried eyes.

"It's okay," I reassure them. "It's not invasive or anything. It's completely safe." I should know. It's my research. "And if it helps find Anton, I'm all in."

I look back at the Chief Guide. "Can we start right now?"

"I appreciate your enthusiasm, but it is midnight, dear. I believe they'd like to start first thing in the morning. They've already cleared your absence from class this week with your professors."

I take in a breath, which I keep forgetting to do.

Then she adds, "One more thing. The accuracy of their signal searching isn't what they'd like it to be. The scientists wondered if you'd be willing to work with them on some ideas they've got."

Holy smokey quartz. The Chief Guide's scientists need my help? "Yeah. I'm in."

EVEN WITH ONLY THREE hours of sleep, I'm wide awake this morning. I've been whisked into a lab facility with people looking at me like they can't decide if they should be annoyed or impressed.

"Right," says a woman with a tablet. "Let's get started."

No small talk or welcome-to-the-team speech is necessary, I guess. I'm putting her in the annoyed camp.

The woman brings me up to speed, sort of, which is funny since most of the background information came directly from my own research. But then she starts showing me the devices they've experimented with.

Seeing my theoretical ideas sitting on a desk, fully formed in a combination of metal alloys and crystals, is surreal. I had planned to spend the next several years of my 2U education creating this.

So, this is what a staff of highly trained scientists and engineers, a fat budget, and the blessing of the Chief Guide can do with an idea?

Bring it on.

By lunchtime, I've been sent into four different rooms with four different groups of random volunteers, and they've identified my personal vibration correctly all four times. Admittedly, it's a small sample size, but we just beat the seventy-five percent success rate of the previous technologies.

More importantly, I tell my ego, now they've got the device calibrated to my frequency and verified that it's working. That was the easy part.

Their working theory? My personal vibration and Anton's might be similar enough because of our close genetics that understanding how my vibration works might help them more accurately identify the vibration they're picking up in Montana.

By mid-afternoon, I'm working with an engineer who specializes in inter- and intra-planal physics, and he's explaining why one of the assumptions I used in my research isn't working. I'm keeping up, but just barely. I don't have time to be embarrassed.

By dinnertime, I've had three a-ha moments, at least six dammit moments, and an aw-shucks or two.

By bedtime, I'm exhausted. I barely have the energy to send a message to Shae telling her where I've been—at least the minimal information I'm allowed to share.

We're a tiny step closer to finding Anton.

FOUR DAYS LATER, Mom, Dad, and I are again sitting in the Chief Guide's Obsidian Chamber.

"We've got him," she says, that genuine grin on her face. "The extraction team just notified us. They're bringing him in. Anton will be here by tomorrow morning."

We're all frozen. We're thrilled, of course. But also terrified. Are they bringing him in trussed up in handcuffs? Is he returning as a... criminal?

The Chief Guide must sense our worry because she tilts her head to one side and adopts a gentler tone of voice.

"What I'm about to tell you must stay within this room for now. According to the extraction team, Anton was being restrained in a government research facility. The specific details of exactly where he was and what they were doing with him aren't something I can share with you yet. You can see him when he gets here for fifteen minutes, supervised. After that, we'll need to debrief him fully, which they tell me could take several days. If that goes well, then we plan to reintroduce him to our community."

This all sounds very scary. Those damned rumors were true after all.

My lungs turn to cold diamonds in my chest.

"Our sincere hope is that he'll be back in your family home as quickly as possible. We'll make our top counselors and therapists available to Anton and to all three of you for as long as you need them."

She clasps and unclasps her hands. She suddenly seems as uncertain us we are.

"I know you're worried," she says, "but we're going to do everything we can to ensure Anton is safe, well, and welcome. From the few facts we've received so far—and believe me, I've already got people looking into that government facility—Anton wasn't there by choice. But he appears to be alert, strong enough to walk, and able to communicate with our team. And when they extracted him from his cell, he could phase in and out on command as they escaped the facility. All of that is good news."

My parents nod slowly, and my mom tries to smile.

My heart is racing.

My brother is coming home.

THE NEXT MORNING, one of the Chief Guide's staff escorts us to the East Surface Gate.

My heart skitters.

The East Surface Gate is one of only three portals from our city to the out-world.

I'm going outside to meet Anton. *Outside.*

Me. I'm actually going to see the out-world.

I know I should be focused on Anton. And I am. I can't wait to see him, the jerk. Except now I know he's not a jerk. Kidnapped. Geez.

But now, for the first time in two years, maybe it's okay to think about something other than finding Anton.

I mean, we're only going to stand just outside the gate so that we can greet Anton when he gets here. It's not like we'll be traveling through the out-world. We won't be seeing cities, windmills, McDonald's, or... I don't know... whales or anything.

But I'll be breathing out-world air, seeing out-world trees. And grass. Weeds. Birds, maybe. A deer? A skunk? Snakes? Oh, I'd like to see one of those cute little horned toads.

I wonder... will I be able to see the outside of our mountain? I've seen photos of it, taken by people who've been out-world for one reason or another. But to see the mountain we live in from the outside, in person? Wow.

I can hardly breathe.

As we approach the East Gate, we pass through several checkpoints lined with crystals. Then we move into the final tunnel that leads to the surface of the Earth. I'm shivering by the time we reach the last checkpoint, but I'm not cold. It's actually growing warmer. The microlayer of tourmaline that lines this section of the tunnel here shimmers for a moment, then we're beyond it.

The tunnel suddenly looks like a lava tube. It's become something raw and natural instead of something we've carved from the mountain's heart.

For a moment, I wish I could have brought Shae here to see this. I already know I'll have a hard time explaining it all to her later. Words are going to be massively inadequate.

Ten meters ahead of us, the lava tube tunnel ends, and the

opening is a bright circle—so bright it takes a minute to see what's beyond the opening.

Then it hits me.

Sunlight. That bright opening ahead of me is the out-world, bathed in sunlight.

As we step around the carefully randomized tumble of rocks on the tunnel floor, I begin to make out colors and shapes beyond the opening. A bunch of people are standing in the sparse grass beyond the entrance—guards, officials, a few senators, someone with a camera, and the Chief Guide. Then I see trees and bushes start to take shape beyond the people.

Then, incredibly, I've taken one last step, and I'm out of the tunnel.

I'm in the bright sunlight, squinting.

And there is Anton.

He's flanked by two guards, but they aren't hanging onto him, and his hands aren't in handcuffs. He's standing there, looking thinner than I last saw him. His blond hair is much shorter than he used to keep it, greasy and tangled. He's got a scruffy blond beard I've never seen him wear.

But it's him. And he's grinning at us, eyes sparkling exactly the way I remember.

Every other thought in my head vanishes. It's Anton. He's back.

Mom lets out a small scream, like it escaped without her even knowing, and she races across the few meters to Anton and throws her arms around him. He wraps himself around her, and they're both crying and laughing and crying some more. Dad and I catch up, and we're all crying and hugging now.

Anton is back.

He's here. He's not a sky-runner.

Not a traitor. Not a criminal.

My brother is back. I can't even process what this means to me, to my parents, and to the people who've whispered about him for two years. And right now, I just don't care. All I can do is squeeze my eyes shut and hold on tightly to my family.

After a few moments of hugging and crying, we start to get our sniffles under control.

I back up a little to give my mom more space because she's still grasping at Anton and turning him this way and that so she can "get a good look at him." My dad is beaming. I just want to watch them for a moment, this fractured family of mine.

I know there will be investigations. The confirmation that our people are being hunted on the outside will shake our city like an earthquake. But that's a problem for tomorrow.

Today, in this moment right here, right now, I swear I can feel the fissures that have been lying just under the surface of our family start to fuse back together.

I know it will take time.

But I feel cracked, jagged edges starting to smooth.

I stand here watching my brother as a strange-smelling breeze sweeps air across my warm skin. I hear that same breeze whisper through the trees around us. Something is chirping—a grasshopper, I think. Or maybe a bird?

At the thought of birds, I look up.

And there's the sky.

The sky!

I stare, amazed. My poor brain reaches for words, but none come.

There is no gemstone quite that color. That changeable, essential, heart-pounding color.

No height to measure.

No ceiling to catch light or reflect shadow or keep us grounded.

My feet feel unsteady, my head tingles, my chest expands like a wish.

A laugh bursts from me.

Our professor told us we might feel nauseated. But that's not it at all. I am disoriented, for sure. But in a glorious way.

I could fall up into that dazzling blue chalcedony sky for ages, I think, and never miss the ground.

My brother is back, my family is whole, and I finally understand out-worlders' obsession with the sky. This is why they call it heaven.

My vibration—my soul—begins to fill my body, my nerves, my bones.

I let my arms rise towards that astounding sky, my feet lifting gently into the sunlit air, my hair drifting on unseen currents of energy.

And I begin to dance.

CRASH LANDING
MARLENE FABIEN STILES

Jumping Jupiter! Riding out this ion storm is nothing like the test in the flight simulator that I aced at the Solar Academy. Junk debris is heading straight for my surveillance shuttle! This kind of space rubble ought to be logged on the navigation charts along with comets and meteor showers. . .

Great Rings of Saturn! A crunched hunk of metal the size of Ohio is coming my way! I yank on the joystick, barely swerve out of the way.

Safe! The scanner shows no other obstacles larger than a pellet. Start to breathe again.

Red lights pop up all over the control panel. Now what? Did space gravel breach the shuttle's hull? Red skull icon flashes. The computer's deadpan voice announces, "Life support will fail in ten minutes."

I'm doomed.

My mouth goes dry as I calibrate the distance to a planet——any planet——near enough to land. Ten minutes will get me to a rocky dwarf with an atmosphere but this nameless world has an X3 rating. Check the stats; it's a desert environment suitable for microbial extremophiles and small creatures adapted to limited water sources and extreme heat like Earth's thorny lizards and dung beetles. But a homo sapiens like myself won't last long in a hellishly hot, dry climate. Do I die on a desolate rock or shoot past it into space?

I'm a procrastinator. I prefer dying later.

The window is lit with unblinking stars in a black abyss as the control panel sets a course. Vog of Venus! This X3 planet borders the sector of our galaxy colonized by Vahmpyrs, Earth's mortal enemy. I can't land there, they'll kill me! But when I try to change the trajectory, my hands freeze to the joystick.

As X3 rockets closer, red skull icons flare. The computer's mechanical voice thunders, "Collision course. Abort immediately!"

I statue by the window and stare slack-jawed as deep space darkness whirls into ochre skies the color of windswept dunes.

Move, idiot! Climb into the safety harness before——

My shuttle slams into hot sand.

When I wake up, I'm slumped in the safety harness. Outside the window it's murky black.

This can't be right! The planet isn't tidally locked in rotation around its sun, there's no perpetual dark side. So why is the gauge on the control panel registering the outside temperature as a cool 10 degrees C? This close to a blue star sun, temperatures should be at the boiling point.

My guts twist. I can't stop sobbing. What in Hades' name is going on? Why has the world gone dark? I should have kept rocketing into space. Now I've crash-landed on a bizarre world that defies physics. Is this an experimental station created by Vahmpyrs? They're reputed to be demonically clever and more advanced than Earth's civilization.

My mind flashes back to childhood nightmares generated by stories of the Vahmpyr invaders who attacked Earth half a century ago. They're hideously winged creatures that resemble monstrous butterflies with two sightless, bald heads atop a stout, tubular trunk that can spout tentacles at will. Their wings are covered with glaring eyes haloed blue and crimson, while their heads appear blindfolded by skin stretched taut over a curved proboscis and long slit of a mouth.

Cold terror claws my spine. Vahmpyrs are chameleons who shapeshift into shadows to ambush their prey. They were only driven from Earth after decades of brutal fighting that destroyed most of our urban centers. Even a century later, most of these devastated cities were never rebuilt and were eventually reclaimed by jungles and new growth forests.

Get a grip! Assessing my situation from readings on the control panel, my best guess is that my shuttle plunged into a sinkhole and I'm in some kind of subterranean cavern.

This is curious . . . the oxygen level is 58%, which is considerably higher than Earth's 21%. Breathing that high of a level of oxygen for an extended period will lead to lung damage, but I can make adjustments to the filters on my space suit's helmet to compensate for the discrepancy. I won't die of suffocation, but I might starve. My shuttle only carries provisions for four days. Surveillance missions are supposed to be short-term.

Four days, and then...? What are my chances that Space Exploration Inc. will launch a search and rescue mission for me?

Leaning forward, I breathe deeply to put a lid on my anxiety. The odds aren't good. Why would they risk lives to rescue a low-ranking surveillance assistant? I'm no one special or important, and I'm easily replaced.

Oh my God, I'm going to die in this pit! I'll never see my mother again, or my friends or the sweet-faced technical assistant who smiled at me before take-off and seemed interested in going out for a coffee when I returned to base. I was so certain I'd come back...

Yesterday I had everything to live for. Now I have nothing, absolutely nothing . . . my life is as good as over——

What was that at the window? I steady myself against the smooth, thermal glass and squint into the eerie darkness. There it is again, a flicker of...bioluminescence? Shimmering specks of blue and crimson abruptly coalesce into a hundred glinting eyespots arrayed on massive, shadowy wings.

My blood freezes. It must be a Vahmpyr——what else could it be?

I cringe as the monster raises its wings and flies up to the window. I try to back away from its two hideous heads, but I'm tied to the safety harness.

One head is smooth and almost serene but the other is wrinkled and snarling. When they open their mouths, strange, rasping noises like raging winds pepper the shuttle's metallic walls. The heads argue in Pokin, the galactic language they brought to Earth.

One voice is rough as a tempest. "Kill the human. It killed us."

The other wafts soft, like a sultry breeze. "This one did not kill us. It is young."

"Kill it anyway. They are all the same."

"No, hasn't there been enough killing?"

I struggle to escape my harness but only get more entangled in its straps. "Please! I mean no harm! I crash landed here by accident!"

Twisting toward me, the gentler face raises its head to my eye level. "If that is the case, young human, then you have landed on this desert world as we did, through no choice of your own. We are also abandoned here and yet for many years we have managed to survive."

"Survive!" The angry face makes a guttural noise that weirdly imitates laughter. "We have no choice but to survive since we have lost all hope of rescue." It makes a snorting, pig-like sound. "You are alive now, but you must decide how long that will last."

The hair at the nape of my neck stands on end. Is this a threat?

The gentle voice sounds soothing. "How fortunate it is that your shuttle fell into this crevasse. You are safe here from the malignancy of this blue sun's light. Neither your species nor ours can withstand the surface heat."

"We are prisoners of this underworld," the angry face growls and shocks the darkness with sparks of luminescence.

Silence settles over the two heads like a long sigh. I shift my weight from one foot to the other. What are they going to do to me?

The gentler one's mouth curls at the edges, resembling a smile. "We are imprisoned here. But it's cool enough and there's water in a subterranean river where we catch eels to eat."

What is the monster trying to say? That it will allow me to live in its underworld and will actually help me adapt to this bleak and sunless environment? The Vahmpyr seems duplicitous with its two heads focused on opposite emotions. Its smooth head seems amiable but the wrinkled head acts like it wants to kill me.

I draw back as the monster in the window abruptly flares into full color, displaying its glittering, eye-spangled wings. A tentacle-like appendage stretches from its tubular body and brushes against the shuttle's window.

Cold terror electrifies every nerve in my body. Is it trying to break in? I close my eyes and tremble, waiting for the tentacle to smash through the thermal glass. When it doesn't wrap around my throat, I open my eyes and see it slide down the glass then retract. The Vahmpyr's scintillating, bioluminescent wings dissolve into darkness.

The creature is gone...or is it? Maybe it was testing the strength of the glass or perhaps it's searching for an easier way to break into my shuttle?

I struggle out of the safety harness and stumble over my own feet in a rush to check the locks on the hatch. They're secure. I'm safe, at least for the moment. But I need to find a weapon to defend myself if the angry Vahmpyr head overrides the milder one.

Just my luck, this surveillance shuttle isn't armed. All I find in the storage locker is an emergency flare along with a liter of water and a small cache of dried seaweed. My lifelong nervous eating disorder gets the better of me. I gobble the salty seaweed and gulp down most of the water.

What's wrong with me? Those were all the supplies I had! I should have rationed them, at least the water. For three years the Solar Academy pounded flat facts into my brain: a human being can only survive four days without water, but can live for up to two weeks without food. My lack of self-control destroyed my two-week safety margin. Now what do I do?

Pus on a Pulsar! I have to decide if I'd rather starve to death or venture into the cavern to find the river that the Vahmpyr described. But was it telling me the truth? This could be a ruse to lure me outside the shuttle so it could kill me.

Trying to put a lid on my panic, I search for a distraction and run a diagnostic on the shuttle's life support. I minimize every system to avoid draining energy.

That done, I can't think of anything else to do, so I hunker down next to the storage locker, knees drawn up to my head, trying not to throw up.

My mouth still fills with bile. Almighty asteroids, I'm only twenty-three! Even if the Vahmpyr doesn't kill me, I can't live the rest of my life in this sunless environment. Do I even want to survive in this underworld, eating raw eels? What kind of life is that? It's not one I anticipated when I signed up with Space Exploration, Inc. Seems like a thousand years ago, I received the highest marks in my graduating class from the Solar Academy and was rewarded with a job and my first solo mission.

Some reward. I expected a career of glamor, adventure, high living...it was all at my fingertips but now the life I envisioned is lost forever. Might as well shrivel up and die but...somehow...I still want to survive.

The Vahmpyr is the obstacle. I can't share this ecosystem with a monster. But I don't have any other option. Killing it is out of the question since it's twice my size and I don't have a weapon.

Tears blind my eyes. "I don't want to die!"

Bioluminescent eye spots light up the window as the Vahmpyr reappears. "You won't die, young human, although you may feel it is your better option at this moment."

"What do you know?" My voice echoes shrilly in the shuttle's metallic shell.

"We know because we too wanted to die when we first crashed onto this planet. But we are lonely and tired of arguing with ourselves after countless years. It cheers us both to speak to another sentient being———even a human who destroyed their planet."

My jaw drops. "*We* destroyed *our* planet? You've got it wrong. Vahmpyrs invaded *our* world."

"Think, human. Your atmosphere was polluted, your oceans over-heated, and the other species who shared your world were on the edge of extinction. We Vahmpyrs are guardians of the unique planets in our galaxy that support life. Your kind had overrun your viable world and turned it into a place of death."

Stammer out an answer. "Earth has always had mass extinctions thanks to meteors and volcanoes, but the ecosystem eventually revives."

"Our projections indicated that the damage done by your kind was almost irreversible. If we hadn't intervened, your species would have made the Earth as inhospitable as this desert planet."

My hands are shaking. Some of what the Vahmpyr is telling me rings true. All the equatorial regions of the Earth are hot and drought-stricken. Life is confined to the Polar Regions. "Are you going to invade the Earth again?"

The angry head bursts into bitter laughter. "We have been lost here too long to know our leaders' plans. But there has been much discussion. Never before have we encountered creatures more stubborn and irresponsible than humans."

I don't know how to answer.

We stare at each other in silence, then the placid head sighs. "None of this matters now. We are all marooned here. We should think of our survival, not theoretical possibilities."

My voice sticks in my throat. "Are you going to kill me?"

"We could, but what would be the point? That would merely ensure that we would be alone again with only our thoughts, and loneliness is the greatest torment that we endure." The gentle voice ebbs into silence then flows back. "When you are ready, young human, we will guide you to the river and teach you how to catch eels."

Angry face grunts but says nothing.

Is the gentle head telling the truth? Will the Vahmpyr help me or will the snarling head override the other's reasoning? Do I dare open the hatch and step outside? Vahmpyrs prefer to kill with a single blow that breaks the neck. If this is a ruse, I will die instantly.

How can I trust this monster? Do I have a choice?

The gentle head seems to understand my hesitation. "As soon as you leave the shuttle, you will find the rocks ahead of you are jagged, but you can balance yourself on the stalagmites on either side. Walk ten steps then turn to your right. You will hear the sound of water."

Water! As I reach for the hatch, the snarling face appears in the window.

Horror yanks me back. "How do I know you won't kill me?"

The gentle face takes the angry one's place. "I will not let you die."

"And I will not let you live!" the snarling one shouts.

My heart sinks. I look from the surly head to the kinder one. "Which of you dominates the other?"

"It depends on you," the snarling head hisses.

"Yes, it depends on you," the gentle one says.

"How does it depend on me?"

"Isn't it obvious?" the angry head asks.

The gentle face softens. "Prove to us that you aren't a monster."

MESS
VERONICA R. CALISTO

My teeth buzzed in warning well before the Assembly security officers cuffed me and dragged me onto the command deck.

Eyes turned my way, the officers hostile, eager. Not Commander Birch, though. He posed beneath the ship's navigation dome, facing away from me like he'd choreographed this scene.

Pricks of blue light winked on the dome above the Commander's shoulders, snagging my attention. The sight confirmed what the vibration in my teeth knew: the fool had brought me back to the Butterfly Nebula–the final resting place of the former flagship of White Star Cruise Lines, the Andersen.

We needed to leave.

"Well, then, Joan Arc." Commander Birch swiveled toward me, theatrically slow. Perfectly pressed Assembly uniform. Posture straight as a crystal's edge. Smirk the only thing off balance on his surgically-homogenized face. "Or is it Ruth Bader? Billi Holly? You've used so many fake names, I don't know what to call you."

He knew my birth name. He wouldn't have brought us here otherwise.

"We need to leave." I gritted the words through teeth I didn't dare open. Not so near the artifact that had twisted me into a creature of sublime appetite.

Commander Birch tilted his head off-center. "Why is it that criminals can never stomach the havoc they've wrought?"

Why did no one ever believe me?

Yes, my family raided the ancient Merconian ruins, and yes, they'd taken artifacts rumored to have been the end of that civilization, but I'd been barely nine at the time. Little more than another artifact my parents had smuggled on board. No one cared about that part. Only that the Merlins had stolen untold riches, escaped on the Andersen, and that something terrible happened in the Butterfly Nebula. I'd been the only survivor and no one believed how I made it back to the cruise launch point, without a ship and covered in blood.

"Three decades, Ursula Merlin, and I've finally brought you back here to face your crimes."

My crimes. Not what was done to me, then through me. Of course.

I tried again. "The Merconian artifact—"

He scoffed. "The whole Assembly has heard your little fairy tale, Ursula Merlin."

I clenched my jaw harder, counter pressure to the increasing throb in my teeth. "Death and blood. The original—"

"Mermaids don't exist."

Not the way he thought of them, as happy benign creatures who only wanted love. "There are reasons every planet has a story about creatures from the darkness consuming entire civilizations."

His upper lip spasmed, like a dog facing a wolf.

The nebula cloud was growing larger in the scope of the dome. Noises twisted out of my stomach and my legs thrummed in anticipation.

Not again.

We were getting too close.

Would no one listen?

I twisted toward the security officer clutching my left arm. Keeping my teeth clenched, I willed him to listen. "If you escape in a pod before we reach the nebula shadow you should be safe."

He didn't turn to look at me. The skin around his eye tightened, though, and he glared. Like he refused to look at me but could not swallow the rage. "My parents were on the Andersen. Their twentieth-anniversary trip."

"They wouldn't want you to die like they did."

Now, the officer turned the glare on me.

He had such lovely lavender eyes in a face that looked like a rusted shovel blade. Pity, that.

"You threaten me?" He enunciated each word with angry precision.

"What my mother unleashed—"

Heat flashed across my right cheek. A slap from Commander Birch that rocked my head to the side.

I swirled my head back to him.

"You are here to face the truth of your crimes." He curled his splayed fingers into a fist two inches from my nose. "No more of your stories."

Rather than dissipate, the burn in my cheek spread. It tickled across the bridge of my nose and caressed my lips. Slithering between my scalp and skull.

We were too close already.

Commander Birch leaned in close enough to reveal the tiny lines where his face had been mangled to this unremarkable-statue version of him. "What do you have to say for yourself?"

We crossed into the nebula shadow.

Its chill clashed with the heat searing through my head, churning my stomach and buckling my knees.

Commander Birch gripped my clenched jaw and pulled my face closer to his. "Speak, Ursula."

My pants ripped in the wake of my legs melding together into one long, powerful, hunting fin. Sensations flooded in, flowing to me on the sea beneath this existence. Eddies of terror riding the abyssal tide that I'd only touched the one time—when my mother broke open the cursed Merconian artifact on the Andersen.

Instinct made me break from the cuffs and catch Commander Birch's second slap before it landed.

Alarm perfumed the air. The security officers released me, fleeing. Other officers followed.

Too late to escape.

Hunger pooled in my stomach and rose. Spilling across my skin and flexing it into plated scales. Cascading the cool subspace-sea through my veins. Strengthening my jaw and lengthening my fingers into claws sharp enough to peel into a ribcage like an overripe melon. My eyesight sharpened enough to see all the tiny, delicious vessels pulsing in Commander Birch's face.

He yanked at my grip on his arm, still too anger-blind to understand.

"Let me go!" He ordered. Like he ever had control.

I smiled, grinning wider than humanly possible. My teeth sharpened. "Too late."

Commander Birch tugged again. Belief, though. Comprehension. Fear finally flooded his scent.

Fantastic.

I bucked upward, swimming both of us to the top of the navigation dome with three swishes of my hunting fin.

I relaxed my jaw, gave in to the war of hot and cold within, and became the monster from my own nightmares.

Blood and cracking bones.

Fear-sweetened hearts spilling their ambrosia across my lips.

Harmonious screams.

And beneath it all, profound and fathomless, hunger.

GLENCOE
JESSICA MEHRING

Across the world I traveled alone
to find tucked into Highland hills
a place that echoed soft yet shrill
and dug the history from my bones
the mud and rage and cursed thrones
the wars of pride in those hulking hills
the Weeping Glen and those that killed.
How does such beauty bleed from stone?
Echoes of years in the cold green brush
deep and somber they stir the heart
and steeply down the waters rush
to cleanse the heart, to soothe, to hush.
Back to the world alone I start
bearing the mark of kinship's touch.

MEMORY LANE

BAILEY FINN

When the alarm greeted me, I reached over the bed and begged Sharon to turn it off. There was no response. Sharon had left for work early. I got home late last night, and she had already fallen asleep. Now she was gone again and wouldn't be back until it was time for me to leave. I pinched the bridge of my nose and groaned at the alarm, scolding it for not waking me sooner. I trudged down the stairs and fixed breakfast for two.

It wasn't the alarm's fault, after all, it wasn't psychic. Nor was it Sharon's fault or mine. Things were just, well, difficult. With my Pa living with us, truly, nothing had been easy. Despite his cheery demeanor, he needed a lot of care. Against the doctor's orders, I snuck a piece of bacon into Dad's toast and egg whites and took it up to him. I only did it once a week. Yeah, it was greasy, but the doc says he's only got a few months anyway, so why not let the poor man enjoy his breakfast? So, I headed back up the stairs with the hot plate in hand, knocked, and opened his door. I didn't want to see my Pa in this state, but if I didn't, who would?

Pa's room was simple. He had moved in with us last year, and most of his things had been sold off. He only kept the necessities and a handful of boxes that contained his favorite items. There was an old ashtray from my grandfather that still clung to the scent of cigarettes, though Pa had long since stopped smoking. On a chair sat an old stuffed bear that reeked of the cologne Pa had spilled on it years ago.

"Morning, how ya doing, Pa?"

"Same as yesterday, Danny, same as yesterday." He smiled at me. His eyes were somewhere on the boundary of hopeful and hollow that people his age often cross. Doctors gave him a week last visit, and that was last month. The truth is, he's lasted longer than they thought he would. I set his breakfast down on the nightstand next to the dinner he hadn't eaten from the night before.

"Yeah, well, sometimes that's the best we can do." I took the spoiled dinner away.

"Do me a favor, Danny boy, there's a photo album in the closet, can you bring it to me?"

I nodded and shuffled through the old box of industrial memorabilia to a cream-colored album that almost looked tan from sun poisoning through the years.

"Here ya go, Pa."

His rubbery hands clasped around the book. It was more of a scrapbook than a photo album. But there was no sense in correcting him.

"Did I ever tell you about the time your Ma and I went to Du-op Hop?" He looked at me with the eyes of a child stumbling across a buried treasure in their backyard.

He had told the story almost every morning this week. At first, I'd tried to explain that he'd already told me, but he was too far gone, and it was easier to listen to whatever he wanted to talk about.

"No Pa, tell me about it." I removed the bear from its perch and made myself comfortable.

"Well, it's better if you see the pictures." He patted the side of the bed.

He hadn't asked me that before. His frame was frail. I wasn't sure he could even flip the pages. I got up and sat next to him.

When Pa opened the book, the pages flipped on their own and accelerated until Pa dropped the scrapbook. His hands were covered in pastel colors and dusted with glitter and stickers. Our lights flickered rapidly, and the room shook. I wrestled a chain of border cut-outs as black ink sprung from the book and covered my eyes. Then, there was nothing. The kind of stillness that accompanies one questioning their existence.

"What the hell!?" I wiped the ink from my face. "Pa, are you all right?" I looked around, but he was nowhere to be found. I wasn't in his room. More than that, I wasn't in my house. I stood at an intersection with a 7-Eleven on one corner and a roller rink across from it. No one goes to roller rinks anymore, was this time travel? Or perhaps I fell asleep listening to Pa? For all I knew, we both inhaled too much dust from the book. It didn't feel like a dream, though. I was aware of all my senses and surroundings, and I wasn't a lucid dreamer. I decided this place was real, and I had to find Pa and take us home. I was just about to move when a young teen in a letterman's jacket approached with an ear-to-ear grin.

"Hey man, what are you doing in the middle of the road? Street-lights are about to go out, you could get hurt. You lost?" He had his arm around a petite young woman in an ankle-length skirt and pearls.

"You could say that, yeah. Name's Danny" I took another glance around.

"The police station is two blocks north," the young lady offered, "if you follow this road, you'll hit it. Sheriff Higgins knows everybody and everywhere. He can help you get where you need to go. Do you want us to escort you, Mr. Danny?"

"No, thanks, I can manage." I smiled, a town like this shouldn't be too hard to navigate.

"Ok, good luck. Come on Billy, let's go. Everyone's waiting at the Du-op Hop!" The young lady pulled the arm of her partner.

"Sure, Maddy." A light chuckle escaped the boy.

That's odd, I thought, Billy and Maddy.

"Are you Billy Reynolds?"

"Hm, you know me? You friends with my Pa?" he asked.

"Uh, yeah, anyway, you kids have fun." I waved them off as casually as I could.

They nodded and left for the roller rink. The Du-op Hop. This was the night Pa said he fell in love with mom. The way he told it, they danced and drank slushes until ten. Their parents busted them for staying out past curfew.

I took care not to be seen and watched them go inside. If this truly was the past, I should try not to interfere. At least that's what people say, butterflies, tsunamis, and all that jazz. They danced until the DJ's last song. Pa ended the night by putting a class ring on Mom after the last song. They roamed the moonlit streets even after the streetlights turned off. The two of them were walking home when two shadows approached and demanded money. Pa never mentioned this part. I forgot this was a memory and leapt forward to help, but my mother, the pacifist, got to them first. She slugged the muggers with her purse. I don't know what was in it, but it was enough to give the assailants pause. She dropped it and ran with Pa.

Pa never talked about the mugging that night. They both must've been terrified out of their souls.

"Oh, terrified, yes but magnificent. Wouldn't have changed a thing. My Maddy was always a spitfire." I heard my Pa, the real one, his voice gruff with age. I looked for him but didn't see him.

"Pa, where are you, what's going on!?" I spun on my heels in a desperate attempt to find him.

"Here, if you thought this night was heart-stopping, let me show you what really scared me." Pa's voice became more distant, and the ground began to rumble. Black ink eked through the cracks in concrete and slowly overwhelmed me.

This time, we were at Ma and Pa's house, my childhood home. My mother looked the way I knew her growing up. She was wearing jeans and one of Pa's oversized shirts. She was laughing and crying on Pa's shoulder.

"Wait, I know this night," I whispered, watching through the window. The younger version of me, full of acne and pizza grease, came down the stairs. He flew towards the door and snatched the car keys.

"Take pictures!" Ma yelled as the younger me shut the door. I hid as best I could as he left and drove off.

I returned to the window, still doing my best not to be seen.

My mom's smile turned to a frown, "He's right, ya know. It's only the movies. He's not even calling it a date yet. You didn't have to call off work for this." She looked up at my Pa, leaning into his chest.

"Bah, he's alone with some girl he stutters and blushes over when you ask about her. Whether he calls it what it is or not. A date is a date, and I won't miss my son's first one. I just hope little Danny doesn't crash the car. Or worse, crash and burn," Pa laughed, and mom playfully slugged him in the side.

"That's not funny, Billy," she scolded and restrained a smile.

"It's kind of funny," Pa countered. Then my mom kissed my Pa with the kind of passion privacy lends to, but also with the class of a woman and mother who loves deeply.

I turned away from the window and started walking down the old road. I didn't remember it being that big a fuss for my Pa. But Pa did stay up all night and was waiting for me. He said he just couldn't sleep, so he came down to watch tv. But seeing this, I knew he had waited until I got home safe. I scratched the back of my head, suddenly uncomfortable in my skin. Sharon and I used to wait up for each other too. But now, we could barely stay awake for ourselves.

"Pa, you..." I whispered into the cool crisp air.

"Of course, I waited for you to come home, ya idjit." Pa's voice replied with loud and robust laughter as the ink swirled around me once more.

In the next round, we found ourselves inside the house. Pa's suitcases were still in the living room. It was earlier this year when Pa had first moved in with us. We'd taken a welcome home photo that evening. I was late getting home.

Sharon shook the milk jug of spare change and eyed a pamphlet about the Serengeti for Safari tours.

"I don't understand, where is he?" She put the pamphlets away and set the table for dinner.

Pa came out of the kitchen with the dinner plates and sat next to her. "I'm sure he'll be here soon. I'm sorry about the trip, hon. I don't mean to be a burden on you both. But I am grateful for you." He grinned from ear to ear.

"No, no, Pa. It's quite all right. We can go anytime." She wiped her eyes and hugged his neck, "and we couldn't be happier to have you."

The Serengeti was meant to be an anniversary trip. We both agreed we couldn't afford it while caring for Pa. I knew she was disappointed, but I never saw her cry.

I wanted to reach out to her. I had to. The me from this memory wouldn't be home in time to console her. She would be asleep, and he wouldn't wake her, let alone know of her distress until much later. I approached them, and Sharon gestured for me to come closer.

"Oh, hon, how long have you been home? I didn't hear you come in." She smiled.

"Just a few minutes," I answered and hugged her, "I know it's hard, and I don't thank you enough for everything. I love you, Sharon."

She cried and melted into my embrace. I still didn't know if what was happening to me was time travel or something else. Now, I didn't care. Sharon needed me. I failed the first time, but I was here now. Pa left up the stairs with a smile. I clung to Sharon in desperate need. It had been too long. Too long since we had embraced, too long since we had had the same work schedule, took long since we had even spoken outside of texting. Too long. The black ink came, and this time I prayed it would leave me be. The magic did not heed my wish, and the flurry of scrapbook material swallowed me.

When I wiped the glitter from my eyes again. Pa was next to me. We were on his bed, in his room. He was just the way he was this morning, except his eyes were shut, and he was still. I shook him and tapped his shoulder.

"Pa! Pa, what was that? Wake up, Pa!" I clung to him and wept, but I knew he couldn't hear me. I called emergency services, and they did their best. It wasn't enough. I prayed it to be some trick of the ink, some Charles Dickens warning, but it wasn't. Pa had already outlasted the doctor's expectations, and he was gone.

AFTER PA'S CEREMONY, I was made to go through his possessions. In the last box, I found his scrapbook again and set it aside. I rose from my knees. Sharon was going to be home from work soon. I went downstairs and pulled out our old suitcases, and began to pack. I'd ask Sharon to go camping with me tomorrow. I mean, it's not Serengeti, but it's a start. If we play our cards right for the rest of the year, we can probably go on Safari next year. The first thing I put in the suitcase was our camera.

We were going to take a lot of pictures.

GOING UP?
JENNA MACFARLANE

Dedicated to all aunts who made a difference.

Madison swam as hard as she could. Anxiety circled as a cool wave heaved her over its spine. Peering into the aqua sea, her yellow and cobalt fins paddled below. A smaller wave blindsided her, forcing brine into her lungs. She coughed in panic and caught her breath. Temporarily surrendering to fatigued muscles, she sighed, reclining until the back of her head rested against the stiff collar of her loaned vest. She admired the rainbow sherbet sky, then tugged at the cruise company's ill-fitting gear, alleviating pressure on her armpits and ribs. Her mind poked her awake. Must get on. No sleeping.

Today was not a good day to die. Not here. Not yet.

Snapping her head upright, she set herself back on course for a sliver of sand and emerald. Its geography bore a marked contrast to the rugged Big Island of Hawaii, where she'd been earlier that day. She pushed hard into a breaststroke, keeping her sights trained on the beach.

That afternoon, when she'd first jumped off the boat, the crystal clear water had created a feeling of vertigo, as if she'd dropped to the bottom of a watery kingdom. Visibility had changed. Her arms and legs were in full view, but the ocean had darkened to a shiny sapphire with the late afternoon light.

Gazing at her arms was a comfort, a reminder that she could swim to safety. Her waterproof watch blinked. Madison studied the back of her shriveled hand. The translucent index nail broke from opening a can of Coke on the boat. A faint aftertaste of roast beef had lingered until the last wave had washed her palette clean.

She squinted over her shoulder at the horizon. The last sighting of her boat had been a sugar cube bobbing in the distance. She panted with fear as sheets of water bandied her about. Her heart sank, noting the island was no closer than the last check.

She resumed kicking.

Madison's muscles contracted and flexed with each stroke. She drew closer to the island. Saltwater glazed her lips—she craved a cold Coke.

That afternoon Captain Clementine's cherub face had puckered with passion as she'd introduced the excursion with the claim that dolphins scanned humans. If they liked a person's energy, they'd make their presence known.

One of the passengers, a marine biologist named Susan, objected. "No research supports that view. Are you saying they can see into a person's soul?"

Clem squinted beyond the group. She wasn't wearing sunglasses, and her freckles branched into fine lines from her eyes. She answered the question with a story. "I used to live in Colorado. When I first visited here, I swam most of the day. I waded in, and the dolphins found me. They saved me. My illness—over time, well, it just disappeared. After that, I moved here. Bought me a boat, so I could share this with you all." Clem's passion was magnetic. She was living her dream.

The marine biologist quietly removed herself from the group, and Clem's assistant followed her. His expression mirrored the glassy surface of the harbor. Madison wondered if he regularly walked the line between science and fanciful thinking. He seemed intent on smoothing the waves before they crested.

Madison, for one, was fine with all that talk. She wanted more and longed for something powerful to take hold and guide her toward a calling. But so far, she'd felt strangely indifferent to life, as if she'd become a passenger, having given up the driver's seat long ago. When she'd lament and share that thought, some of her well-meaning friends would say that she should take possession of her life, followed by a "You know?"

Should.

Madison agreed. The trouble was, she didn't know how.

"I heard they aren't monogamous," piped up one of the passengers, nodding out to sea.

The assistant had returned with a portable cooler full of Cokes and a coy smile. "If you see them together, they're doing it."

Madison thought about that—carefree creatures unencumbered when it came to mating, building a house, getting a job, and paying bills. They lived inside every moment, pregnant with possibility.

After some safety guidance and a rundown of the day's schedule, Clem retreated to the helm and fired up the engine. The assistant darted from cleat to cleat, untying ropes and hopping back to the deck.

Madison leaned against the railing and opened a can of Coke, chipping her index nail. They were on a three-hour tour. The beloved show, *Gilligan's Island,* had been a mainstay of her childhood. Hours were spent devouring tales of the unlikely group surviving on their wits and determination.

Clem opened the throttle, coasting out into open water, the Big Island firmly in the rearview mirror. Madison sipped her drink. Fizz tickled her nose; salty breezes tugged her hair. She lifted her face to the sun, thinking the moment was perfect.

After about fifteen minutes, dolphins chaperoned the boat in twos and threes, breaking the surface and arching in tandem. Riveted by one of the animals surfing starboard side, Madison moved to the bow for a closer look. He appeared to be looking right at her.

One of the female passengers sidled up. "It's like they're checking us out."

"I feel that way too. Can't wait to get in the water." Madison kept her eyes locked on the dolphin gliding below.

"I'll be tempted to pet them. I know I will."

Madison stayed silent, not wanting to scold the woman. At the same time, she sensed that if a person did reach, the animals would keep their distance.

Fins speckled the churning surface. Madison's heart rose in anticipation.

"My god, are we going to be in the middle of that?" asked the woman.

"Oh, I hope so." Madison ached to connect—to hear what they had to say. She'd been isolated in life—no long-term boyfriends or family ties. Holding a job had proved challenging. Maybe the dolphins could help her heal.

Clem slowed the boat, announcing the first stop. "Whatever you do, don't touch 'em," she said. "Keep your hands at your sides at all times." Then she resumed the dolphin sex ed. Some of the passengers, preparing themselves for snorkeling, looked confused. Madison didn't much care what the dolphins did so long as she could swim into their world.

Clementine glanced at the two younger people in the group and explained that dolphins were prolific procreators. "They're romantics."

Madison wished to hear about the far more interesting topic of evolution. Dolphins and whales were among the few species to evolve from land back to sea when the earth was young. To think that a little dog, venturing into the ocean for food, eventually stayed and adapted, albeit over millions of years. But still.

Madison pulled on her fins and mask and penguin-walked to the edge. The animals churned below, swirling water into figure eights. Ever since Madison was a little girl, she'd dreamed of meeting dolphins. From her childhood home, she'd watched the daily sunset and imagined the fireball lounged underwater overnight drawing a myriad of sea creatures.

Put away foolish notions, Madison's Aunt Clara had always said.

The female passenger from earlier was the first to jump. "Bonsai!" she yelled.

Another, a man, broke the surface, gulping air and fluttering his arms as if doing the twist. Several others followed. The marine biologist hung back in a huddle with Clem.

Lowering herself down the ladder into the velvet aqua water, Madison was relaxed and confident. Every cell in her body vibrated. How natural it was to be in the ocean, even though it should've felt foreign.

Madison adjusted her mask and snorkel, submerged, and peered into the dappled indigo. Freeways of dolphins intersected at least twenty feet below. The sound of a thousand soft tuning forks coiled towards a common pitch—their language.

Her shipmates swam in tight donuts around the boat for the first couple of dives, each about twenty minutes long. Madison ventured further out to no avail. The animals had kept their distance. Clementine explained that was normal. They sense our unease, she cautioned.

In between swims, Madison sat on deck, giddily scanning the surface for fins. Nursing a second Coke, chilled condensation pinged her upper legs with each sip. She couldn't remember when she'd felt so free.

When Clem announced the last stop of the day, Madison took a moment to orient. The Big Island was a hazy mound in the distance. Determined to make contact with the dolphins, she eased into the deeper, darker water and kicked her fins hard in the opposite direction of the group. Dolphins darted in the distance. Highways of aqua-tinted bodies crisscrossed several stories below. Some coupled at the midsection. Others spiraled and played. Madison marveled at how they could hear each other through the layers of sound. What were they saying?

If a connection could be made, they'd adjust their pace so she could keep up. The question was, would they?

Her skin tingled with gooseflesh—a champagne moment. Even if they hadn't approached, she felt included in their world—loved in a way, though the thought surprised her.

After several minutes of paddling, three dolphins barely brushed her arms, emerging from nowhere. They hovered barely out of reach. The dolphin in the center stared, his body horizontal while the others kept their backs turned and bodies curved into a comma. They formed a tight unit, inches away from each other.

Captivated, Madison couldn't take her eyes off the center animal. And though she lacked words for her feelings, she knew that he wanted her to join. No sooner than she'd acknowledged the thought, he pivoted, swimming at a pace she could manage. Madison followed eagerly, obediently keeping her arms at her sides.

After a few minutes, the dolphins accelerated and were gone. The effect of sudden loneliness was jarring. Madison rose to the surface to regroup and get her bearings. The boat had disappeared, her ship-mates and captain along with it.

CLARA WOULD HAVE LIKED to die with a smile on her face, but that didn't happen. The viewing had occurred several days earlier and was attended by only one person—Madison.

Though she hadn't been at her 104-year-old Aunt Clara's side when she passed, Madison was told it had been a peaceful affair.

In her youth, Clara had worked at UCLA Medical Center and would swim at the beach after work with a group of female friends who called themselves Gulls. Clara loved the freedom of the open water, stretching her body lean against the current.

Madison loved her great-aunt fiercely. Clara was wise, strong, and direct. Most of all, she *saw* Madison for who she was and believed in her artistic ability.

Clara was born on the Saskatchewan plains, becoming a natural-ized American citizen in the 50s. She'd adapted well to life in Los Angeles during its heyday. The photos of young Clara depicted a beauty and confidence that Madison had always lacked.

For the last two decades of Clara's life, Madison would visit her in the desert and they'd sit on her patio at sunset, sipping gin and tonics, musing about life's mysteries. Clara would regale her with stories of her life in old LA.

On one occasion, Clara insisted that the opposite of love was hate. Then she'd confessed to having had an abortion in her twenties before she'd had her girls. "They don't know," she'd said.

Madison had been too shocked to respond to either comment, though she'd disagreed about love. The opposite was indifference— not mattering, being invisible. She'd felt that way in her family—with everyone except Clara. With Clara, Madison existed. And that made all the difference.

Just then, Clara set her highball glass on the table with a click and turned to face Madison. "I don't think they treated you right."

"Who?"

"Them. Your parents, your brothers—my sister—*all* of them. They abandoned you, and for what? Because you didn't do what they wanted." Clara cleared her throat as if she might spit. "That's just dumb."

Madison took a swig, hoping for the alcohol to soften her mind. "We've gone over this. They didn't want me to talk to you and the rest of the family. Grandma got mad at me because, well because I was there and Mom wasn't. Maybe she was mad at herself, I don't know."

Clara swiped the air as if the statements were nonsense. "My sister was a terrible mother. We all knew when we saw you kids dressed in clothes way too big."

Though they'd previously discussed Madison's childhood, Clara had never passed judgment. Madison's stomach tightened. "We had a lot of family secrets. I told you about those—the ones I remember anyway. Mom might've gone a little nuts over it all."

Clara's gaze drifted passed Madison. "Norma used to send your mother to school when she was too sick to move. That poor child."

Madison's heart sank, thinking of her mother, and how tough it had been for her growing up. Later, she'd been the one to divulge the abuse, all of the things Madison couldn't recall. "The secrets—I have to forgive those. I survived it all. That's the main thing. I survived. And you. I got lucky with you, Clara. I'm so glad you're in my life."

Uncomfortable with compliments, Clara waved Madison's words into the desert breeze, then stood. "Your grandmother was meant to be an actress. The worst thing my mother ever did was pull her out of the theater." Then she rattled the melting ice in her glass. "Another?"

Tears had stung Madison's eyes as she turned down another drink. Still reeling from the admission about Clara's abortion, Madison downed the last of her cocktail and gazed at the fading sky behind Mt. San Jacinto. That marked the first time any family member had acknowledged something real. Numbness and fear coiled in her stomach. Unable to name her feelings, Madison watched Clara about to open the screen door and asked the question that had tormented her: "I turned out all right. Didn't I?"

Clara paused, her back turned. She bowed her head and turned slightly towards Madison. "Maddie, you have talent. Your paintings. You must paint."

Clara loved art, especially Madison's. Though Madison had sold many of her works, she downplayed her ability. But Clara didn't. Madison's painting of a poppy was proudly displayed in Clara's living room, feet from where they sat. When it had come time for Clara to downsize and move to assisted living, Madison's painting had been one of the few possessions that made the cut.

Paint. Clara's words echoed in Madison's heart.

Clara's life had been fueled by curiosity, confidence, and cold gin. She loved men, gambling, and horses in that order. Likewise, she despised self-pity, excess, and Democratic presidents, in that order.

How different Madison and Clara were.

And now, the only family member who understood her was gone. Madison felt broken and watery inside. Dammed grief threatened to burst.

MADISON WAITED in a marbled reception area. Despite the triple-digit heat wave outside, the mortuary was frigid, neutral, and without scent. The place had a peaceful air—tomb-like. The Latino family sharing the lobby with Madison smiled. Everyone was there to acknowledge loss, but their youngest, a girl of about three, toddled over with a used handkerchief, extending it to Madison. Madison hesitated, and the family nodded politely, pulling the child into their fold.

The mortuary had been Clara's choice, one of many details arranged before her death. She didn't want her daughters burdened. So, in her later years, the organization of her affairs became a priority.

Clad in a navy jacket and skirt despite the heat outside, the receptionist motioned Madison to follow her down a shiny windowless hallway. "You're the only one coming." She opened the door to the room. "You'll have fifteen minutes."

Madison nodded, indicating she'd see herself out, and pulled a seat up to the coffin. Struck by Clara's appearance, Madison felt she was in the company of a stranger. The white gauze dress was clearly padded to mask the boney outcroppings of Clara's ribs and hips. Her skeleton was draped in crepe paper skin, hands resting across her tummy. Veins pooled purple between tendons attached to delicate fingers. A Band-Aid covered a bruise on her forehead from the fatal fall. A frown deeply etched into her face was a full half-circle of lips and cheeks working in tandem to express disappointment. Clara's skin was cold.

Though Clara would've disapproved of her frown, the overall effect was honest. At 104, the journey had taken too long, and she'd been impatient. Despite the disapproving expression, she was lovely until the end. And her wavy platinum hair lined eyebrows, and clear polished nails were perfect.

Your talent. Clara's words echoed. *Paint.*

Madison quaked with grief and doubled over in great, heaving sobs.

Tears intermingled with salt water as Madison paddled towards the mysterious land mass. Must preserve hydration. No crying. Imagine this is the 1950s, and I'm my aunt. I'm a Gull. I can do this.

With all her might, Madison pumped her muscles, heaving shelves of water out of her way. She shifted into survival mode and renewed her course for the shore. The rhythmic strokes and no holds barred force lulled her into a meditative state.

An object moved in the distance—a person or animal. As she swam closer, the figure, clearly human, swept half-circles with her arms overhead.

Madison gave her all, pulling through the tide, thrusting forward until her feet scuffed the bottom. She heaved herself up, shoving water aside until her quads shimmied free of the current. Madison staggered up the beach, out of reach of waves, and collapsed on the sand.

A young woman squealed with a mix of delight and concern. She sidled close to Madison. "What can I do?" she breathed.

Madison pulled her mask away and stretched her finned legs. Unable to respond, Madison coughed out the last bit of salt and rolled to her side in the shadow of the woman above.

"Are you alone?"

"My boat—" Madison said in a raspy tone. She squinted at the woman. "I had people. On the boat. I was swimming with them—the dolphins. The dolphins. And then no boat."

The woman's rounded nose and full lips were vaguely familiar. She shook her head. "I didn't see a boat."

Madison struggled to lift her wrist and squinted at the time. "I could've sworn it was only a few minutes that I was with them...You know, they slowed down and all. But I kept up, then they disappeared. I'm so thirsty."

The young woman's eyes lit up. "I have something." And with that, she took off.

Madison was too out of it to pay attention. Her eyes fluttered closed to the rhythmic waves and warm sun.

"Here."

Cold hardness pressed against her forearm. The woman held a bottle. Madison sat up thinking she must be dreaming. The woman deftly removed the top and handed Madison a Cola. "I always bring a sixer to share with the Gulls."

Madison straightened and tipped the bottle to her lips. She guzzled the fizz until the carbonation burned her throat, and she caught her breath.

The woman sat down and drank with her. They sipped in silence until the bottles were drained.

Between the sugar, caffeine, and hydration, Madison gained focus. "It was after lunch, our last dive of the day. Maybe two, two-thirty?" She pointed at her wrist. "It's five-thirty. Something happened."

The woman appeared surprised. "Isn't that the queerest? For me, it was about the same—I get off around five. Well, I was waiting for the gals, the Gulls. I must've drifted off. When I opened my eyes—the city, cars, everything. Poof."

"So, my watch and your work schedule are about the same, right?"

She hummed affirmatively. "Seems so. I parked up that hill." Clara gazed over her shoulder at the jungle.

Madison's skin prickled with gooseflesh. She wanted desperately to call Clem, convey her whereabouts, and request a rescue party. "Do you have a phone?"

The woman looked over her glasses at Madison. "A telephone?"

"By the way, I'm Madison." The Coke had revived her.

"Clara. Pleased to make your acquaintance. We do find ourselves in a pickle, isn't that the truth?"

Madison brightened at the mention of her aunt's name. "Do you have it with you—your phone?"

Clara nudged her glasses in place and hugged her knees. "That makes no sense."

Madison was mystified. "No mobile?"

She frowned. "What do filling stations have to do with a phone? Please, you're frightening me with these questions."

Madison's heart raced. She had to get out of there. Gathering her fins, she rose to her feet and inhaled. "I'm almost afraid to ask—what year is it?"

Clara stared at the jungle as if she'd heard a sound. "Well, I'm a secretary at the medical center. Oh, and this is Los Angeles." Clara whirled around. "What was the question?"

Madison tried again. "Clara, when were you born?"

Clara smiled coyly. "People say I look young for my age. 1916."

Madison gulped. The year Clara was born. "Okay, so here's the thing. I'm in 2020. How did this happen?"

Clara flashed a wry smile, then bolted down the beach and splashed into the current. Compelled to stay with Clara, Madison dropped her fins and reluctantly followed, stopping at the shoreline and digging her toes into the soft sand. Cool water pooled at her feet.

"Joining me?" Clara yelled over her shoulder, slumping when a shelf of water broke against her chest. "Olly Olly oxen free!"

Madison felt her brows knit in irritation. She marched into the water up to her waist. A flash of Clara's arms appeared above the surface. Then she was gone. "No, no, no!" Madison yelled herself hoarse, slapping at the surf in frustration. Defeated, she returned to her fins and mask and lay down utterly spent, on the beach. "Clara, Clara," she cried, surrendering to heaving sobs.

A cardboard carrier with the other four Cokes lay undisturbed. Madison polished off one, then scuttled down the beach to discover Clara's worn baby blue towel and brown pocketbook. Searching for clues, she fished in the handbag for the wallet and found her ID. Madison studied the photo on the old California license, noting the resemblance to her face. Her blue eyes and bright smile stared confidently back. The birthday matched her aunt's.

Madison looked up at the late afternoon sky as emotion welled.

Madison stuffed the wallet into the purse and scuttled towards the forest. She stood at the edge, listening. No bird or animal sounds. Step by step, she treaded over vines and sand. Foliage scuffed her arms as she picked her way toward a light patch ahead. Madison picked up her pace until a clearing appeared. An object resembling a spiral staircase made of intertwined branches twisted into the clouds. Madison strode towards it, caressing its roughness.

A twig snapped. Clara was there, welcoming Madison into her embrace. Madison fought tears as she stepped back and studied Clara's young face. "What's happening?"

Clara held her arms. "Oh, Maddie. You know it's my time."

"I saw you. In a casket. I can't believe it. Oh, Clara. I don't want to let you go."

"Were my nails done?"

Madison laughed for the first time. The question was so Clara. "They were perfect."

She nodded, satisfied. "Maddie, listen. Time is short. You must promise to paint."

"Okay," said Madison without conviction.

"You must paint." Then Clara backed away from Madison. "And you must climb. Simple and yet—" She sighed. "If you resist it'll be hard."

Madison released the makeshift staircase and reached for her aunt. She ached to hold on.

Clara frowned, reminiscent of her face at the mortuary. "This is what I wanted to show you." Clara took Madison's hand. "Go now. It's your way back to where you were and where you'll go, Maddie. It's my time. You have to let me go."

Madison hesitated, still gripping Clara's hand. "But I don't want to. Can't I stay here?"

Clara pointed upward. "You don't have a choice, my dear. Make your masterpiece." She mocked her serious, brow-knit expression "I'll do what my mother used to when people weren't doing right—I'll whack you over the head with a rolled-up newspaper."

Madison let out a small chuckle and smiled through tears. The story of her great-grandmother, Gammy, was never far from her mind. Gammy whacked people in her day and got away with it.

The staircase pulled loose from the sand, roots dangling as it hovered a few inches from the ground. She stepped up and turned to see Clara mouth the words *I love you*. And then she was gone.

MADISON LIFTED HER HEAD, sensing someone's touch. The mortuary's receptionist tapped her shoulder and asked if she was all right. Madison lifted her head from the casket, noticing a smeared makeup imprint on her forearm. Requesting another minute, Madison rubbed her skin and sighed in relief. "Fell asleep."

She took one last look at her aunt's body. Clara's halo of white hair and gauze dress lay in stillness like before, but on her rouged cheek, lay a glistening spec. Madison lifted the tiny object to the light. A single grain of white sand.

She looked overhead, suddenly feeling watched. With her free hand, she located the little girl's handkerchief in her pocket and carefully wrapped the grain, tucking the bundle into her purse. Finally, she stood, inhaled sharply, and smoothed her clothes—it was time to go.

Madison strode through the blazing parking lot, slipped into her car, and winced at the white-hot seat and steering wheel. She cranked the engine and waited for the air inside the car to cool. She turned on the radio, merging onto the main highway towards the coast.

Cactus and sand stretched under an uninterrupted azure sky. It was approaching the time of day when she and Clara would have watched the sunset, drinking gin and tonics. Clara's stories. She'd miss that too.

Depending on traffic, there might be just enough time to pack for her Hawaiian trip and grab a swim before bed. She turned her thoughts over to the coming days on the Big Island. How hopeful she was to see wild dolphins. A mental picture flashed. Madison exhaled, realizing she'd had a heavy dream while leaning over Clara's casket. Her childish vision of the sun setting into the sea crossed her mind.

Then she remembered the painting she'd started of an island. It was vaguely sketched out, the underpainting of sea and sky in place.

Clara's voice echoed. *Paint.* This time it was louder, with a drum-beat of thoughts. And this time, Madison answered.

I will.

ANNIE'S SNOW
CATHERINE DILTS

Annie reached across the console and placed her hand on her granddaughter's arm. Withered, faded flesh contrasted against the girl's firm dark skin.

"I can't thank you enough for busting me out of jail for the day."

"Grammy Annie, your retirement home is very nice." Kiara flipped the turn signal. The tock-tock-tock sounded until they turned onto the county road. "You shouldn't think of it that way."

"I know, I know." Annie heard the slurry of snow and road soil shushing under the SUV's tires. "I should be grateful. The Lord knows plenty of folks my age are struggling to get by in terrible conditions."

Not that there were many people her age. At eighty-three, she was a member of a dwindling generation. Annie tugged the insulated container of a fancy coffee drink from the cup holder. Her hand shook. Grasping her cup with both hands, she barely managed to raise it to her lips. She downed a big swallow of the warm, sugary coffee. Perhaps that would steady her grip.

And her nerves.

"I'm surely comfortable, but comfort isn't everything." Annie waved a hand in the general direction of the surrounding mountains and pine trees. "I miss this."

"You have a nice view from your balcony," Kiara said.

The SUV bumped off the last of the asphalt, onto gravel. Annie struggled to return the coffee container to the cup holder.

"It's not the same." Annie hoped she didn't sound like one of the whiney old ladies in her retirement home. Most were younger than her, and had a whole list of complaints they aired on a daily basis, from health to neglectful family to past wrongs they nurtured like house plants. "I know it's silly, but I wish I could hike those hills just one more time."

"We can get out and walk around a little."

Walk. Was it that many years ago when she hiked, climbed, and ran the mountain trails? Annie glanced out the side window, hoping to hide her disappointment from the child. She felt trapped by her traitorous old body.

Kiara pulled the SUV into a parking lot. Not many people were out on a chilly weekday. Two passenger cars sat near a wooden sign.

"This nature trail is smooth enough for your walker." Kiara pushed a button to turn off the engine. "I hope it's not too cold for you." She twisted to grab a jacket from the back seat. "Maybe you'd better put this on."

"You know what, honey? I'd rather go up to the top of the hills. Get a nice view of the valley. If your car can handle a jeep road."

Kiara laughed, a rich sound full of youth and strength. "Grammy, this IS a Jeep!"

Annie sniffed. "It doesn't look like any Jeep I remember. With leather seats and all those buttons and dials like an airplane cockpit?"

Annie often teased her offspring about their ridiculous luxuries and comforts. Really, though, she was proud of how her extended family had prospered. It hadn't been easy in her youth for a black couple to get ahead, but her husband Clarence had been determined and persistent.

"Tell me where we're going, and I'll plug it into the GPS." Kiara started the engine again by pressing the button. A display like a TV screen lit up.

"It's just an old logging road the hunters use. Probably not even on your little computer. I'll tell you when to turn."

"An adventure." Kiara smiled. "Ok Grammy Annie, I'm game."

The road was rougher than Annie remembered. Perhaps it hadn't been maintained. Or maybe her old bones were more sensitive to the bumps and sharp turns than they'd been fifteen years ago. Kiara drove with confidence and skill, which surprised Annie. Maybe the kid was tougher than she looked.

As she half-listened to her granddaughter chatter about college, Annie realized Kiara wasn't just being charitable, donating precious time to her helpless old grams. The trip was the child's chance to communicate with the oldest generation in her family. The generation she might become someday if she was so blessed.

Or cursed.

Truth be told, Annie couldn't understand half of what the girl said. She had no touchstone to connect to the experiences of modern youth. Their language might as well have been Greek, full of technological references that had passed Annie by long before the cellular telephone became as essential to life as air and water. She sat up as straight as her crooked old spine would allow, and focused on Kiara's voice.

"My degree is just about guaranteed to get me the job I want," Kiara said. "I just need to get through this really tough math class." She tilted her cup, draining the last of her coffee without spilling a drop, despite the bumpy road. "But I'm doing all the talking. It must be the caffeine. I was hoping to hear some of your hunting stories."

"I don't want to bore you."

Annie had noticed her grandchildren's glazed eyes when she got on a tear telling stories during their infrequent visits to her home. They were educated but had a softness to them — city folks. To be fair, some of her progeny hunted, hiked, and even ran crazy long races through the mountains. But most seemed comfortable among throngs of people.

"No, really Grammy. I want to know. Was it so different back in your day?" She shrugged. "I try to convince myself I'm tapping into something primeval when I go hunting with Dad. Our equipment is more high tech. But so was yours, compared to what people used a hundred years ago. The gear might change, but the experience is the same. Right? Hunting and fishing take us back to our ancient roots."

"Well. Ancient. I suppose I qualify." Annie chuckled. She had spent more time in the 1900s than she would in the 2000s. To young people, that might as well be the Stone Age. "Let's see." She studied the steep wall of the cliff the narrow dirt road wound past. "One time, your grandfather and I tracked a herd of elk all the way to the top of a ten-thousand-foot mountain before we realized what we'd done. Wasn't even hunting season. We tracked them for the pure fun of it. We were in good shape back then."

When she and Clarence were youngsters, they'd had endless energy. White hikers seemed startled to see black folks out in the woods. Clarence charmed people with his eagerness to share wood-lore, pointing out signs of wildlife they had overlooked. Then one day, the kids were grown and gone, the mirror reflected an old woman's face, and cancer took down Clarence in an ugly battle. It might be a sin, but sometimes Annie wished they'd fallen off some remote cliff that spring before the diagnosis. The good Lord didn't reveal the future to anyone but His prophets. Ordinary folks went through life like a person walking a trail on a moonless night with no flashlight. Maybe it was a hidden mercy they'd gone through those times blind.

"Look at the diversity of the tree population," Kiara said, a tone of awe in her words. "This forest is really healthy. And old."

"You know a lot about trees, for a city girl."

"I took a forestry class," Kiara said. "I liked it more than I imagined I would. I'm so glad people in your day had the foresight to set aside old growth forest. Preserving it for future generations."

"That's not what saved these trees. You notice how rugged the terrain is. They were too hard to get to, much less haul out. There was plenty of forest all around here easier to log."

"My instructor didn't mention that," Kiara said. "Makes sense, though — the economics behind conservation. I'll have to bring that up in class next semester. I'm going to take more forestry classes. All those family hikes and campouts must have influenced me."

Countless summers they took their kids, and later their grandkids, to the mountains every summer weekend. Looking back now, it was amazing they'd had so few mishaps. Other than a few skinned knees and bug bites.

"You weren't born yet," Annie said, "but one time your uncle Jerrod walked barefoot through the campfire."

"On purpose?"

Annie shook her head. "Jerrod was worried his baby sister – your Aunt Gloria was still in diapers at the time – well, he saw her reaching for the plate of s'mores and just headed straight for the picnic table. No thought at all about the fire. He didn't want his sister getting all the treats."

She smiled at the memory. Kids and camping. Often it was a lot of work, but now some of her fondest memories were of those times.

"Uncle Jerrod was ahead of his time," Kiara said. "Firewalking is a thing at motivational seminars. It's supposed to get you over your fears."

"Fear of what?" Annie asked.

Kiara shrugged. "Whatever's holding you back, I guess. I've never done it. Did Uncle Jerrod burn his feet?"

"They say the Lord watches over fools and children. He must have been working overtime that camping trip, because Jerrod didn't get burned. Not one little bit."

"It's a physics thing, Grammy. Anyone can walk on fire if they know what they're doing. Uncle Jerrod got lucky."

Annie pretended to listen as her granddaughter explained away the miracle of Jerrod's feet with a tedious science lesson.

The drive seemed to go on and on, and her bones ached with every jarring jolt. Annie covered her discomfort with a smile. It wouldn't do if Kiara thought she was too frail for the rugged road, and took her back early. Before Annie was done.

One wrong turn and a few miles later, Kiara put the Jeep into 4-wheel drive. The vehicle crawled to the top of a hill. Trees circled the crest like a fringe of hair on a bald man's head. The view was just like Annie remembered. Like the last time she and Clarence had been here, in his dented pickup. Annie had fashioned seat covers out of old blankets to cover the cracked vinyl bench seat. They'd gotten a lot of miles out of that old truck, long after they could afford fancier vehicles.

Kiara parked so they had a view through the windshield. That's not what Annie wanted – to sit and look. She could watch a nature show on her television at the retirement home if all she wanted to do was look.

Annie grasped the door and pulled the handle. The Jeep was cocked at a slight angle. The door swung open suddenly, helped by a gust of wind, nearly dragging Annie out of her seat.

"Grammy! Let me help."

Kiara rushed around the vehicle and grabbed the door. "You shouldn't be out in this cold wind." She squinted at the gray sky. "I don't like the looks of those dark clouds. The snow wasn't due until tonight, but I can see it falling on the far peaks."

The child had an eye for the weather. She drove a vehicle capable of handling rough roads. She had knowledge of the forest. It would be a pity if this experience soured Kiara on her obvious love of nature.

Annie started to slide out of the Jeep. Kiara grabbed for her like she was a delicate bird falling from a nest.

"I don't think your walker is going to work up here."

Annie waved her hands in frustration, probably confirming her resemblance to a bird. "Help me get to that log."

A tree had been felled by a lightning strike. Decay softened the contours as it returned to the earth from which it came. She and Clarence had undoubtedly seen it, maybe sat on this very fallen tree. And now it was nearly gone, like the fading memories of her beloved husband.

Kiara grasped Annie's arm as she toddled over the uneven ground, her feet in danger of going out from under her at any moment. It seemed like just yesterday she could hike these hills all day, with a heavy pack and a rifle strapped to her back.

"It hasn't changed," Annie said, her voice a hushed whisper like she was in church services. "Almost the same exact view." Kiara helped Annie lower her bottom onto the fallen log. "I'm ashamed I can't walk by myself. Just doesn't seem right. Thank you, honey."

"Don't you think like that for a moment," Kiara said. "How many eighty-somethings in your home could manage a trip like this? I'm proud of you."

Annie had lost some vital padding over the years. She wore old lady blue jeans with a stretchy waistband. The lumpy bark felt rough through the material, and mildly painful. But the discomfort reminded her she was really here and not in a lovely dream.

Kiara seemed to sense that Annie needed a moment. She wandered off to stare down the steep side of the hill, where the earth had crumbled eons ago to form an abrupt cliff. Annie hated to burden her like this. Was she taking unfair advantage of her granddaughter's good nature? Or would she understand?

The tree providing her seat had been sturdy, had weathered winters, housed birds, witnessed predators taking down and consuming prey. Rare few animals died of old age out here in the wilderness. That was a human convention – to outlast your usefulness and become a burden to others. Like an old dog that couldn't hold its pee anymore. A pet owner might have the decency and sense of mercy to put an old dog down. Doctors just pumped old folks full of pills to keep them going way past their natural expiration dates.

When the opportunity came so unexpectedly today, it seemed as if the Lord had answered Annie's prayers. She couldn't keep a firearm in the retirement home. Her son had distributed Clarence's hunting rifles to family, and kept Annie's in storage. Annie didn't take many pills, and nothing that would kill her. This was her best option.

The clouds thickened and drifted down lower. Sunset was a ways off, but the sky darkened. The first flakes swirled on the wind. Kiara returned from the cliff edge, wrapping her arms around herself despite her nice down jacket.

"What an amazing view. I'm glad you talked me into driving up here. There are birds flying below us. I love that feeling, like you could just spread your wings and join them."

"Freedom," Annie said. "That's what you feel. Like you can just leave this old world behind."

Snowflakes landed on Kiara's long, dark lashes. She blinked.

"Grammy, it's snowing. We'd better get down off this hill before we get stuck here."

Annie did her best to look pitiful. "Just a few more minutes?"

"Okay." Kiara seemed reluctant. "I'll get a blanket. And the thermos of hot chocolate. I don't want you freezing to death."

Annie waited until Kiara's bootsteps crunching across the dried grasses faded. She pushed her hands against the tree bark, damp and cold with a dusting of snow. She struggled to her feet, grasping onto the spindly trunk of a pine growing from the ruin of the fallen tree. So far, so good. Now if she could just walk across the uneven ground without tripping over a clump of dried grass or breaking an ankle in a ground squirrel hole. She risked a glance at the SUV.

Kiara stood at the open backend of the Jeep. Her attention was focused on digging out the promised blanket and thermos.

Now was the moment.

Annie carefully worked her way to the edge of the cliff. A stand of aspens clung to the rim. She grasped the smooth bark of a sapling.

Below. Below was the same jumble of broken rocks she remembered. Below was rest and sleep. Annie felt dizzy. Like she was already falling, even though she still clutched the aspen. No one would think anything of an old woman taking a tumble off a mountain. They would say her balance was off, which was normal for a woman her age. People at the home fell frequently, sometimes breaking their brittle old bones. A fall would not shock anyone.

What would be shocking was the location. Family members would be angry with Kiara for taking Annie out in this weather, letting her dodder around on a mountaintop until falling to her death.

"Grammy!"

Snow muffled Kiara's voice. Heavy flakes came down faster and thicker. Annie could barely see her through the curtain of white.

"Grammy, you're so tiny, that wind could sweep you right over the edge. Wait for me."

Annie imagined the feeling of soaring over the hills. Finding Clarence. Roaming the wilderness for eternity, hand in hand. The snow swirled around her, erasing the view of the surrounding hills, softening the mountaintop. She imagined herself youthful again. Strong and healthy. Her heart soared.

Lord, if it's Your will, take me now. Take my hand.

Annie relaxed her grip on the aspen. The wind buffeted her, pushing her a step closer.

"Grammy, don't let go." There was an edge to Kiara's voice, like she was dancing on the edge of panic. "Those rocks are slick."

Annie assumed the fall would be fatal. But what if it wasn't? She imagined her broken body writhing on the rocks, her granddaughter facing that gruesome sight. Would the cold kill her before help arrived? Would the coyotes start picking at her before she was completely gone?

"It's my time." Annie barely managed a whisper.

"I can't lose you. Please. Take my hand."

Her granddaughter's words jarred Annie. Was that the answer to her prayer? She peered down the cliff at the rocky base, blanketed by snow.

"You know these mountains," Kiara said. "What you said about the old-growth forest. You gave me all kinds of ideas about things I didn't learn at the university."

"You young people carry around all the knowledge in the world in your fancy cell phones," Annie said.

"Knowledge maybe." Kiara took a step closer. "Words and facts that happened to get recorded. Not wisdom. What you know is important. You and Grampa laid the foundation. You were there. How can I take things a step further if I don't have solid ground under my feet?"

Like the pine growing from the rotting tree trunk. The young growth taking nutrients from the old decay. Not the way Annie viewed herself, but maybe that's what she'd become. A fallen tree, rotting back into soil for the next generation of pines. The wind gusted, swirling the curtain of snow aside for one last glimpse of the valley below.

"I miss you so much." Her whispered words swept away on the wind.

"I miss Grampa too." Kiara's boots squeaked across the freshly fallen snow. "I was so young when he passed. Your stories are the only way I know him."

Annie closed her eyes. A fallen tree could pass along its worth through its death. But a human? Perhaps her work wasn't yet done. *I'm sorry Clarence. You'll have to wait for me just a bit longer.*

She took a step back from the cliff, reaching blindly behind her for the hand she trusted was stretched toward her. Kiara's hand grasped hers.

"I thought I'd lost you." Kiara wrapped a blanket around Annie, hugging her fiercely through the wool. "I haven't heard all your hunting stories yet." Her words stuttered past her lips. "And Grampa's favorite fishing spot? How am I supposed to find it this summer?"

"Winter's only half gone." Annie buried her face into the wool blanket covering her granddaughter's shoulder. "And you're planning for summer?"

"Yes." Kiara wrapped an arm around Annie and tugged her toward the Jeep. "And you're taking me fishing."

Youth had no concept of time. Annie didn't know if she'd still be around come summer. But another summer didn't sound too bad.

ABOUT THE AUTHORS

Alicia Cay

Alicia Cay is a writer of speculative and mystery stories. Her short fiction has appeared in *Galaxy's Edge* Magazine, and in several anthologies including *Unmasked* from WordFire Press and *The Wild Hunt* from Air and Nothingness Press. She suffers from wanderlust, collects quotes, and lives beneath the shadows of the Rocky Mountains with a corgi, a kitty, and a lot of fur. Find her at aliciacay.com.

April Benson

April Benson is a hometown Colorado mountain girl with a deep-rooted passion for the philosophy of life and the pursuit of happiness. Much of her personal writing evolves from her love of travel and adventures across the world, ranging from cross-country U.S. road trips to European escapades. In 2022, she leveraged her writing skills in the U.S. Army to author articles on multinational combat medicine across Europe. While stationed as a soldier in Germany, she also pioneered an internal outreach program to continue the powerful narrative of saving lives on the battlefield. If you ever meet April, she will make you think twice about the meaning of life and likely rope you into her travels.

Robert Spiller

Besides being a master of space and time, Robert Spiller is the author of the Bonnie Pinkwater mystery series: *The Witch of Agnesi, A Calculated Demise, Irrational Numbers,* and most recently *Radical Equations and Napier's Bones*. His math teacher/sleuth uses mathematics and her knowledge of historic mathematicians to solve murders in the small Colorado town of East Plains. A retired mathematician, Robert lives in Colorado Springs, Colorado with his wife Barbara.

Jean Alfieri
When Jean Alfieri's eyes locked with those of a smooshy-faced little dog who sat inside a kennel at the Humane Society, it was love! He captured her heart. She captured their many adventures in short story poems starring Zuggy the Rescue Pug. An author, speaker, and advocate for the adoption of senior dogs, she and her husband currently live with their three fur kids in Colorado. They joke that although the humans pay the mortgage, it's really the dogs' house! Jean finds much of her writing inspiration from her "vintage puppies" and work at the Pikes Peak Humane Society.

D.J. Davis
DJ Davis is a Colorado native with mountains in her DNA. She is obsessed with the forests, lakes, and craggy peaks. The rugged high country and rich history of the state set the scene for her stories. When she's not writing or photographing the wildlife, she frequently disappears into the wilderness with her husband and dogs. You can find her at Mountains of Dreams (https://djdavisauthor.com/).

Barbara Preslier
Barbara Preslier grew up frolicking on the beaches of Miami, Florida. She graduated with an English degree from Colgate University in NY, and continued on to the Goldman School of Dentistry in MA. She practiced general and forensic dentistry in South Florida for over thirty years. After raising twin daughters, she retired and moved to Colorado with her husband. She has focused on her writing career, and is currently finishing her fourth novel. Her publications include short stories and professional journal articles. When not toiling at her desk, she enjoys geocaching, crocheting and traveling.

Bowen Gillings
Bowen Gillings is an award-winning author who writes to bring more joy into the world. His debut novella *A Night to Remember* reached

#9 on Amazon.com's Top 100 for its subgenre. His work is featured in *Fresh Starts* anthology, *Allegory* e-zine, and on *Stories Live!* and *Stark Reflections on Writing and Publishing* YouTube channels. He is an active member and former president of Pikes Peak Writers and a member of Rocky Mountain Fiction Writers and The League of Utah Writers. He holds a Master of Education plus five martial arts black belt certifications, is an Army veteran, loves travel, cooking, and a fine adult beverage. He lives in Colorado with his wife and daughter. Follow him on Facebook at BowenGillingsAuthor and learn more at storiesbybowen.com.

Bill Bush

Bill Bush grew up in Yates Center, Kansas, and is a graduate of Yates Center High School and Tabor College, where he earned a Master's degree in Accounting. He is a dad, runner and pickleball players as well as a writer. His desire to write comes from his mom, Phyllis Roth Lewis, who was a published author and wrote numerous short stories, poems, and books. He took a step toward becoming a full-time fiction author in 2018 by joining Kansas Publishing Venture as a newspaper reporter. Now he writes nonfiction during the day and fiction at night. You can learn more about Bill at billbushauthor.com or snader-publishing.com, his publishing company.

John Arthur Neal

John Arthur Neal would first like to thank Deborah L. Brewer, editor of the anthology. Debby made *Seafrog* much more readable. John has written three SF novels and is drafting the 6th novel of his *Collinsville Crime Series*. John has also written two novellas, twenty-one short stories, and several screenplays. John's college thesis was a novelette, and he later completed a *Writer's Digest* correspondence course. John participated in two critique groups over the years and has attended hundreds of seminars. He seeks agent representation for his novels and is submitting stories to contests and magazines. Feel free to visit johnarthurneal.com.

Steven Anderson

Steven Anderson is the author of the Reunification series of science fiction adventure-romances and other speculative tales. A passionate fan of science fiction since age six, Steve began creating his own worlds once he was old enough to pick up a crayon. He put his creative skills to work as an aerospace IT professional for many years before writing full time. Steve lives in Colorado Springs with his wife and an aging collection of parts that's sometimes a car. He can often be found somewhere in the Rockies exploring local history and scenic wonders.

Jeff Schmoyer

Jeff Schmoyer sequences words to create short stories, novellas, plays, and computer programs. A recovering tech entrepreneur, he tries to find humor in the everyday world around him. Find more at Jmars-Ink.com.

CS Simpson

CS Simpson is a multi-genre writer of several short stories, some poetry, and a novel. Her work can be found in *Shoreline of Infinity,* the Pikes Peak Writers Anthologies, frontiertales.com, and her own self-published books, The Fable Triad. When she's not writing, editing, or stressing about writing, she's either devouring other author's books or playing The Sims and watching movies while sipping Diet Coke. She also enjoys short hikes with her husband and dog under the Colorado skies she calls home. Keep up with her writing journey at authorcssimpson.com.

KK Quinn

KK Quinn resides in Colorado with her husband, two dogs, three cats, a hamster, and a fish. She writes Fantasy and Sci-fi with a strong passion for world-building. When she's not writing or reading, she spends her time gardening or making home-made soap.

Wendy Oliver

Wendy Oliver has broad interests, from astronomy to Zelda, which are reflected in her writing. She's written a couple middle grade novels, romances, sci-fi stories, blogs for multiple non-profits, and dozens of newspaper articles. Wendy sings, plays oboe, hikes in the mountains, and travels. For fun, she dresses up in medieval clothing and recreates historical crafts. She also works for the US Forest Service. Wendy lives in the Colorado mountains with her husband and dog, plus the deer, pinyon jays, and occasional bald eagle that hang out nearby. At night, she's often outside gazing at the stars. Website: woliverbooks.com

Kelley J.P. Lindberg

Kelley J. P. Lindberg writes award-winning YA and adult fiction, and sometimes admits to having written several best-selling how-to books in her early career. Her fiction and essays have appeared in literary magazines such as *The Baltimore Review*, *The Citron Review*, and *99 Pine Street*; in anthologies including *Bizarre Bazaar* and *Chicken Soup for the Wine Lover's Soul*; and in the Tellables app for the Amazon Alexa platform. She has received awards from the Rocky Mountain Fiction Writers Gold Rush Literary Awards, the YARWA Rosemary Awards (Romance Writers of America), and the Utah Original Writing Competition. When she isn't writing from her home in Colorado, she's traveling as far and as often as she can. Visit her at KelleyLindberg.com or follow her on Twitter at @KelleyLindberg1.

Marlene Fabien Stiles

Marlene Fabian-Stiles enjoys writing in multiple genres and has published a science fiction novel "Moon Life" in partnership with her geneticist brother Hank as well as a first person Alzheimer's account "Elderchild" based heavily on personal experience. She and writing partner Alice Hill will be publishing their children's book "Tulip-o-mania" and "Sistors," a narrative of sibling rivalry. Marlene also publishes short stories and poetry on storystyles.com. As President of the nonprofit, "The I Will Projects" (theiwillprojects.com) Marlene supports innovative approaches to education including a family care-giver program developed in partnership with Hospice and an aquaponics program with the Boys and Girls Club.

Veronica R. Calisto

Veronica R. Calisto (she/her) is a massage therapist, an alto, a writer of speculative fiction, and a big nerd. One of those rare Colorado natives, she has a degree in Molecular, Cellular, Developmental Biology and is a two-time American Idol reject. Veronica is best described as a walking musical who might also be a figment of her own imagination. She is the author of several books including *Diary of a Mad Black Witch* and the first two in the *SparkleTits Chronicles* series.

Jessica Mehring

Jessica Mehring is a Colorado-based author, copywriter and entrepreneur. She believes that history and nature are our greatest teachers, yet she is also endlessly fascinated by technology and the human brain. She loves reading, walks in the woods, and creating and collecting art. She lives with her husband, two daughters, and more pets than she'd like to admit to—and her growing collection of books and office supplies are slowly taking over their house. You can connect with Jessica at jessicamehringauthor.com.

Bailey Finn

Bailey Finn is a speculative fiction author who enjoys stories that bring magic into the mundane. She works full-time in crisis intervention helping families through the worst of times. When Bailey is not helping those in need, she enjoys ballroom dancing and getting the gang together for a round of tabletop gaming. Bailey resides in Colorado Springs and is a member of Pikes Peak Writers where she is always happy to connect with fellow authors and readers, as well as dancers and gamers.

Jenna MacFarlane

Being a late bloomer in nearly every regard, MacFarlane got her start writing short stories in her thirties. Years later, her short story, *Old Debt* was published in 2017 in the anthology *It's About Time*. In 2019, while on a road trip in the west, MacFarlane penned her first draft of the novel *Hardware Stories*. Having experienced some of the trials as protagonist Claire, a misplaced westerner working at a southern hard-ware store, MacFarlane was inspired to bring the characters to life and make good on a lifelong promise to publish. She has plans to adapt the novel to a screenplay. MacFarlane's first book, *Hindsight* will publish in 2023. *Hindsight* is a memoir detailing MacFarlane's long road to love and is an inspiration for the indie film *Adopting Audrey* which premiered in August 2022.

Catherine Dilts

Catherine prefers writing cozy mysteries and short stories surrounded by flowers on her sunny deck, but any day – and anywhere – spent writing is a good day. The first in her new Rose Creek series, *The Body in the Cattails*, has a May 2023 release date. Author of the *Rock Shop Mystery* series and the stand-alone *Survive Or Die* with Encircle Publications, Catherine also writes for Annie's Fiction, contributing three books for the Secrets of the *Castleton Manor Library* series, and two for the *Annie's Museum of Mysteries* series. Her short story *Claire's Cabin* appears in the Alfred Hitchcock Mystery Magazine March/April 2023 issue.

ABOUT THE EDITORS

Kathie Scrimgeour
Project Manager, Editor

Kathie writes under the pseudonym KJ Scrim. She has been the Project manager for PPW's first three anthologies, *Fresh Starts*, *Dream*, and *Journeys into Possibility*. In addition, she serves as secretary on the Board of Directors with PPW, was the previous Manager Editor of *Writing from the Peak* (PPW's blog) and has been a long-time volunteer at their annual conference held in Colorado Springs. You can follow her on her website, KJScrim.com and on Facebook. When she's not writing you can find her somewhere in Arizona biking, hiking, or rock climbing.

Deborah L. Brewer
Editor

A volunteer with Pikes Peak Writers, whether blogging, editing, or working at the conference, Deborah finds satisfaction in helping fellow writers achieve their writing dreams.

Kim Olgren
Assistant Project Manager, Editor

Like many writers, Kim Olgren is a voracious reader. She's worn many hats, but writing has been her constant companion. In her "free" time she is a house renovator, PPW volunteer, maker, traveler, and loves hanging out with her family and faithful sofa wolf. She is a published mystery writer but writes in many genres.

Kim has been a volunteer with Pikes Peak Writers since 2018. In addition to her duties as board president, she has been the editor of the PPW newsletter, non-conference events director, and is a contributor to Writing from the Peak, the PPW blog.

Josh Clark
Cover Design

Josh Clark is a writer, graphic designer, and bookseller. His short fiction has been published by Pikes Peak Writers, Black Hare Press, Trembling with Fear, and received a Silver Honorable Mention in the Writers of the Future Contest. As a graphic designer, Josh has worked at the Professional Bull Riders, a local newspaper, an automotive advertising agency, and as a freelancer. His life is filled with words professionally and recreationally, so if he's not writing or reading you're likely to find him at author events, science fiction conventions, writing conferences, or out in nature brainstorming his next novel.

You can find him on Twitter @joshofclark

ABOUT PIKES PEAK WRITERS

The non-profit organization, **Pikes Peak Writers,** began as a conference founded in 1993 by author Jimmie Butler under the auspices and sponsorship of the Friends of Pikes Peak Library. The inaugural conference centered on "Useful Tips for Writing Commercial Fiction," and enjoyed sponsorship by the Friends of the Pikes Peak Library District and The Kennedy Center Imagination Celebration.

The conference has achieved a top ten ranking among U.S. writing conferences by Writers Digest Magazine.

After many years of successful conferences, a core group of volunteers formed the parent organization, **Pikes Peak Writers**, as a 501(c)(3) nonprofit organization dedicated to providing quality education for writers year-round.

Since Pikes Peak Writers' founding in 2001, non-conference events have blossomed to more than 40 free and low-cost events, including monthly Write Brain sessions, writing workshops, and a host of other fun and educational meetings and events. PPW has also published three outstanding anthologies featuring stories by members of the organization.

Membership in PPW is over 2,000 and growing. The organization is governed by an all-volunteer Board of Directors and maintained by a dedicated group of volunteers.

TALES FROM PIKES PEAK WRITERS

Fresh Starts anthology

Dream anthology

Journeys Into Possibility anthology

www.ingramcontent.com/pod-product-compliance
Lightning Source LLC
Chambersburg PA
CBHW060428180626
46817CB00007B/2721